BIG AS LIFE

ALSO BY MAUREEN HOWARD

Novels

Not a Word About Nightingales
Bridgeport Bus
Before My Time
Grace Abounding
Expensive Habits
Natural History
A Lover's Almanac

Memoir

Facts of Life

BIG AS LIFE

Three Tales for Spring

Maureen Howard

OUACHITA TECHNICAL COLLEGE

VIKING

VIKING
Published by the Penguin Group
Penguin Putnam Inc., 375 Hudson Street, New York, New York 10014, U.S.A.
Penguin Books Ltd, 27 Wrights Lane, London W8 5TZ, England
Penguin Books Australia Ltd, Ringwood, Victoria, Australia
Penguin Books Canada Ltd, 10 Alcorn Avenue, Toronto, Ontario, Canada M4V 3B2
Penguin Books (N.Z.) Ltd, 182–190 Wairau Road, Auckland 10, New Zealand

Penguin Books Ltd, Registered Offices:
Harmondsworth, Middlesex, England

First published in 2001 by Viking Penguin,
a member of Penguin Putnam Inc.

1 3 5 7 9 10 8 6 4 2

ILLUSTRATION CREDITS: Page 75: *Livre de la Passion*, Vatican City, Biblioteca Apostolica
Vaticana; 127: © Collection of The New-York Historical Society; 138: John James Audubon
Museum, Henderson, Kentucky; 140: From *Audubon the Naturalist* by Francis Hobart Herrick, Appleton, 1917; 149: Ernst Mayr Library of the Museum of Comparative Zoology,
Harvard University; 164: Collection of B. L. Rathbone, Liverpool.

PUBLISHER'S NOTE: This is a work of fiction. Names, characters, places and incidents are either
the product of the author's imagination or are used fictitiously.

CIP data available.

ISBN 0-670-89978-X

This book is printed on acid-free paper. ∞

Printed in the United States of America
Set in Electra
Designed by Nancy Resnick

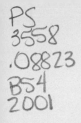

To Kate Howard Fudge
and
Christopher Kearns

Acknowledgments

It's a pleasure to thank my gentle, though I trust strict, readers of these tales—Joanna Scott, James Logenbach, George Kearns, Rebecca Goldstein. In imagining Ballycarne, a village of my construction in the West of Ireland, I am grateful to Maura McTighe for her great knowledge. There's no way to repay the McTighes for enveloping me in the past mysteries and present joys of Sligo. In writing my fiction I am ever so thankful to the many interpreters of Audubon's life and work, in particular Christopher Irmscher, Shirley Streshinsky, Carolyn De Latte, Alice Ford, Theodore Stebbins, Gerry and Ann Weissmann. Don Boarman, curator of the John James Audubon Museum in Henderson, Kentucky; the Audubon Museum at Mill Grove, Pennsylvania, and the Peabody Museum of Harvard University unraveled some myths and set me right. The Berkshire Athenaeum and the Chapin Library of Williams College were helpful to a mere weekend resident. Once again, Mary Witkowski of the Historical Collections, Bridgeport Public Library, for her continuing assistance; as well as Natalie Charkow, Mike Daly, Janet Marks, Brad Morrow, Patty O'Toole, Gloria Loomis— always; Paul Slovak (my patient editor); and will I ever stop off with thanking Mark Probst—never.

BIG AS LIFE

APRIL

Children with Matches

*What force is there in the thing given which compels
the recipient to make a return?*

—Marcel Mauss, *The Gift*

SOUNDS

Imagine carp—flickering metallic orange, not gold. Their movements
delightful to behold as swamp grasses swaying on the edge of an ornamental pond. Natural, by design so natural. The carp are the idea of
George Baird, President of Baird Bank and Trust. He has caused the
gutting of this pond, the cementing of its retaining walls to simulate
crags and timeworn crannies. He believes his carp to be old, that the
same stock performs for him these twenty years, flashing like dancers in
the Burly-que over in Troy or hovering in tranquillity like their gilt im-
ages on a Japanese screen. His fish are that versatile.

George Baird is set out by his fish pond, tucked up in lap robes. He
is dying. The day is resplendent with the warmth of false Spring, so his
doctor allows this excursion. Baird has sent his nurse back to the house.
In a feeble pantomime he has asked for a cup of tea. Free of her fussing
at last, with difficulty he wheels his invalid chair closer to the black wa-

ter, the better to see his treasures, for they have emerged from their Winter torpor.

During the Winter the carp do not feed. Banker Baird, as the mill hands once called him, does not feed. The taste of milk toast and junket is abhorrent, nursery food spooned out at life's entrance and exit. His flesh hangs pale and bruised from his bones, though he is so thoroughly swaddled only one hand moving fitfully and his bulbous head topped with a jaunty fedora can be seen. The overseers and engineers who came to his office, caps in hand, knew him as the broad barrel of a man with a thicket of unruly hair who let their notes run till next payday.

He knew you as Canuck, Polack, Irish.

On Sunday you took the wife and kids on the trolley to Baird's place—a good walk past the end of the line—to picnic on his back acres.

You believed he was like you—that he was uncomfortable buttoned into the worsted suit pulling at his shoulders and high belly, that he had once earned his living by the labor of his hands. It was memorable, the crushing grip of his handshake granting your first mortgage—the small lot you would proudly build on in town.

His ring, set with diamonds big as headlights on his touring car, was an affront to the town merchants and to the lawyers educated at Williams and Harvard, who'd lost the Yankee art of cutting a shrewd deal. They went, when invited, to Baird's showplace beyond sidewalks and city water, although by arrangement, let's call it an arrangement, the phone and electricity lines extended to his world.

He contributed to the Congregational church but did not enter its pure whitewashed walls.

His raucous baritone laughter broke the sanctimonious whisper of cash counted out in the mighty hall of his bank.

From his post by the pond, George Baird cannot see the grand house which lies behind him. Insofar as he can ask, he has asked that his back be turned to that investment in shingles, lime and bricks. His son now lives there with his pickle of a wife, a mean spirited do-gooder, and their two little girls, Lily and Rose. They have taken possession, filled the rooms with their discontent. The sour wife dusts and mops and scours. No servant save the nurse, Miss Wipe Arse, an annoyance.

In the mighty brick mills and factories along the Housatonic it has been launched—the next downward cycle—and how will this son survive—his second son no better than a clerk at the bank, a mild, evasive man not party to his wife's spiritual ambition. If the patriarch had words, could spew forth more than clotted vowels, he would say, *Do not foreclose. By Jesus, boy, I did not shut down in the Great Depression of '07. And in a period of recovery built this damn house you have never enjoyed.* In his mind, which is clear as the sky above, the big house with its gardens and stable was built for his first son. The pond intended as a watery diversion for the weary soldier home from the Great War. And didn't that brave fella love to spot the biggest fish—supple, iridescent, leader of the pack—though the soft-finned koi could lose them all, slip away without a ripple. George Baird was planning ahead to a tennis court when the golden son died of the Spanish flu in 1919.

Such a bustle in the water plants provided for his exotic minnows. The females laying their eggs. He will not live to see them hatch. He fears he will not live to hear the insistent comfort of Spring peepers. A flash of graceful tail, the rare koi, an arrogant fellow much like the gilded fish suspended in calm waters on his Japanese screen which that woman has folded away in a crippling Christian gesture, that woman (pretending he can't recall her name), the woman married to his son, the clerk. Not the glimmering fish she counts sinful, but the seductive brush strokes of the pagan painter, his boat adrift with many beautiful maidens posturing in their embroidered kimonos, tending to their luxurious hair.

The gentle slap, slapping of water on concrete in the wake of some minor disturbance in the reeds, and in the distance the lopping of limbs, his son working in the woods, forging his solitary trails. George Baird locates himself in the day—midafternoon. The bronze doors at his bank are locked to its unhappy clients. His son should be there tending to desperate business, not plotting his folly. George Baird, President of the failing bank, cannot in the end, knowing it's his end, pass on his title to the woodsman who can't tell good ash from chokecherry, who, with a dainty silver lead pencil, takes notes on the weeds underfoot—skunk cabbage, bedstraw, cancerroot. And then the repetitive tune, his granddaughters home from school, the gangly girl, Rose, her high shoulders hunched over the spinet, playing her scales, obedient *da-deedle-dum-dum, deedlee-da*, his insufferable daily penance. Banker Baird, strictly commercial, has never been afflicted by the arts, the spinet in the parlor purchased as furniture in 1910, along with his wife's Limoges, the Tiffany tea service, the mahogany dining room set. In that same year he procured the Japanese screen, the only thing in the lot he cared for.

Midafternoon. A long shadow stretches across the lawn, the turret of his house catching up with an old man, chilling his bones. How often his wife climbed the back stairs so narrow and steep to that useless rotunda, freeze your tits off in Winter, hell in the Summer heat. *To read. To sew.* She held with that story. *To absent yourself, Miss High and Mighty.* She has been absent now for some years, at rest in her family's vault, a fancy dollhouse of death. George Baird has instructed that his remains be stuck in New England earth with no marker. *Da-deedlee-da-da, deedlee-dum-dum.* His carp shimmering now, strutting their stuff in vaudevillian procession. With the good arm he wheels closer, closer down the grassy slope into the mire, as if to join them in play, peeing himself with pleasure. He has always marveled at how they survive, dormant, unfed in the cold; burrowing into the mud in a dry season. He hears the death knell of Nursey's tread on gravel, the tinkle of cup and saucer, the snap of her starched apron, but has one moment left to himself, mumbling the undeliverable message, a gargle of *o, o, o's*—*Do not foreclose.*

Dum-diddlee-dum. Diddlee-dum-dum. Rose has turned the page, progressing in her Czerny Exercises. Lily, dull as a dumpling, colors another picture for Grampa, red for the King's cape, yellow for his crown.

Dum-dum-diddlee-dum. In the woods—*lop, lop*—a split second of silence between the cut and thud on the ground. And then *peep, peep, peep, peep,* the first sweet amphibian cries of the season, but it is the enduring silence of fish the old man yearns for now that he is at a loss for words.

In 1907 scrip was issued by the Berkshire Clearing House as emergency currency. In 1933, as the snow held fast to the peak of Monument Mountain, scrip was issued again, with nothing behind it but the town's desperate belief in Banker Baird's son. It was Spring, and Julian listening for the crazy courtship flight of the woodcock at dusk, for the rustle of the red fox emerging from his Winter lair, did not hear his father's garbled order, but Julian Baird made good on every note of the funny money. He did not foreclose.

CHILDREN WITH MATCHES

Spook house. Attractive nuisance. Children in the neighborhood no longer wonder at shutters banging off hinges, the flutter of curtains at blank windows. No way a thrill in their tough street life. Spook house, only attractive to me. Wind sucks down through the chimney, a fierce April shower splashing out of gutters—what's left of them. Silent carpenter ants work away at the listing veranda, labor endlessly at their hills of powdery decay. I am in the tower where my prince will find me.

Yes, that sort of wide-eyed story with a prince.

If he cares to find me looking down from a modest shingle turret, which as a girl I imagined to be a tower high above the sweeping lawns and woods—the family land. *Once-upon-a* . . . In those days a stone floor was exposed to the elements where a carriage house once stood. *Children with matches.* The charred ruins had been cleared away. I scoured the Belgian blocks for treasure—worn chips of glass, mysterious brass fittings. And what did they know, two old women who kept me in the gloomy tower? How could they possibly know, with their doors bolted, their shades drawn, to blame children with matches? The only wicked child in clear view was me. The horses gone before their time, long gone, Dobbin and Rascals of their legends, the illustrious names dusted off for a moody girl, though they recalled each automobile driven out of the carriage house—the Auburn, the DeSoto, the dark green Lincoln with opera windows. As though I cared, a kid they were stuck with for a season, gave diddly-squat for their fancy garage, their uppity *porte cochère* which held fast to the house over a circular drive so that in some tiresome dead time they were sheltered from the scalding sun.

And from the softest Spring rain, wasn't that so? Old girls checking glories of the past.

Peonies round the gazebo. That would be Lily.

By the tool shed. Correction came by way of Rose.

More *children with matches*, for this house stood alone, ungarnished by outbuildings. When I was first closed in the tower, I saw at a glance that in their vast garden there was no place to hide. I'm up in that drafty room again, listening for the squeal of a hinge, creak of stair tread. No place to hide if he comes, the man I'm determined to kiss into life. No craggy frog prince—believe me, he's handsome, smooth. You may think him too old to be my lover.

As a child I was called Marie Claude. From below I heard their anxious, lilting voices, "Marie Claude! Marie Claude!"—the chirping of those creatures who held me hostage in the tower. Eventually I might go down to supper and not sulk, make one of them, most likely Lily, the stout one in bangles and gossamer scarves, huff and puff up the stairs to the door of my chamber, bumping her head on the low lintel. Eventually, but for the punishing moment I narrowed my eyes, despising a clot of cement in the brown lawn and the dark tangle of woodland. To the East, they told me, lay the fish pond now dry, and to the West *Daddy's Timber Trail*, schooling me in their sacred geography.

To the West the sun burnt its way through the pitch pines and birches where final hillocks of snow clung in darkness to matted leaves.

Beyond the woods, white chimney smoke rose, wavered through the fiery end of day, and oh!—if only I, too, might be carried by the wind, dissolve in thin air.

"Marie Claude!" It was Rose stooping in the doorway, the tall whiskered one come for me, the one dressed all in grey flannel like a giant mouse in *Nutcracker*, which I was taken to with much ceremony and dress-up by my mother. That was Christmas, a glittering evening in the city, and now it was Spring—mud season in this Northern industrial town. I had been dumped, an angry child with a permanent frown, abandoned to these witches (elderly aunts), confined to the tower (sewing room of a rackety old house) while my mother (on an amorous adventure?) flew away. One night, before the door to the tower was pawed open, before the great mouse with bristly grey hair smiled her nibbling smile, Marie Claude, as I was then, scooted out, down the steep back stairs once good enough for serving girls. Out through the chill solarium, off to the shadows and glowering branches of the forest. A nasty escapade, not a story to tell my silver haired lover.

When I came back to the tower, just weeks ago, and looked down, the trees were gone, one ancient pine left, darkly drooping as a widow. Hans, Hans Gruen, settled on the window seat to a stack of old *Life* magazines. The very spectacles sliding down his nose were distinguished. How amazing that Hans Gruen came with me to the spook house, a man busy with his conferences, his corporate boards. Unwilling to reveal the cruelty of a childhood prank, I didn't tell him of that night long ago when I ran for the dark woods. Terrifying, though often in the Brothers Grimm a child encounters a helpful bird or tattered peasant with a loaf of bread, no more marvelous than Hans coming with me to this ghost ridden place. Looking down through the rattling sash windows, I saw a small yard with that mournful tree and exhausted forsythia blooming wearily over a chain-link fence that sets the house apart from a few rinky-dink trailers to the East, a strip mall to the West.

"They locked me in this tower." They, poor maiden ladies. In the dusty Spring twilight, I examined a skein of grey wool, in its strands tiny curls of dead moth worms, brittle and dry. I fingered a bit of rose chiffon, a limp scrap of violet sateen, and heard them again, the harmless old crones who have willed me their house — "Marie Claude! Marie Claude!"

Hans paced the room, circling the cutting table, a trunk with trans-Atlantic stickers, a Morris chair in full decline. "You can make quick work of this."

His voice betrayed no impatience as he tapped a Singer sewing machine, gilt flowers girdling the swell of its Victorian body. His tapered fingers tap, tap, tapping.

Prince. Lover. Piss-poor abstractions.

Maddening — his manicure, exquisite haircut, the denim work shirt he affects. His generosity seemed programmed at that moment, self-aware, and I found nothing more to say to this curried specimen I'd brought to view my miserable inheritance. That's where your disappointment gets you, Claude, slops over to this admirable man. Unclear what I expected from a desolate house, discarded even in memory, but hadn't I hoped for something, a sentimental shard — one cut glass goblet, a weightless teacup with faded gold rim?

"Quick work? I have to come back for the lawyer." And for Spero's Quality Homes. Tilda Spero, the real estate woman already entrusted with my sale, had greeted us at the busted iron gate and handed over the keys to the house now mine. A woman professionally suited up for work, but her station wagon waiting at the curb in a downtrodden neighborhood was full of children in Catholic school uniforms — punching, shoving each other in some hilarious game.

Not a chatty sort, Tilda Spero forced a smile — "This is no longer a residential zone" — then, looking from the unruly kids in the car to the shattered windows of the house, "more of an attractive nuisance, I'd say."

I made it clear that Mrs. Spero's duties were over for the day, but as I wandered the echoing rooms with Hans he picked up on her theme: the dangling electric fixtures, rusted heating vents were a menace.

Though the leaded glass, the green tiles framing the fireplace—lovely Arts and Crafts. "If only," Hans said, "twenty, thirty years ago . . ."

"If only they had died earlier?" I'd thought that as we drove upstate, and if only the company in this company town had not left for cheap labor, then my great-grandfather's house with its parklike acres would still be intact. "They lived to an inconvenient old age."

"How old, Claude?"

"Sorry!" His age a running joke between us. Our May/December problem no problem at all, and there was my admission what with my mother dead, my father practiced at keeping his distance, I wanted to be no one's daughter. "The aunts were old when I was a kid. Especially the great mouse."

"The artist?"

"That was the roly-poly. She did something fey with pillows and silk scarves. Sold them to my mother's horror in the parlor of this house."

"A commercial property then. And the other one?"

"Music." I was reluctant to speak of the other one, a tall drink of water bundled in grey sweaters and stockings, her steel wool head bobbing over the yellowed keys of a spinet, spidery fingers stumbling through flashy arpeggios. Each night, after supper, I had been her captive audience while the artiste readied the sloppy desserts to be served in the library, some ritual that went back to Daddy or to Dobbin's day. A story too foolish for this serious man; still, I laughed outright at the memory—"Blancmange! Bread puddings!"

"Hungry?" Hans checking his watch. Always checking the time allotted.

"Desperate. I bet there's no place fit to eat in this town."

A bet I lost, for Hans can find the one perfect restaurant in Keokuk or Belgrade and found it on the mostly deserted main street: an old German couple proud of their schnitzel, their prune whip. On our way back to the city, I slept the heavy meal off, but later that night roamed the tidy rooms of my lover's apartment, still unfamiliar to me, worrying that I had shown him too much or too little of my past. The house on

Park Street pitiful, no more than a dreary picture of domestic decline—not a sea of sweltering tents in the refugee camps of an African country Hans Gruen had recently advised, as though in a land laid waste by tribal wars and AIDS, he must propose a faint hope of economic prosperity. With that decent thought, I believed I was no pouting princess. Just lucky for once in my life. I switched on the light over his desk to see what hour of the restless night. There was the kidskin calendar embossed with his name, a full calendar with his departures to mostly foreign cities; there, too, the dead wife, handsome—the grown sons with merely pretty wives, the gap-toothed grandson in a sailor suit. All perfect in their silver frames, untroubling to me, this family he had scheduled in. How my Hans suffers his sons' suburban success, the chill embrace of their admiration. A little late in the day, he's discovered there's no way to bridge the gulf. I bathe in his contrition. Look, I have captured my prize, we both know it. And there, set apart, the photo ops, my economist with men of state—with Kissinger, Carter—Hans, almost boyish—with Thatcher, Mitterrand, with the Pope for God's sake. His sharply cut features are now smooth as the profile on a worn coin.

But what had I not told him? That I had been deposited in the spook house for a short season between the convent in Montreal and the *lycée* in Paris, a packing up, moving on time, moving to the best post my father would ever have. And that my mother had sublet a tiny flat in New York, a *pied-à-terre*. Molly Montour would toss that term at the Baird sisters, her weird half-sisters, a generation older. They were to look after Marie Claude. Yes, to help with my lessons, but truly to keep me with them for some weeks to get the feel of family, of home, the place her people came from. This plot was presented by my mother as a gift to all parties, and then she skipped off to an interim affair. How did a kid know that for certain? Know the smell of Havana cigars in her clothes. My father did not smoke. Know the gold link bracelet never worn, hiding in its velvet pouch at the back of her dresser drawer. Know that in Molly's wandering life, I must wait for her in odd places until she turned up once more.

Listen, it was never Christmas holidays, Summer visits. For one cold season I was given over to childless women who hadn't a clue. I wasn't a prisoner in their tower, merely sent up to answer simple questions in workbooks of math and French. I never saw the aunts again. When my mother died, they sent a sympathy card to the hospice on the Maryland shore. How the news of that death came to them was unclear. Their card was signed in the big open script of good children. Aunt Lily. Aunt Rose. There is no mystery in the lawyer finding me in the age of accessible identities from which no one can hide. When I flipped through my mail and discovered the letter with the postmark of this town, I was shamed, the wounded shame of a naughty child. Now I'm simply mortified that these poor souls thought of me at all. Thought to please me with their gift.

So—waiting for Hans to come get me.

I've set a rusted pot under a leak in the ceiling. A downpour veers to the West, flapping the sheet-metal roof of Jimbo's Bakery. My day begins with a cruller and cup of weak coffee at the counter of this greasy shop nestled between a laundromat and a nail salon. Each morning, crossing the tarmac, I think *Daddy's Timber Trail*. Slow work, my business with the lawyer and Spero. I never guessed how slow the other business—memory, a swiping at dust in unreachable corners. I soon lost track of the week, then counted—this is the day he will come, if he comes. Testing him, testing, an old habit with me, testing—one, two, testing—to see if my claim rings true. Hans Gruen must drive right under the *porte cochère*, sheltering him from the Spring rain, isn't that so. Ridiculous, we will drive back to the city in a convoy of two. But first he must climb the stairs to the tower to find me, listen to the ping, ping, ping of water in my pail, then take me home. Home, his spare widower's apartment.

Or home, the cramped room and a half, two blocks from the community college where I teach. If you asked me a while back, I'd have said it would take a miracle to get me out of my safe nest. The home of my childhood was nowhere, as you may have guessed. My father was

State, Foreign Service, honorable, The Honorable Jack Montour, to put the best light on his career. We moved about. In her final days, my mother confused the houseboy (Bogotá) with the cook (Ivory Coast). She insisted the chaise longue was lost on its way to Marseille. We knew it was the Shaker bed.

Awful for us, her daughter and husband by the bedside, Molly's fevered mind recalling the many households we presumed she did not love. It came to me then that her beauty had led her astray, may have masked much ordinary life that she cared for. In a way we banked on her ripeness-is-all, her extravagant body to let Moll go her way and to keep us in line. Now her prattle was of Wedgwood bought at Harrods, of the Portuguese soup tureen—all broken in transit. Awful, so awful we believed it was the morphine speaking, easing the constriction of her failing heart. In what seemed a final aria, she raved about State's warehouse in Istanbul, *like a fire sale at Macy's*. How clearly she remembered the vast display of recycled domestic goods—abandoned chairs, tables, double boilers, baby cots—from which she chose the rattan couch to overlook the Bosporus where Russian tankers with more than oil sailed by, ships in the night.

"Which you reported on, dutiful Jack."

"Now, Molls," my father said to stop her spilling the beans, open secrets no longer buried in the files.

The hairdresser came in the room with brush and harmless hair spray. Imagine Molly Montour waving her away, no longer vain or interested in the dignity of her dying, her hair a fright of white roots gaining on ash blond tangles. Taking our turns, we waited. Toward dawn, she roused herself. I was alone with her in the room. "That house was the best," she said, "stairs to the sewing room, high, so high. . . ."

I knew at once it was the tower she spoke of, the best house was the spook house where she once left me. "Why the best?" I asked. "Please tell me!"

"But you were too often away, Marie Claude, too often away at school." Scrambling the years, my mother gave me the only clue that she ever missed me. I'm grateful—too grateful don't I know it—for her final words.

Long ago, I dropped the double moniker given to me by my Francophile father. *If you would only straighten up, Marie Claude.* My mother, who carried her breasts high as an endowment of the gods, could not bear my schoolgirl slump, the downward cast of my weak eyes. Molly Montour, née Baird, did not live to see the fashion for narrow-chested scrawn and scholarly glasses. She would have taken little pleasure in her daughter pecking at the edges of academic conferences. You do see that I have been a determined disappointment. But lately, there's this dear, deluded man, who transforms schoolmarm into sprite, sees me as gamine. I'm waiting for him in the high round room, prison or primal palace, that my mother's thought turned to in the end. And if he does not come, Molls, I will have lived in your leaky tower at last, launched a paper missile, the frail trajectory of my story.

TOTAL NETWORKING IN THE ENTREPRENEURIAL CULTURE

You may wonder how we met, your daughter and this serious man who often travels with a State Department visa, who may be seen with glib television pundits mourning the slippage of whole banking systems into default. How does a player of that mark tie up with the little brown wren?

Hans Gruen arrived at the community college where I teach without escort. An urban campus surrounded by parking lots half empty in the lull between day and night classes. He found his way through the crisscross of walks, not a scrap of the red carpet he was accustomed to, the welcome of deans, provosts, Nobel economists. Skidding cross campus, he headed toward the dowdiest building, figuring some authority in its age. Ugly red brick with colonial façade houses our administration. In our muddled architecture you can read a history of public education— WPA moderno, Fifties Bauhaus bunker, glass box of the Sixties, Post-modern student center with its giddy, gaudy references coming full-circle to colonial revival. Teachers' to junior to community college.

In the empty hall of the administration building, Gruen encountered himself on a Xeroxed flier the color of bubble gum, his flesh pixelated grey, hair rubbery, a case of pinkeye. The title of his lecture alarming: "Total Networking in the Entrepreneurial Culture." What the hell did that mean? This gig put on his calendar by an intern from the Kennedy School, a fast-tracker who made it known he was overqualified for the Summer job. Hans Gruen was booked months ahead. Perhaps this trip to the inner city foretold grazing pastures to come. As his name reached the upper limits of the Foundation stationery, might he be eased off the tougher assignments? Goodwill missions to such modest campus settings were the duty of junior officers or advisers *ex officio*. Yet his calendar was always full. Next week he would be back in West Africa, check the program investigating the managerial impact of transnational corporations. The poster informed him that he was an hour early. An hour of Hans' time is costly.

No one about, he read notices of career opportunities for specialized skills, workaday jobs a good distance from entrepreneurial. Later, he would tell me he'd thought to speak to the students about his recent travels in Africa, bring them up to date on the poverty problem—call the selfish man, *homo economicus*, into account. What models do we press upon the post-colonial world with our aid, material goods versus quality of life? That sort of thing. What cultures lie beyond the extended instructional reach? This lecture played well in small liberal arts colleges, but Hans had little knowledge of my students, decent kids aiming to enter a world of commerce more parochial than global. His distinction between patronage and the spirit of contemporary philanthropy would mean little to them. He looped back to the Elizabethan Poor Laws, the outset of social responsibility in the West, networking, for it was always a trustee of the Foundation who pressed him to visit elite venues where a son or daughter . . . Why would students at this blue collar school receive the Foundation's lofty agenda, the support of good causes in hopes that the state, if there exists a responsible state, will take on population control, the gas line, clean water? Money laid out for distant, unpredictable profits.

Eerie, the empty hallway, scuffed walls of institutional cream, many doors, shadowy figures moving behind frosted glass in a dumb show. Gruen succumbed to panic, the sudden divestment of his purpose, of himself as the rosy pretender on the poster. For a mere five minutes out of time, his precious time, he loitered on the stained industrial carpet. In a disturbing projection not new to him, he saw himself apart, as though on a screen. Out-of-body, the spiritual fakirs call it, as though his lethargy in the blasting steam heat of this deserted passage was a spell cast on another Hans Gruen, a boy dead to all feeling, hiding in the dark, a scene that faded quickly as in a movie land dissolve. Later, he would tell me that lost memory was like capital never recovered.

But on the day of this misadventure at our humble campus, his hosts came upon him with elaborate apologies. Hans returned to the reality he was cast in. Inaccurately introduced: his years at the World Bank overlapping his run at UNESCO. A conference table, no students. Apparently he was to hold forth for the edification of the faculty and their colleagues at neighboring institutions. The young scholar in Trotsky beard and glasses who muddled the introduction had cribbed "Total Networking in the blah, blah, blah" from the annual report of the Foundation. Hans so blind to home grown pomposity, he hadn't recalled the invention of an illustrated page on which liberating computer screens circled a classroom of sub-Saharan students (many of them now dead of starvation). I sat doodling at the far end of the conference table between two women sociologists. Disguised in a floppy black sweater that swallowed me up, Gruen sensed I didn't belong, a kid too wise for my years, smiling at my colleague's tedious bid for his day in the sun as darkness fell on the obscure campus. I worried the spikes of my elfin hair. *If you would only soften, wash and curl, Marie Claude* . . . Doodling at the conference table, I was bored, bored as Hans Gruen had been the previous weekend watching the pre-game show to the Super Bowl in a hotel room, popping a can of beer from the hospitality bar.

You'd like us to move on to the Hyatt, to the neutral bed hastily rented?

But Hans first set eyes on your daughter in a classroom where he scrapped his encouraging talk for privileged youngsters to instruct needy academics on *valid technologies replicable across multiple constituencies*, his words airy as bubbles stretched thin. *Let us take African initiatives, Zimbabwe. Let us take free markets as opposed to an agriculture of protectionism. Let us take the erosion of GATT by the EU deflationary cycle.* Gruen had an easy sell with this crowd, delivering applied economics, fancy pants experiments in hope more uncertain than the answers to the weekly quiz I give my classes. Now he directed his words to the little woman in black with the wry smile. I wasn't buying.

The Hyatt?

First the dull reception where Hans Gruen caught my name with the French spin on *Montour* I was trained to. He would have caught at any favor.

"Montour?"

He had known my father, of course. In Brussels at a NATO conference? Perhaps earlier? The Paris years. In any case the honored guest escaped the wine and cheese post-mortems with me, not rudely, for didn't we know how to duck out? Diplomacy in our bloodlines. And the networking left behind, when it came down to it, was in-house academic, career opportunities in the tristate area, a limited constituency.

In the Hyatt lounge we were blest, the cocktail hour over, dying refrain of a Cole Porter tune. The plump old maestro of the piano bar bursting the seams of his tux bid farewell to the regulars, a nightly confraternity of businessmen and minor mafiosi who control waste disposal in Newark. Later, Gruen would say he was thankful that he had not, as was his custom, requested a driver, that he'd tooled himself through the Holland Tunnel to come upon the humbling occasion of this lecture.

He knew the greased palm of the doorman, the official car parked outside the Ritz, Hassler Medici—name your philanderer's Plaza—the chauffeur napping through a lengthy assignation. Knew of, for Hans had been a fairly good boy, no frivolous flings. His single passion for a courageous journalist was not steamy enough to unglue him from wife and kids, though his nobility pleased neither woman. The strong minded journalist moved on to her Pulitzer. His wife, chin up, wounded eyes, did not conceal the scourge of her forgiveness.

This little piggy cried wee, wee, wee. . . . I can't count my lovers on fingers and toes, adolescence extending well into my twenties, years in which I competed with you—Molly always fairest of them all, Marie Claude a mere crack in the mirror. In Washington, Cambridge, New York, I lay deathlike on the analyst's couch, the spell broken at last by the mercy of your decline. Having mercy, I cut off the fruitless game, the blood sport between us. As though switching electric currents with one of the clever transformers you traveled with to blow-dry your golden hair, I flipped from body to mind. Making up for lost time, as though I could erase the cluttered pages of my passport, I consumed the history of the country I did not grow up in. Painful to Molly Montour that her bookish girl was hard at her studies, dry as a pod at thirty, yet as the end came I was teary and kind. *Ever so kind,* that was your compliment to me. As we endured the last weeks of kindness, you gave up on the beauty tips, remedies for my dull brown hair and spare figure. The years have ticked by. In my concealing sweaters I'm boy-girl strutting in tights and Shakespearean jerkin, the disguise unconvincing, confusing my colleagues studiously hip to all sexual variations. What is it they should know about this woman of forty?

Night of the encounter?

We slipped in and out of character, the visiting dignitary and the schoolmarm negotiating the night. First dispensing with Jack Montour, his Cold War frolics at the embassy in Paris. We spoke of my father as if he were dead. He is in Chevy Chase, a condominium within the beltway. On a clear day he can see the Pentagon, the upper floor of Defense in which he was last briefed. Jack wears his British blazer, club tie (St. Elmo's) for cocktails and a few rubbers of bridge after dinner with the old crew from State (those still intact). Light patter about the treats given up. No longer brandy and soda, the nightcap you surely remember. He drives the swirling cloverleafs home at a decent hour, the signs for Dulles reminding him that there will be no further arrival for orientation, no departure to the next post. My father sits up late in his study, propped in the wing chair bought at auction in Montreal during a painful transition. You had taken off to New York with me in tow— Marie Claude your hostage, your pawn. He bid too much for the Chippendale chair which proved to be fake. Each night Jack Montour falls asleep in its worn comfort perusing *Foreign Affairs* or the *Statesman's Yearbook* as though he is still in the game.

The Hyatt, a deserted lounge, I must get on with it. TV muted, graceful three points from downtown—fourth quarter, clock running, the bartender hoping the old lech will score, old goat buying drinks for a college girl.

Mocking my father, I *didn't give a fig* for his precious protocol, cookie pusher diplomacy. "Such a pooh-bah, wasn't he?"

"Powerless really. Jacques Montour was a Company Man."

"Jack. He was plain Jack. He came off a potato farm in Maine." Enough said: why make a point that he went to college on the GI Bill, dirt poor Catholic boy converted to elegant living.

"Sworn to affairs of State," Gruen said.

"Some of them dubious."

About teen time in Panama, when you shipped me to the boarding school in Geneva, I discovered that many of my father's dispatches fed no policy as to trade restrictions. On home leave in D.C., I presumed that even his talks to Rotary Clubs were bogus. Second Secretary, Chargé d'Affaires, Minister of Trade—titles on his calling cards were half true. My daddy was a spy, wholly true in the dim confessional light of the cocktail lounge far from academic toughies jostling for position. Yet, remembering your indiscretions, I was cautious, did not review my father's career with this intimate stranger who toyed with the ring on my finger. Moll, in your cups, you could scare the striped pants off plain Jack with a wink, a whisper of disclosure.

I fluffed my feathers, preened in the smoky grey mirrors. "So what the hell was I doing there today? I know nothing about monies shuffled from player to player in your global shell game, no more than I read in the papers."

Hans asked what I did know.

"Dowries," I said, "cows, fields, barrels of rum and guana."

What a seduction!

Shit—the droppings scraped from the dovecote, highly valued in the marriage portion, but that was in France, a footnote picked up from my father. Early American dowries, you will understand my need for specialization, I said, in the careerist plot I pick over, a dusty half-acre in the light of your global enterprise, but mine, my own back yard, so to speak. And I spun my yarn as an enchantment, a story got out of musty church basements, flaking town records. I had enchanted myself with the bitter romance of the hope chest, its quilts and embroidered finery, girls hoping, hoping that their handiwork would elevate them to a lifetime of domestic chores. There was bite to the lecture spilling from my mouth pursed tight as a rosebud, demanding that he listen. And Hans Gruen listened to me; after all, I'd half listened to his gloss on the economics of inequality, and he thought me a pretty imp when blessed with belief in my subject—a dusty corner of history, it seemed to him— the privileges and restraints of the colonial marriage settlement.

The contractual, I said, the list of *chattels personal*—goods, plate, money, real estate—that determined a woman's status. Take the case of Eliza Tibbs, take Eliza, a schoolmistress like myself, her refusal to sign over her brick dwelling-house to the widower Jonathan Gee. But Gruen wanted to take Claude Montour, wondering what he might find hidden under the voluminous turtleneck sweater that cupped the delicate chin, held my thin neck in a vise. Lightly, he touched my thigh under the table.

"Eliza Tibbs knew her Latin." I was wistful, longing for Hans Gruen to take note of my wavering independence, my thin hand with blunt boyish nails groping for his. "Eliza knew her Greek, not that anyone cares."

If this was my idea of sweet talk, he'd never be good at it.

"Don't be coy," he said, "it doesn't become you."

I sipped at the drink I'd forgotten. "Am I one more score on the great man's rounds?"

"No," Gruen said, "that wouldn't be true."

At long last, the key to the room. Now close the curtain as far as my mother is concerned. Her concern would be with strategies, the heart primed, all too ready. I must go it alone without her prompting or faint praise running in my head. At long last I lay naked on the neutral bed waiting. *Come, come here.* The yearning in my voice out of practice. I beckoned Hans back to the life of his body, but he was ridiculous, fumbling with his pants like a boy. I laughed, held out my arms to him, and he was amazed at the pelts of unshaven hair, thick as my bush. *Here*, I said again, grasping his smooth white hair, drawing his mouth to one small breast, then the other, wanting him to taste my hard pink nipples in the dark, then guiding him down my taut belly. I was greedy for his arousal. Often Hans Gruen wondered what had become of him as a man, but now he was easy. He had asked me what I knew and I dodged him with domestic economies, my Miss Tibbs from the archives. He could not have imagined my specialization in lust, that I was an old hand at this bedtime story. And I could not believe his wariness, a Boy Scout earning his merit badge after all his travels in the miserable world.

In the weeks that followed there were disclosures—that doubling of himself in the empty corridor of the administration building, his paralysis of emotion. Such incidents came upon him as visions of himself enacting the dread moment, but devoid of feeling. In Helsinki: whipping his scalded flesh with birch branches in the cold, blood rising as he watched a woman's delight in this healing prosecution, observing her pluck even as she turned from him, walked naked across the simulated tundra, ending their long affair. He thought now of that journalist who dumped him in the spa of a first-class hotel, of their encounters in one city or another when time allowed. He had been cautious, unable to ruin himself for the love of her. Connecticut: in this state of detachment numb to the melancholy bedroom when the closet was cleared of his dead wife's clothes, the girlish tennis outfits, proper suits and matronly gowns which so defined her. Stranger still, the Situation Room: the aura of doom—his bright young face begging for recognition as he spelled out to Lyndon Johnson the budgetary pit of escalation in Southeast Asia. Each place, public or private, was revealed in all its humbling details. Each failure of his sorrow evoked a dim sanctuary in which a boy, Hans, hid from the light of day. He felt cheated, for always, as the memory was about to surface—the memory that would make him whole, not a spectator of his absent emotions—the scene faded.

I told Hans Gruen as much as was good for us of my career as a party girl, a troubled past which seemed ordinary in the telling, more ordinary than my solitary life in the archives. Though I had sworn to keep to my story, I could not leave my mother out, recalling the bright glimmer in her eyes at a likely prospect and the inevitable shadows of regret, how Molly's great love was being in love, an endless affair. So—neither of us in the dark. Hopeful.

Given that hope, we contracted, high on the discovery of each other—distant dignitary who fell through the Holland Tunnel to wonders in New Jersey, uptight teacher once reckless in the heart's acrobatics—within the weeks that followed we contracted to wed: his last go at love; my sensible shoes kicked off for the pinch of a glass slipper. Well, that takes us far beyond the Hyatt, settles us in. Might as well publish the banns. But we will be married by a justice of the peace, if we marry at all.

I'm waiting for Hans who may not turn up, may abandon the project. As though, in Foundation speak, Gruen sees our romance as development disaster. Overreach of my entrepreneurial.

Never. Not for a single moment did I project long-term designs on

Hans Gruen with my rap on Eliza's control of every petticoat and pound sterling upon marriage to Jonathan Gee. So many widowers in need of a wife, that was the simple truth, the death rate of women in childbirth horrendous. Not advertising myself as a likely prospect, such calculations out of the question. On that threatening Winter night, I had planned to slip away to my snug apartment, correct papers, my students' parroting of the week's lesson. But the weather held and I was in for it, the fancy guest lecture, the lecturer bewildered by his audience. My colleagues not in his league, nor was I, Claude Montour hiding behind the skirts of Eliza, her quaint feminist narrative with subtext of rebellion. In the morning—

After the complimentary breakfast, we deserted the love nest. Snow during the night, the gas stations and convenience store, the ramp leading up to the Jersey Turnpike—all fresh and silent. We dug out Gruen's car, silly the both of us, like kids awarded a day off from school. The whole world pure, soiled only by our footprints, as though we were the first man and woman to ever misbehave. Sinners in the eyes of an angry God? For pity's sake, we were two unfortunate souls who won the lottery. A roll in the hay, bundling, a month of bangs. More than a month. More. April, mid-April, Spring vacation and I have returned to the gritty town to attend to my business—the lawyer, Spero, probate. Returned to my house.

Hans had said: "I want you out of here."

My trashed house. Did you think for a moment it wasn't trashed? That on our first tour we had not noted along with lovely Arts and Crafts, neat details of molding and fenestration, the stained mattresses on the floor spewing kapok, velvet sofa in the parlor knifed, the kitchen implement still implanted in the victim? Sharp ammonia stink of cat everywhere, strays who bedded down in the initialed sheets of the linen closet, in the frayed tea towels of the butler's pantry, in the cozy litter of papers in the library—oh, doesn't the library, which I revisit each passing day, bring on the tears as it had when we first viewed the war zone of my inheritance—pages ripped from the Waverley Novels, from old Latin texts with notes scribbled in the margins (*Thisbe shy, love made her bold*), broken spines of the local writers, Melville and Hawthorne, the great composers' grey wigs stained with the bloody binding of *Compton's Musical Encyclopedia*, copyright 1937. To what purpose cigarette burns in the *OED*, as though to torture words, set them blubbering for mercy. I cried over so much spilt ink. A crime that I would never know who read these stories, who hunted for definitions. Certainly not Molly whose packets of mysteries and French *Vogue* were forwarded in the diplomatic post to wherever in the world. But when I ascended to the turret with Hans, we discovered only the sewing room scraps, *Life* neatly stacked, the skeletal remains of a houseplant upright in its pot. All was orderly here, magically preserved.

Though it was simply more likely that the vandals had not braved the last flight of stairs, the dark winding passage that led up from the kitchen where the plates and saucers were cruelly shattered.

"Every scrap in place, the castle where time stopped."

"Come off it, my dear!"

I deserved his gentle belittling, for couldn't I see the gas tanks squatting beside the trailers, the patch of back yard, the salacious swag of red curtain in the nail salon, see that this mini-rotunda, pitiful Parthenon cracked open to the elements, this tacky excuse for a tower was too scary, off limits, removed from the ordinary rooms below that were all too available for crashing, boozing, screwing, doping, whatever the creeps saw fit in their despoiling of a rich man's house? Yet each night I sleep here, in this matter unfaithful to my lover. Here in the chill of damp Spring nights, I stretch out in the Morris chair as though in a safe haven. Not safe. *Children with matches.* This big tinder box would go up in glorious flames.

The little door to the tower stuck when first tried. Then it came back to me, the trick of pulling up on the latch. *Stoop down,* I said, as the door creaked open on its hinges. We crouched like sneak thieves. Hans brushed the cobwebs from his pristine work shirt. Looking down from the tower, I had remembered the wicked child, Marie Claude, the night of her escape, running off through the forest. This was my first secret.

And I have not told my father about Gruen, could not bear his blustery satisfaction. I speak to him of my work, where we leave off in our telephone call each week.

"How's Miss Tibbs?" Jack takes a respectful interest in his daughter's career, such a turn from her ill spent youth, this busying herself with each baby step of promotion, earning a pittance.

"Eliza, delightful as always. Her signature changes, fat swirling capitals after she ties up with Jonathan Gee."

But I do not speak of Hans Gruen, the Winter months of our considerate passion, the care we take with each other in bed, the days of his full calendar in which I continued my classes and did not abandon my scholarly project, at this stage a reckoning with my notes on a black female under contract for seven years to Eliza Tibbs (maiden schoolteacher, aged seventeen). An indentured servant not unusual, but I'm troubled by this listing of human property. The historian is happier with a strict accounting of paraphernalia:

> *a churn, washtub, two pails, sauspan, peper pot, Looking Glass, fleshfork, one boughten Bed-Tick Bolster & Pillows containing 9 yds at 65s & 3yds @ 55s pr yard. all L38-17-6 &c and about 42lb of Choice feathers put therein @ 45s/pr lb.*

All these goods given to Eliza by her late father as well as the gift of her learning, for she listed the flowers in her garden according to the classifications of Linnaeus, though no name or age is given for the black female. Still so much to be learned if I take Eliza (calling her by her first name always) beyond a paper to be delivered at a sectarian conference, a monograph on one bright exception to the rules of coverture, this girl who would not assign her goods to Jonathan Gee (widower, aged thirty-three, father of two children), would not give over so much as a saucepan to him at the publishing of their banns. If I examine every scrap of evidence I believe I will find the name and age of the black woman who Eliza taught to read, to do sums. I imagine the servant planting bee balm, which the books say brought the hummingbird, and that she cured the healing roots of tansy, showed Eliza how to fold lavender in with her linens. Though Eliza had little use for fancywork, I suppose she instructed her friend in the use of the needle and in all manner of Berlin and Dresden embroidery, in transparent and filigree painting on glass. I reject a dark figure bent over washtub or churn, sleeping on a straw pallet, poking the fire before dawn while Eliza and Jonathan dream on in choice feathers. What a story I might tell of the servant's achievements, of her mistress awarding the black woman her "freedom dues" long before the end of the contract. Escapist romance, for I'm well aware that I'm testing my man like that girl (b. 1745) who would not sign over her coin silver teaspoons or the female who was her rightful property. Testing Hans to take me as I am.

Claude Montour with my spoiled goods.

True about Eliza's bold signature, but it's a cover, a way of not saying to my father—Hans Gruen is my intended. *Intended?* A carefully chosen word that would send Molly into hoots of laughter.

Hans has confessed to his sons with unnatural lightness that he is "seeing someone." A lying phrase, but how to put it? An earnest young woman who blossoms in the bedroom. The Gruen boys conceal their embarrassment, never having countered the intentions of their illustrious dad. They are in mergers and acquisitions, micro-economics in their father's grand schemes for a profit-sharing world. A tricky season both global and domestic. They presume it's a glitch, this "someone" will pass.

Might as well be having an affair.

No, we are sworn to each other. We have declared our intentions.

ECONOMY

Spring vacation. I came back to settle my affairs. The will was to be read in the lawyer's office. The will of Lillian Baird *in accordance with the wishes of her guardian, the predeceased Rose Zak.*

"Zak! Zak!"

Chris Sheedy, a new-minted lawyer, had the quick answer, like my one bright student, the kid way ahead of the pack in U.S. History to the Civil War, "Her legal name, Rose Zak. The sister, *being of unsound mind* . . ."

"Eccentrics!" I thumped Sheedy's desk, would not listen to this assault on two foolish ladies who pulled the shades not to see what I knew as a child, that the neighborhood had gone down long ago, that the two-family houses built in the Twenties were cheap rents, lived in by the workers at GE, by the crew rolling out newsprint down at the mill. Rose Zak was a hoax, a trick played on me from the grave by my mother.

"Somewhat intrusive"—Sheedy, shifting papers on an elephantine oak desk, ducked my rage—"my handing the keys over to Mrs. Spero."

"I want to sell the damn place."

"I should think so."

"Why? Why would you think so?"

"Listen, we don't have much business in that part of town. These women, your aunts? Some old connection with the head of the firm."

"The head of the firm?"

"Passed on." A touch of solemnity here. "I'm the new boy, cleaning up loose ends of his practice. See," Chris Sheedy easing into the personal, "I didn't hanker after the big firm, the big city." Real estate law, his area of expertise, old towns coming up for the tourist trade, converted factories on the Housatonic a nice start—your espresso bars, local crafts, discount outlets. A cabaret, *Time and Again*, opened last Summer in the paper mill. Flustered by his promotional line, he suddenly Xed one of the papers I must sign, sign for the shambles, now mine.

"It's not that bad," I said, "the big city. Whole neighborhoods free of the tourist trade, like the part of town where you don't do business."

With an amateurish clearing of throat, Sheedy explained there was a lien on the property. Several years the old girl, Lillian Baird that would be, had not paid the taxes, being, as it were, *non compos*. By way of apology for the slight misfortune of back taxes—not the dark secret of Rose Zak or the pitiful tale of Lily—he offered his client lunch, steering me through a brick alley to a small square with a dry fountain. A few civic buildings hold their own with dignity against the brazen façade of an ubiquitous discount drug, a shabby five-and-dime, the gutted department store. In a handsome commercial structure, The Till, a nifty café: terrazzo floors, marble pillars supporting an arched ceiling, all newly refurbished, like my lawyer dolled up in his new suit and Polo tie. He's soft, chunky but not a jock. I figure hours of sports on TV, no runs along the river.

Again Chris Sheedy, eager and awkward, pleasant and rude, called to mind the shuffling posture of my one student engaged in an anxious love affair with historical documents merely cited in the easy-read textbook. Rashid, a boy whose body has filled out, his black hair already receding. He comes, oh so politely, to the lady professor's office with the sources—sermons, journals, letters—and cannot contain his outrage, as though it's last night's local news—Narraganset children held hostages by the New England Federation, young male Mohawks shipped to Bermuda, delivered into slavery. I spend hours with this bright boy reading Governor Bradford's *History of Plymouth Plantation* though the course skips on, high-dee-ho, to Salem Witch Trials, French and Indian Wars. After Spring break full speed ahead to the eve of the Revolution, by May we must get to the Civil War. Rashid will be stuck in the "Articles of Agreement with the Niantics," coming by with his amazing discoveries of a harsh Christian state. I looked up his application to the college: Muslim, born in Jersey City. Last week he scheduled his usual appointment, but did not come gently knocking at my door. I wanted to ask where his people came from, what Mem Sahibs—British, French—

trouble his mind. So rare that a student poked beyond easy assimilation to the dominant culture. I waited, waited for Rashid until there was nothing to do but wonder at my disappointment.

Lord, I'm the prim teacher to these boys, Chris Sheedy talking on at me, how he's missing law school, moot court, arguing the complicated appeals, when all he'll be up to for some time is grunt work—closings, petty claims, wills. Politics, he thinks politics in a town like this, in a few years run for City Council, though first you get married.

"To run for City Council?"

"Hey, only kidding."

The restaurant mostly empty, a few tables with small town professionals, fussy Italian food. I thought of the honest meal with Hans cooked by the old Germans. Listening to the prospects that lay ahead for my young lawyer, I thought, too, of Rose Zak, impossible to think of her as other than the great mouse, to imagine her apart from Lily. Yet cruel, whoever was to blame, discarding her history. Whoever—Molly. And why did she never tell me that Lily was simple? My mother, their little sister who beat them both in death.

Sheedy was in the Governor's Mansion by the time the dessert menus came. I flipped to see the kiwi sherbet, the cappuccino cheese cake I would not order. On the menu a photo in sentimental rotogravure of the large room in which we sat: *Baird Bank and Trust, 1895, built in the neoclassical style of local granite and Vermont marble. The handsome central vault with Italianate detail* . . . and so forth, a bit of civic lore for the tourist trade and for the woman whose great grandfather built this temple of local commerce. Across the vast room, the polished gears and shafts of a massive safe were set up on a plinth like a futuristic sculpture, a still shot from *Metropolis*. Sheedy ordered his *dolce*. His broad body will run to fat. When he campaigns for State Senate, his wife will make him turn down the goodies.

I wanted to ask how can you plan it all—wife, 2.4 children, politics. Just politics, not even a party. A moderate, fearful of public confrontation. When it was my turn in the do-si-do talk, I did not suggest we were idling in the hallowed hall of my family's bank. I spoke of my work in the archives, of Eliza Tibbs who would not assign her worldly goods to the widower Jonathan Gee. How few women in New England, I said, exercised a degree of independence, but listing Eliza's comfortable dwelling-house of brick, her adjoining lots and silver plate, I noted Chris Sheedy faking attention. The flicker of eyelids, forward thrust of the chin seen when my students doze through my lecture.

"A woman of property like myself, an instructor of the young." Should I have said that like Eliza, I'm marrying my widower? That Hans is neither Jonathan Gee to be brought into line, nor a boy out of a fairy tale with silver skates, a magic ring. He is a man who instructs financial ministers, confronts dictators of rogue nations, who hankers after the big cities—Paris, London, D.C. That he's old enough to be Sheedy's father, not my father. And that we need each other's bodies. I will give him my youth, what's left of it. What use flogging the kid lawyer? Sunlight streaked through arched windows, warmed the veined marble pillars. The Till was a chapel—user-friendly—only the faint clatter of plates being cleared. A small white mist hovered over the teller's cage at the end of the espresso bar like a blank thought cloud, a clean page to write on. *I will not give up my house. The spook house is mine.* I inscribe these words to pay back my mother for silence. For silence read lies. I thought I had done with her, had played out my perversity, that we drew back to kindness.

"Eliza wore galoshes," I said, "the streets were not paved. What a mess in the Spring. Listed in the dowry: *galoshes, two pairs with wooden soles and leather strapping.*"

"Interesting," Sheedy said.

"Very. It is very interesting." Looking to the rosettes in Banker Baird's Italianate ceiling, I saw they were perfectly replastered, regilded. I will not sell my house with a tower, library, solarium, *porte cochère*, the back stairs spiraling down to the kitchen.

"Call off Spero."

Sheedy splattered his tiramisù. "Hey there!"

"The back taxes? Give me the bad news."

Half my meager salary at the workaday college. The head of the firm, once powerful, now deceased, had stalled the posse, whoever reclaims property in this town.

"Politics," Chris Sheedy flashing his credit card, "same old story, *noblesse oblige*."

I did not correct, in teacherly fashion, his misuse of the phrase. No tax collector in Town Hall was obliged to let the bill run for the insolvent Bairds. My lawyer by default suggested the best move was default.

"I'll pay up, every nickel."

"Sorry for your troubles."

"So am I."

My windfall of troubles compounded. I never disclosed the unhappy news of the spook house to my father and still feared the swaggering pride in Jack Montour's acceptance of Gruen, as though I had come to my senses, come home to his world. Waiting for Hans, I can't imagine how to tell him I've heeled in, that this house with all its ruined paraphernalia, its blighted romance, will continue to be mine. A woman throwing good money after bad; perhaps he'll count me a negative return on his investment. For all his gift at negotiation, Hans can not get beyond "seeing someone," tell his sons he is a truly smitten man. White lies of omission. Molly the mortal trouble, my mother who never told me Lily with her dippy scarves was, to put it kindly, not all there. And that a man once loved, at least married, Rose. Rose Zak, poor woman. Exactly how poor?

VISITORS

The terrifying sights of the rooms below do not rule out Spring in the air. April—the promise of Easter lies ahead, bunnies and bright eggs, a plastic cross twined with lilies displayed with Lotto, six-packs, detergent in the window of the corner market where they once shopped each day,

Lily and Rose, as I remember, remember them carrying paper bags across the street to their grand house. Carless, confined, I now understand, by their poverty.

When the rain lets up, the neighborhood children spill off the school bus, puffy Winter jackets flying open. Little innocents and tawdry teens, all shipped away from Park Street. I presume *away* is a better world. The yellow brick public school I so desired, wanting to be an ordinary child with lunch box, milk money, a mother walking me to the schoolyard. That dear dowdy building boarded up, every window. Graffiti faded on those designated doors—BOYS, GIRLS. I envied the unknown girls, their bright parkas and slacks, the nifty sneakers. Hated the navy blue skirts, British brogans, the plaid robe and the prim convent nightie that I wore each morning in this house as I watched those kids go to school. Peeking out to the street life, life anywhere but the stale parlor. And when I was dressed, brushed, plaited, sent up to this room, I snapped up the dark linen shades to see the deserted street.

A boy stands in the doorway of Jimbo's Bakery, nestles a sack of doughnuts next to his heart, runs for his bike thrown in a puddle, varooms down *Daddy's Timber Trail*. A boy, not off on the yellow bus. Truant? The twitch of teacher in me, uncontrollable. I am hungry for my cruller, for my cup of pale coffee, for the few words—cheerful, guarded—with Jimbo. His withered flesh darker than his coffee. A curiosity these days at his counter, the woman living in the ghost house, driving in and out through the chain-link fence, the locks gone, long gone on all but the front door.

Jimbo clamps fist to stomach. "Love my cookin', it don't love me." Each day of the week: "You in the big house?"

"Yes."

"Doin' fine?"

"Fine."

"Miss Lil made my mamma's church hats."

This discovery is tremendous, but he remembers nothing more, not a sight of the parlor strewn with silk roses and ribbons. Jimbo's tale hearsay, hand-me-down history. His mother died when he was four. I'm left to imagine naked hats waiting for a sprig of flowers, veils, a plume.

On the day the letter arrived at the history department, my campus address, announcing my right to the property of Lillian Baird, I noticed the green tips pushing up by the war memorial to students dead in two wars, for the first time marveled at swollen buds on the lone magnolia. Walking in Central Park, Hans had shown me the tufts of garlic grass, the heads of early daffodils in their papery cauls. The natural world of my country was foreign to me. I had moved about, post to post. In Turkey, Jack nurtured lemons in a pot. Spritzing their shiny leaves, he wore gloves on the hands that once forked into the earth for his family's spuds. In Bogotá, Molly instructed the gardeners to do their thing. My father drove us to view velds, savannas, pampas and once a rain forest that lay far from the embassy in Panama City where Spring was a non-season. I do remember his complaint that the cherry trees blossomed so late in Montreal. Paris—on the first balmy days in the Bois, I rode under ancient trees I could not name. Fleeing the disarray of my parents' marriage, I cared only to control my horse, his canter and trot that might set me free. Though once a New England Spring assaulted me with all its natural terrors. On that clear cold night I heard every twig snap, rabbit in the brush and the call of peepers. The night I ran from this house into the dark woods, my sturdy shoes sucked into the swampy path underfoot, heart thumping with fear at the rustle of new leaves overhead. My great secret of that night? Not just another cop story.

Cop story, not to be confused with the hoopla of last night's sirens, a gaggle of patrol cars. Nine, ten o'clock—I ran down all those stairs from the turret to say I was legit.

"My house, O.K.?"

From the rotten front porch, proclaiming to the assembled crowd—neighbors, my neighbors huddling in bathrobes and blankets against the cold, an outraged mother clutching a baby to her breast in fear. No reason to fear a lone woman in her house, but one of them had turned me in, had reported the dangerous flicker of my candlelight in the windows. The men in blue, bored with domestic disturbance, barroom rumbles, were costumed in bullet proof vests for a shootout.

Turning to the old cop in charge, "I belong here." Unsettling that even this grizzled man had no memory of the Bairds. Of their *position* popped into my head—what a word.

"Two harmless old ladies?" I prompted Captain Abriola in a bit of local history.

No recall of Lily or Rose. I belonged to a vanished tribe, a people lost to the culture of Park Street with no park, no trees. He called his boys off. Their disappointment and the angry dismay of my neighbors as they drifted back to more satisfying television dramas. Abriola wrote a number to call.

"My house has no phone."

"Girl, you best move to the motel out of town while you settle your business."

I'd lost track of my business and had a wizard of a cell phone in my car on which I spoke to Gruen's secretary, tracking his movements in Africa. Now I reckon this is the day on which he must come, if he comes. Testing, my old habit. Hans Gruen must drive right up to the door in the vintage Mercedes, must climb the stairs to find me moping, the ping of water seeping though the queer conical ceiling and then, then he must take me home. If he comes, he must come in at the end. But isn't that the way children dictate who will enter and when exit, who must live on in their stories?

Cop story, the real thing. Dusk then, as it is now, though with the woods gone the sun doesn't flare in brilliant flashes through the trees. A bloody red streak is swiped across the sky, background for the strip mall and for the spur to the shopping plaza with fast food that will soon put Jimbo out of business.

When, as a child, I ran into the woods, the day's dying enchanted me as in a book of tales, folktales I read to myself in a particular book that traveled with my white bed and china reading lamp from post to post. Billeted with Lily and Rose, I should have been gobbling preteen series—spunky girls with their horses, dogs, best friends—stories which preach simple lessons of loyalty, endurance, the groundwork for love. My book that I would not outgrow was dear to me, its apple green cover of durable cloth, its gilt lettering traced endlessly with my finger. *Tales of Olden Times* was a favor dealt out at an official Washington Christmas party celebrated in the ballroom of a glitzy hotel. As I ripped the wrapping, I knew the gift was meant for an older child. The girls my age were tearing into dolls of many nations. I had been distracted, watching Molly vamp a plump fellow with a round head smooth as a honeydew melon—who turned out to be an Under Secretary of State. He had stopped by, the way those heavies stop by at a party, and I dipped into a Santa sack meant for grown girls with pierced ears, real stockings.

I had just learned to read but the words in these tales were beyond me, so I looked long at the pictures and made up stories of the children in greasy brown rags, of children in richly embroidered costumes dancing round and around in a pretty village square. My stories were always of children, the parents—whether kings or farmers, queens or hungry travelers—were left out. The best picture—a cherubic girl sleeping in the woods, her curly head cradled by a stone that lay to the side of a path littered with twigs and leaves. The skeletal limbs of barren trees were no protection, no comfort. Shadows in the foreground where one boot had fallen off in her flight, poor flap-soled boot, poor torn stocking. I had no doubt it was cold, the damp cold that seeped through my snowsuit when the Sisters in Montreal let us sled downhill at the convent. But in the background the glowing end of day. Some woodland creature of Disney perfection would nuzzle this child awake, lead her through the starry night toward safety. Safety was a rustic cottage with warm light in the windows. At times the door would be half open to welcome me. Then I could see the table with bread and a peasant's hunk of yellow cheese on a white plate with a blue rim. I had no idea who waited in that humble house, but I knew that I was hungry.

By the time Molly left me with the witches—Aunt Lily, Aunt Rose—
I had read Perrault's fairy tales, not fully aware of their arresting sexual
violence, their ambiguous morals fit for a royal court. I understood that
my own story ended in the middle, cut off before a just or happy ending. Still, I believe it was that picture of the sleeping girl, blessedly
alone, of sunset burning through the woods that sent me down the
steep back stairs, out through the solarium over shards of broken glass
and pots. I ran from the queer old sisters, past a dirty puddle once their
fish pond, straight into the woods.

At first I found my way to a clearing, paths leading from it this way
and that. I tried one that came to a swampy end in the fading light and
turned back to find a second path that led once again to the clearing
where peepers screeched at my invasion of their amphibian world.
Now that it was night, I saw the white bark of the birches. Though there
were many trees, I knew only birches and pines. Trying another path, a
fallen trunk blocked my way, its thick brown bark scratched my legs,
tore at my skirt, a plaid skirt left over from the convent I would no
longer attend. The moon dove in and out of the clouds and in a flicker
of light I discovered a bench, so I would not have to lie upon the cold
ground like the girl in my story. I could not have weighed much, but its
rotted arms and legs gave way as though it had balanced there for years
waiting to trick me. All tricks—that maze of woodland paths senseless
as a board game in which fate is determined by a throw of the dice.

Fear of an owl's hoot? Surely he hooted at me, would devour me on
the spot. Now, in this season when I am preparing Thoreau for the
classroom, I think that clever woodsman was right—hope had been
abandoned in the owl's melancholy *hoo hoo hoo*. But in that dark moment I cursed Molly, whatever frivolity she was up to in New York. *Sa-
lope.* At the convent I had learned to curse in two languages, and I
cursed my father, his crooked smile like a healed cut across his compli-
ant face. In Canada, he had seen us off at the airport. We would not be
with him again till Paris. He spoke to us obliquely of important matters
that detained him in Montreal. Paris—his grand promotion. Too

worldly for my years, I understood his evasion as well as my parents' embrace. They held each other too long, too dearly at this parting. Silently crying out to my mother, *Mon cul*, not to reply to the owl's hoot, to the wind now batting the bare branches. *Merde*, I was lost in the woods. Way off on Park Street, I heard the plaintive honk of a horn. The woods had sloped down, down, and when I looked back I could no longer see a light in my tower. Pure shit. There would be no cuddly creature to rescue me in this forsaken place. I ran on till I found the cottage.

A hut. Through the one window patched with plastic, the faint glow of candle stubs.

What do I remember without embroidery, without imagining that night? A family—mother, father, two kids. The woman skeletal, an effigy in a hunter's checked shirt. The man fat, belly big as a beach ball riding his belt. Mr. and Mrs. Jack Sprat in reverse. He asked, rudely, what I wanted. I wanted, their unwelcome visitor, wanted nothing more than to get out of the dark and the cold. The magic cottage was one room. There they lived in the sweltering stink of a kerosene stove. The boy, nine or ten, more or less my age, flipped a jackknife into the wooden floor, perhaps to impress me with his show-off mumblety-peg game. The girl was pink-cheeked with a seraphim's ring of blond curls and I thought she could not belong here, that she was part of my foolish old tale.

"That's our Sissy," the woman said with a maternal smile, her teeth showing brown, several missing.

Sissy took me by the hand. She wore only a scrappy undershirt that rode up her rosy bum when she squatted to show me the bed she had made for her doll, a flat faced creature with orange nylon hair. After long silence the man asked where I came from.

"From the house, other side of the woods."

Then he lurched toward me and cursed, words never heard in the convent. He was, both were, father and mother, drunk as lords, my father's expression. They were not lords, not servants, not farmers—travelers I suppose on a long route of desperation. The man continued to curse, his face ruddy, swollen. I believe that he was once good looking, his big body athletic, and that the mother was a sweet thing in the fleeting manner of high school girls, but that is conjecture—no more reliable than one of those most-wanted portraits fabricated from a victim's inaccurate memory.

The mother and her children paid no mind to his ranting and I understood that I was not to fear him, to keep out of his way and play with Sissy. I did not ask if he would take me back to Lily and Rose. Then silence, his stumbling into the single chair, his meaty face sinking down nose-first on a kitchen table. His wife turned his head gently to the side and finger combed his thinning rusty hair.

"You hungry?" She dealt me saltines and warmed up tomato soup that sat in a pan on the stove—delicious. It was as though I belonged, a lost child in a lost family. The boy showed me how to flip the knife. I failed and failed until at last it cut swiftly into the rotted wooden planks and then he took it from me. Here and there the floorboards were worn through to the dirt the hut sat on. The boy was his father exactly—the vacant good looks, but no temper in his eyes, a deepset passivity, an acceptance of his addiction to the flinging knife. He had a long red scar on his wrist as though once, when distracted, he had missed with his weapon. One of the gaunt woman's hands sported the angry white blister of a burn. I was bloodied on my knees, one eye tearing, whipped by a bare branch. Only Sissy was apart from us—a perfect child, unmarked by the dangers of this woodland world.

"They will come for us," the mother's words rasped in a whiskey voice, not unkindly. I could not imagine Lily and Rose finding their way through the woods. One candle stub guttered, hissed good night.

"*Now I lay me?*" The mother's question to Sissy was no question at all. The child went at once to the cot, pulling me with her. Her trust in a stranger did not seem odd. I believe her life was full of strangers, that she had learned who to trust, who to fear. That's afterthought, not part of this story. We lay side by side with that naked plastic doll. *Down to sleep and if I die.* The child lisping the prayer with her mother. *My shole to keep.* The mother slurring her words. Cradled with the child who was perhaps three years old, I breathed the sweet-sour smell of her and felt her soft curls brush my chin and the warm trickle of her pee down my leg.

In *Tales of Olden Times,* the little girl who has fallen asleep in the woods lies with her brother. I had written the boy out. Now I heard the constant fling of the knife, its slice into dead wood. The moon, our only light, filtered through a cloud. The mother stood by the single window waiting. She did not look to her husband, simply waited for what would come next.

They came for us with searchlights, sirens and an eager wet-nosed hound straining at the leash. To my shame, that dog had sniffed my dirty underwear and socks which a huge cop dangled from his paw. We stood in a phalanx as though for a family photo.

"Kelso," the cop said.

"Mickey?" The father smiled in a besotted stupor.

"Yes, it's Mick." The cop slipped his gun back into its holster.

"Squatters," Aunt Rose said. She wore a long grey coat, a man's coat of another time. She was, as always, ashen. "Come, Marie Claude."

The first colorless light of dawn. I had no idea how long I was lost in the woods, how long Mr. and Mrs. Kelso had taken me in and cared for me. In the squad car, buckled into my seat belt, I turned to see the Kelsos herded off. They took the jackknife from the boy and for one fierce moment he howled. Sissy, decently covered with a blanket, had her doll.

The next day my scratches scabbed over. The gardener's shack was torn down.

"When we had gardeners . . ." Lily began brightly.

When the Bairds had gardeners, the little outbuilding in the woods was lived in from early planting and pruning in the Spring till the gardens were put to bed after the first frost. No more than a shack, not properly heated. Water must be fetched from a stream. The outhouse long gone. Now all was demolished. Firemen came to safely burn the dry timber.

"Peonies by the gazebo!"

Rose would have none of Lily's nonsense. For days she did not play the spinet, but sat with me over my schoolwork. We were into the future perfect—*elle aura prospéré, ils auront prospéré*—when she pulled her raveled cardigan about her. "Those children will be far better off in a good foster home." She spoke as though that lesson was in the workbook before us. Better off? I did not think they would prosper.

A fireman smelling of destruction, stood at the front door. We had not finished my French lesson. He said: "Those boards soaked with kerosene burnt like hellfire. It spread right into the woods. We got it under control."

"I thank you," Rose said. Lily was inconsolable.

Waiting for Hans, I have taken a trick path, nasty tale of olden times, little princess escapes from the tower. I had turned the Kelsos in, led the cops to them. At least the bloodhound was thrown a bone for a fine performance. Hans Gruen will be on the highway now, home from his attempt at economic intervention—prescriptions to end tribal wars that seem to be but are not of another historical time. Not costumed speculations as to the petticoats and nameless black servant of Eliza Tibbs. If Hans comes, he must drive right under my *porte cochère*. I suppose I must tell him at once that for the past few days, for no sensible reason, I think I will keep my ghost house. The best house, Molly said.

DADDY'S TIMBER TRAIL

Imagine Julian Baird kneeling to the first trilliums. At this turn in his path their purple trumpets opened for a short season under the umbrella of their grey green leaves natural to these woods. He had not placed them like his primroses for a random show of color—yellow, red, violet—surprising in the dark woods. Next week his primulas would flower. Next Fall he must gently pull their clumps apart, set them in a clearing, doubling, tripling the display. In Winter, he dreamed of a bench he would build to set among them, a rustic bench under a sugar maple that defied the white pines, spread its limbs as though planted on a front lawn for shade. One Spring, when the sap was running, Bro Baird slashed the trunk, inserted a hollow sumac twig as the Indians had for their sugaring. He hung a pail and one day, when it was full, threw the sap on the snow, scooped the sugary spill to eat like a child of another century. Up at the house they laughed at his sticky hands, the empty bucket—his wife and his father joining for once in their ridicule of the pioneer, though not his solemn daughters, Lily and Rose. In his office at the bank, he sketched the twig bench to be set in the clearing at the very heart of the woods not his. The woods were his father's, left for effect by the landscape architect who settled in Albany, a protegé of Frederick Law Olmsted.

When, as a boy, he was transported to this elaborate establishment far from their comfortable home on Elm Street with neighbors, sidewalks, the milkman and grocery boy, dog's bark and the cheery call of the postman as he came up the front walk, Julian Baird would not enter the wrought iron gate. He looked down the lonely dirt road and wanted to run back into town where some neighbor would take him in. He'd do chores, earn his keep, tutor the dumb Prescotts. Bro, as they called him, was top of his class. This vision of independence was fleeting. He would not be set free of his father's big house for years to come.

Bro, the younger brother of George Jr., was frail. He suffered a mild bout of TB, recovered in a chill Adirondacks sanitarium, but never lost the sunken chest that cradled his cough, the splotch of red painted on his cheeks by the disease. The good times he yearned for in town— pickup games of baseball and snap-the-whip—in truth, he was only a spectator, settled by his mother into a wicker chair on the porch, on the sidelines watching George Ulysses Baird Jr. wham a homer into the Bigelows' vegetable garden, watching Mrs. Bigelow come round the fence in her fresh apron never stained with cooking spills, baby mess. Glo-Glow Bigelow, her amber kiss-me-again eyes lingered on his big brother's body as she handed him the ball.

When, after his illness, Bro was allowed back to school, he watched his brother hoodwink the teachers. Stern Dr. Mallory smiled at George Jr.'s every prank. That young Baird was an American boy from the pages of *Collier's* magazine—tall, carved symmetrical features with the slightly effeminate mouth illustrators favored at the time. One dark lock escaped the oiled wavy hair. Ladykiller, glad-hander. Bro watched his brother please Papa with his insolence and went back to his books, his only sport. His mother rocked on the porch next to the sickly boy she named Julian, after a highly cultivated emperor of Rome—a staunch pagan, had she known it.

Transplanted to the sticks, mother and son longed for the sights and sounds of their lost neighborhood. Secure in his investment, Banker Baird proclaimed the town would come to him. But now the son he cared for, the one deserving of his magnificent grounds, was always in town with a fast set of sports. In the Irish barrooms. In the lobby of the drummers' hotel. To his mother's shame, his bike was seen daily in a certain yard after the kiddies were in school. Glo-Glow of the radiant hair (Mrs. Fanny Bigelow) came to the side door in her wrapper to greet him.

On Sundays, Julian accompanied his mother to the Congregational church, driven in the Locomobile by Gus, the German chauffeur, for all to see the shattered pride on Mrs. Baird's gentle face. At night, Julian, boning up on his Latin, heard his mother at the top of the house, the round room at the farthest remove from her duties. She had given the turret over to the dressmaker and paced through scraps of georgette and muslin, the soft materials she favored Summer and Winter for her gowns. Or he may not have heard his mother sobbing as she threw herself in the Morris chair, for the walls and ceilings of his father's house were thick plaster bound with horsehair; he may only have imagined her distress. This went on for some years, not the matter of Fanny Bigelow, but his brother's dissipation and his mother's sorrow, the years of Julian's high school studies, when he began to classify the ferns that no one cared to see in his father's woods. When he was sent across the hills to Amherst College, the professor of botany was stunned by Julian's knowledge of *dryopteri* in their many forms.

Dear Mother,

We are propagating the oak fern by both root cuttings and spores to test the strength of the offspring, child's play but great fun. I take more delight in my project with the wood anemone, attempting to alter by means of pollination all lavender specimens to white. I will not trouble you with the Latin name. It is the common windflower of Father's woods that blooms in April and disappears as though by magic, though science is never magic as we know.

Written from the turret, April 1917:

Dearest Julian,

The mills are investing in triple deckers out our way. Cheap rent for the workers. Your father is beholden to their business and cannot prevent it. Dr. Prentice and the Howes are building toward the river where the country club will be with golf course and pavilion. The club house will have a ballroom which will suit your brother fine. He has run off in the flivver to New York City. We have word of him by way of credit extended to him in a Broadway hotel. Your father has sent Gus to fetch him from these latest exploits. He will return as always, with an unhealthy complexion and aimless eyes. I am a great sinner, for now that we are in the war I pray Georgie will be conscripted to save his soul. Julian, I thank God they will not take you.

To console his mother, Bro wrote of his success in propagating a subspecies of *Adiantum pedantum*, maidenhair fern.

. . . but not the flirty strumpet of my father's woods, a tall slender lady with replenishing frond clusters, her pinnae red as ripe strawberries, shy, hiding her fruits under the fold of her pinnules. I like to think she will live outside in the cold underbrush of the Holyoke Range.

The irony not lost on Julian, that his brother was reckless with his seed while in the college hothouse he studied asexual plants. He did not believe that his family, forever rent in two, would be healed by the war, though his mother declared Georgie, so handsome in his puttees and overseas cap, a hero before his troop ship sailed out of Boston. And if his brother was suddenly manly, brave at the front, he knew she would dote on that son. Though he delighted in Ovid, all the poet's beasty half-humans, Julian, recording each careful step in the cross-pollination of his anemone, did not believe in such easy transformations.

Claude Montour is at a loss when she discovers these letters in the battered trunk with the Cunard and French Line stickers. Bro (Julian), George Jr., good son and bad, a tried-and-true script. *I am low in my mind with the war news,* that in the delicate hand of the mother, a fili-gree of words reminding Claude of the paper doilies that Lily served under teacups in this house, *so low I want to fly across the hills to you. How I long to see the lovely fern case in your room with its dewy world all safely enclosed.*

Claude is lost in this family agon of mother and sons, though she remembers her grandfather Julian Baird as a very old man seared by the desert sun, his face rutted like a pecan. Those trips to Arizona, a stale air-conditioned condo, watching nature programs on TV in the spare bookless den, a communal swimming pool, withered old people chattering in the sun, far from the snowbound convent in Montreal. Not the same year as Spring in the spook house. No, she was younger, still sucking her braids as her last molars came in and her grandfather led her by the hand, made Marie Claude look at the spidery pink flower sticking out of a cactus, this strange single flower among all his bristly plants in a plot of earth allotted to him. His voice was soft, dry as sand sifting in her tin pail, as he told her the name of the big cactus, that you could cut its flesh, drink its juice if you were lost in the desert. Daddy, his wife called him, his second wife. Yes, Claude patches together the missing pieces of family, the crumpled old man touching her finger to the sharp thorn of the ugly plant, and though her grandmother had passed on the smoky green eyes, the ravishing smile, she could never have been a beauty like Molly. Her grandparents seemed not to mind that she was there in Arizona splashing in the shallow end of the pool, their days all dedicated to pills and naps and skimpy suppers after the nightly news. Mostly, it was only her mother who flew to Arizona to visit her aging parents and came back with Indian dolls and turquoise trinkets. "Lord," Molly cried, "they do have a dull time of it."

The puzzle is not Daddy of the Timber Trail, father of Lily and Rose who did not blossom, nor of the late child begot of a happy marriage, the *bel esprit* who roamed the world. It is the story never told in the few letters, Bro, having moved through his senior year at Amherst, uselessly watching ferns dust the soil with their spores while his brother crawled through broken French earth turned to fluid clay, farmers' fields that spread from the rivers Georgie could not name, fields carefully irrigated by drains and ditches which collapsed under bombardment into a sea of mud and slime, every shell hole a pond. Julian, the scholar, would graduate with honors, winning his prizes that Spring, *I am to be awarded the Wilmont Prize in Botany, Mother, and the Belmore for my translations from the <u>Georgics</u>*. . . . Virgil's advice to farmers and heads of state, and thinking of the brother he could never better, he copied out this passage:

> *Hearts of heroes beating in small breasts,*
> *True to their cause, not victory*

Till the Huns turn in flight—
Passions—a handful of dust laid to rest . . .

To trim the soldier now beloved of his mother, cut him down to size, for the poet's heroes were nothing more than buzzing bees performing their role in the natural order.

Close the lid on that trunk with its stunted story. On poor Bro, who planned to study at Harvard with Oakes Ames, botanist extraordinaire, caretaker of the glass flowers taken from life models, more permanent than live specimens in Asa Gray's Museum of Vegetable Products, the famous glass flowers which draw over a hundred thousand tourists a year with their gift-shop beauty too true to be real, stunningly accurate in all details—780 species, 164 families as well as simulacra of lower plants or Cryptogramma, illustrating the complex life history of fungi, bryophytes and the ferns so loved by the dedicated student Julian Baird. Every stem, leaf, frond, pod, ovary the art of the Blaschkas, father and son, glassmakers of Dresden. Imagine their studio surviving that war, in Belgium no less, their fragile artifacts not blasted to hell, and for some years not shipped across the Atlantic to be bullied by U-boats and submarines, though now they are an endangered species, the powdered enamels of Rudolph Blaschkas' invention pulling from the surface to bare glass (even the *Anemone patens*, the pasqueflower of seasonal redemption), all endangered, the famous glass flowers of the Aga Institute at Harvard, reduced to kitsch by the wonders of time-release photography and the digital camera. Yet somehow endearing, this lost craft of flora replication, as an old man showing a child a cactus blooming in the desert. Bro Baird, a rare species, the gentle man who found his way out of the woods.

He married the first time foolishly, let his heart go cheap to a flirt from the old neighborhood selling Victory Bonds in the town square. The last summer of the war; he was three weeks out of college. She wanted to marry up and took Julian, the second-best Baird. Languidly touching his *Pteridium latiusculum* in the tropical heat of the solarium, pursing her mouth in a pout when he told her it was plain old Eastern bracken, that they could make a meal of it, truly, or burn it to ward off the devil, untruly. She must not believe that on Midsummer Eve it gave birth to one bright-blue flower with a fiery seed which, if you caught it, made you invisible. But they were flesh and blood in the hothouse, propagating before the False Armistice, before poor Bro fully understood that he must write to Professor Ames to say he would not be joining his team at the Institute, that he must work in his father's bank while awaiting the return of his brother from the war. He awaited Rose, a baby with long angular limbs, and in a few years the plump package, Lily. They rented a flat on the street where Julian was born, which did not suit his wife, nothing much did. She had captured a rich man's son, a dull boy given to books and botany. He would have none of the smart set his wife longed for and began to hack out trails in his father's woods, an amateur horticulturist plotting his loop-the-loops of pine needles and cedar bark. When at last they moved out to the Baird house, Frances Baird considered it a shabby inconvenient place, carpets worn to the nap, faded loose covers on the monumental sofas. She was to care for the old man whose wife and favored son were both dead. And where was the money? Her husband was selling off land, all those old fields and woodlots Banker Baird took as collateral from dirt-poor farmers, parcel after parcel almost given away to save their precious bank. Selling, selling off.

Julian Baird's wife did not catch him weeping in the woods as he listened to the reedy tremolo of the hermit thrush and the coarse racket of the pileated woodpecker, birds of the deep forest that would not survive in mere patches of a gentleman's wood. His wife had turned bitter, inward, yet in her way remained social, organizing bazaars and raffles for the Suppression of Commercialized Vice, a detention home for delinquent girls, a dance hall that would serve no liquor. Claude, searching through the litter in the library, can not imagine a Frances Baird who scolded young people in letters to the *Eagle* for running to the movies with their last dime. Her book plate in many tracts on moral improvement pictured Christ in the garden of Gethsemane praying the burden shall pass from him.

"They were a two day scandal." This much known by way of Molly, who delighted in her father marrying when the ground had not settled on his wife's grave, marrying her bog-Irish mother, his secretary at the bank. "You know," Molly said, "my mother taught herself shorthand when she worked in the mill." The sort of tale she loved to tell when the guests were particular as to class. "Not the looms, the paper mill. Not the stinkers where they make newsprint, the mill where they pulped the rags. She made money, my mother did, the American currency you're after."

Jack Montour covered with a laugh too hearty, "Your father and his mill girl, they spoiled you rotten."

When not away at school, Marie Claude sat at table watching the Jack and Molly show, her mother troubling the icy waters of officialdom, her father's distress mixed with pride. Jack was not such a stick after all, and when it became *de rigueur*, he did a little turn of his own — how on his mother's side he was one-eighth Algonquin. A frank American family with such an exotic past. And Molly was right, their guests were after U.S. dollars, though Jack's prospective deals in chemicals, farm equipment, passports, intelligence were not served up with the meal. For all her breaking ranks to hang with junior staff, slighting the Ambassador's wife, Molly observed protocol, at least the easy rules, made out the little place cards. The ranking guest sat to her right.

I loved to laze in the pillows of my parents' bed leafing through *Social Usage Abroad*, which lay on my mother's night table.

> *In countries where English is not widely used, a Roman typeface is preferable for calling cards. Block letters may be chosen for countries that do not use the Latin alphabet. Copperplate Gothic is a handsome choice.*
>
> *Mr. and Mrs. John Quincy Doe regret that a previous engagement . . .*

A woman's wardrobe must include a black dress and appropriate head covering for official mourning.

Informally, a smile, "Hello," or a spontaneous response such as "How do you do?" are proper.

THE VILLAGE

Hans Gruen cradles a woman in his lap. He has carried her across a dirt road from the airstrip and now sits on the curb. The bones of her body seem too light to be human, more like the airy weight of a small bird. Her head is bleeding, no longer profusely, the wound congealing in the heat under her matted dark hair. Her eyes wander from his face to the sun overhead, then blink and return to him. She is concussed, does not see him. Gruen sits on the curb unprotected. There is no cover. Across the road a corrugated-metal hangar is buckling in flames, the grinding death of a giant tin can. Through the black haze of smoke, he makes out little soldiers, a whole company of children running after the last plane as it bumps toward the end of the field and slowly rises out of range. The children carry lightweight automatic rifles. Gruen, expecting to make it out on that plane, was stopped by a runt of a boy with rickety legs. The kid, spun off from his gang, taunted him with a *Bang, bang, you're dead* of the playground. The woman he now carries in his arms fell in Gruen's path. He had tripped heavily onto her body and they lay on the ground in an awkward embrace for a long moment. He remembers watching his attaché case skim across the weedy asphalt. The child screeched a war cry and ran off to join his comrades at the command of their leader.

Gruen speaks to the woman in English. "You'll be all right. I don't know why I say that." Most of the food distribution workers speak English, though this crew he believes to be French and Swedish. She looks to him early middle-aged, one of those good souls searching for purpose. Perhaps one life over and the next sought out. Her breathing is even, childlike, as though she is taking a nap in his arms. Well, they will either make it or they won't, no place to hide. He hates the curb of concrete bricks he sits on. He hates the system of incompetency and graft that has lined the unpaved roadway with this city curb and side-walk as far as he can see.

Holding the woman in his arms, he starts to walk with the sun at his back. The best scenario would be a UN patrol car coming this way. Gruen presumes the plane has contacted the observers' headquarters in town. If the children with guns come after them, there is the faint hope of appealing to their commander, the enormous man in paramilitary costume who sat in his jeep at the airfield and coached the boys as if sending them out on a playing field. Gruen has no business being in this country rich in oil and diamonds no use to the starving. His arrival in this coastal town was not on the agenda. Gold coast? Slave coast? The thick scab of colonial culture grown over a village. In his years at the Foundation, he has never taken risks, never struck out on his own in this manner. With a photographer covering the peacekeepers' de-parture, he had crossed the border to this country, which has consumed $1.3 billion of aid. A heavy silence as he walks down the road with his burden, then an explosion. When he turns to watch the flames lick the bright blue African sky, he sees the rebel jeep with the kids head off in the other direction. So many little boys stashed in that vehicle, like cir-cus clowns stuffed in a VW Beetle.

"We are to be saved. I don't know why I say that."

The photographer was on that plane. He must have seen Gruen stumble over this woman's body, their bodies splayed on the runway like corpses. Perhaps they are presumed dead. Two weeks back, a UN charter plane had gone down in the hill towns which rise from this coastal area. It may be fortunate that Hans Gruen is walking toward the unknown with nothing but a shanty in sight. The woman has closed her eyes. He lays her down in the shade of a tree. The trees look to him

European, the legacy of the colonial government that left these people to their oil deposits with no industrial structure, to disease, tribal wars, the tainted gifts of their freedom.

When he helps the woman to her feet, begins to lift her once again, she fights him off. "Thanks, I'll walk." She is American, huffy, has no idea why she is deposited on this stretch of road with a stranger.

Gruen sees beyond the lone dwelling set in a mud-baked field to a sea of shanties fashioned of cardboard, tin, palm leaves, sliced tires, tar paper and plastic sheeting. They are not far from the outskirts of the town he had come to with the photographer, a brash young man from a cable network aiming to make his name. They met up in Cabinda where the delays flying out were ten, twelve hours if not the next day. His urgency was to keep his appointment with Claude. He'd risked his life driving hell-bent up the coast of Africa in an abandoned Ziff. In Soyo, he paid his last American dollars for a half-tank of gasoline. Claude wanting him in that wreck of a house seems an absurd demand, an idle exercise in loyalty. The photographer had said there were planes going out by the hour that would get him to Air France in Marseille, but he had been wrong, a sunscorched kid full of press corps gossip. With his credentials Gruen could get on a UN charter, keep his date, get back to his life.

Nothing new about the disparity between here and there, switching from political crisis to domestic entanglement. Once, when Gruen came home to Connecticut from India, where he witnessed the mouse people who do not have homes, cook in the sun, he found his wife obsessed with the tile floor in the new kitchen, apparently too porous, hard to keep clean. The mouse people roasted their vermin on the white earth. They lived in a southerly province where the sea salt seeped up through the ground, seasoning their tidbits. It was not his wife's fault and he did not relate this disturbing story to counter her distress at the oily blotches in her terrazzo. But he would tell Claude about the barefoot children in ragged khaki shorts, their red berets aping the guerrilla headgear of their commander. He had always reported horrors to the woman he should in honesty have called his mistress, the armed escorts and bullet proof vests of his missions to Guatemala and Peru gathering statistics for the World Bank, the chilblains in Siberia while searching out worthy projects for the Foundation. They had traded stories and she trumped him. The first woman to reach the sequestered Dalai Lama. When Qaddafi had been at his most inaccessible, she interviewed the despot in his tent. With Claude his stories would not have that edge of competition — just setting the record straight, as in her history lessons. Eliza Tibbs is not the expensive kitchen floor, but neither is she a killer in her lair.

The woman asks reasonably, "You are?" She remembers nothing of the provincial airport, the molded plastic chairs piled with luggage as they shuffled about in the heat, watching the last plane taxi into position for takeoff, then shoving through the revolving door eager to climb into the safety of its belly. She remembers nothing of the children scrambling out of the jeep.

"I was running?"

"Both of us running."

The curb stops where it might be useful, the asphalt sidewalks crumbling into the road. Women and children come out of the shanties, then out of more respectable cement bunkers, to look at the white man in a bloodied suit walking with a bloodied white woman on the road to town. The woman is strong, walking ahead of him toward the traffic circle where the last of the UN observers picks them up.

At breakfast, there is orange juice, English marmalade, heavy bread native to this country. "The flour is stolen. It's ours." "Ours" — the outfit Terry Coyne works for, the food distribution organization authorized, but not controlled by the UN. She sits with Hans Gruen in the empty dining room of a resort hotel overlooking a promenade with palm trees, even a vendor of cashews and sweets, the striped awning of his cart flapping in the ocean breeze. A number of late model German cars are parked along this boulevard.

"Cars of corruption." She is tart in her judgments, not a frail burden as Gruen had thought, and not as young. Terry Coyne from Evanston, Illinois, her last son off to college.

"Thus Africa? Good works?"

She is guarded, as though having lost the hours before and after the child soldiers, she might blurt out a secret, some personal revelation. She speaks of the rice, flour and canned milk parceled out to underweight women and children each day.

The two-inch gash in Terry Coyne's head was dressed at a clinic. "Not a bullet," the medic said, a young black man in a stained white hospital coat sure of a bullet wound when he sees one. "A sharp object." He shaved away a large patch of the injured woman's dark hair, painted the area with scarlet antiseptic. In the speckled hotel mirror, she had looked to herself punk, an aging fan of Seventies noise in a black tee shirt and tattered jeans dealt to her by a weary State Department officer.

Hans Gruen told this man their story. "The incident," the official repeatedly calls it, "scare tactics. Not friendly fire, those kids pockmarking the runway. We will protest the incident while it is still fresh. We'll see you have safe passage out of here."

Terry Coyne says, "Not out of here. I'm going back to my station. I came to see a friend off, a Swedish nurse going home for R & R."

Gruen is sure she is lying, that she still draws a blank, but the man from the embassy, this demoralized chap who represents what's left of the U.S. presence, simply checks her passport again, writes down the name of her boss. "If there's fallout from the incident."

He is a fleshy second-level man who exudes exhaustion, more with his dreary assignment than with the thirty years' war in this country. "Stay put," he says to the wounded woman, "I'll get you transport." With Hans Gruen he makes a show of respect, the Foundation, the stunning connections, everything possible will be done. He reaches for the marmalade and spreads it thickly on a chunk of bread, though he has not joined his compatriots at breakfast.

When he waddles out to an official black car, Gruen says, "Just a fat boy with food, any food."

The helpful man from the embassy does not drive off. He sends his driver, a huge smiling man in gorgeous native dress, to their table with Gruen's attaché case and a suitcase tagged with Terry Coyne's name.

"Apparently I was leaving. My friend is French."

"It will come back." Gruen doesn't know why he says that, or when she will recall time prior to the incident. He takes her trembling hand and places it firmly in his own. They might be a long-married couple on holiday in this resort dining room on a tropical boulevard—pink, cream, aqua hotels, paint flaking off, their welcome signs in German, Portuguese, Spanish faded, all but this one boarded up. "It will come back. The loss is temporary." Terry Coyne found a scarf in her bag and together they fashioned a turban round her head to disguise the scarlet wound. He has never felt such ease with a woman and remembers yesterday, the light weight of her in his arms.

"My friend is French. I believe we came to an impasse. I was leaving her."

"To go home?" The luggage tag reads Evanston.

And then she is gently crying. Gruen wipes her tears with a fine linen napkin which bears an imperial crest.

"Go back to my post. Fill in the blanks."

They wait in the empty dining room for rescue. He asks about the children with guns. Terry Coyne knows them—one day in the lineup for rations, the next taken for the army, whichever faction. Volunteers. Kidnapped. Abandoned. Hans Gruen has read of them in reports which come to the attention of the Human Development Program.

"They're malleable," she says, "don't question orders. Like the scare tactics today."

"Yesterday."

"And if they are killed? You see, they're no one, with no place in this world. They swarm, sting. They call them little bees."

The lone waiter has disappeared. They sit quite comfortably together in the post-colonial dining room, playing with the crumbs. Plastic sheeting and posters of rock stars cover the shabby decor of empire. Now and again they sip bottled water. A van comes with the protective insignia of World Food.

"My people."

They embrace, cling to each other long and hard.

She finally asks him the simplest question, "Going home?"

Hans Gruen, carrying her bag to the curb, does not answer, though he has told her of the death of his wife and something of the spunky woman journalist, about the reports that come his way on mercenaries as well as kid soldiers some of them eight, ten years old, here and in Asia, in Latin America. Their cause has not been of concern to the Foundation. Not yet, he says. But he doesn't answer her final question, offers nothing about the young woman he believes he will marry, about his schoolboy desire to please Claude, which got him into this mess. Their mess, his and Terry Coyne's, the incident like a movie scene with rounds of blanks fired by extras.

The Chargé d'Affaires arrives in a Caddy all gleam, bullet-proof windows. Old Glory and the flag of the recognized government fly from twin aerials. He is a neatly barbered Brooks Brothers man in a comic safari outfit, dead serious about his assignment, about his failure to negotiate any semblance of peace between factions so splintered, the situation heeled in, no longer fluid. Gruen takes him to be decent, a skillful career diplomat sent into a tricky situation.

"The little boys? They are not all boys," he says.

"Spraying bullets in the dust?"

"Blanks, they fired blanks. That faction, smart in their maneuvers with these children. Guns and butter, they want access."

"Access?"

"Power, cigarettes, beer, television." The Chargé d'Affaires is cynical but not unfair, admits he can't unscramble the byzantine alliances. Most he can do is sort victims from predators. He seems annoyed with his gloss on the endless conflagrations, more comfortable with the business in hand. He has been out to see the destruction at the airport, but has not been fully briefed, is mortified that Hans Gruen . . . and so forth.

The stewardess presents a half-bottle of Crozes-Hermitage, '91. *Bien*, it will do fine with the *steak pommes frites*, but he wants the wine at once. First class out of Marseille is fully booked, good times all around, tourists and businessmen absorbed in their reading, spreadsheets, laptops, best sellers. The glittering lights of the Riviera lie beneath them in the night sky. Hans' efficient canvas grip, miraculously delivered to Air France from the chubby commuter plane in Africa, is stowed above his head. He does not open his attaché case to look over his proposals: Conference on Advance GNP per capita undercut by demographic nightmare; Evaluation of Migratory Insecurity; Culture of Gender Disparity? The purpose of his mission now distant, the globe turned inside out, no end to the disasters of the emerging bodies politic. And though he slept like the dead last night on a lumpy pallet in that deserted hotel, he finds no rest in the ample comfort of first class and drums idly on the body of his briefcase. Some minutes before he notices the bloodstain on leather, the strand of dark hair caught in the brass fixture at one corner. Terry Coyne was his victim. Tripping on her body, he'd struck her a blow so wounding she had no memory of heading home. And he told her it would come back about her friend, the French woman she was leaving. He had not watched himself with Terry Coyne in a freeze-frame of their parting, the way he'd so often seen himself dead to the heightened moment. At her leaving, he wept unashamed, the Chargé d'Affaires adjusting his dark glasses, turning to look out to the dazzling sea. Now he plucks the black hairs loose, smooths them with reverence. These few strands are a relic he must believe in, a sacred token of his conversion, and so even as he accepts the attentions of the stewardess, the *steak pommes frites*—it's then he remembers.

Hans in a shadowy place from which he watched a shy girl, a class-mate he cared for in a childish way. An outing, field day at end of the school year. She lay white and still on the grass as the gym teacher cut away the leg of her jeans. The crushed bones of her knee, the neat slice of flesh down to the ankle. Boys solemn, girls weeping are all ordered to stand away. The mangled wheel of a bicycle, constant moan of the deliv-eryman who ran the girl down, soda pops and sandwiches in his wagon meant for this special day. Hans withdrew to the sidelines, then ran for the storage hut with the athletic equipment— baseball bats, soccer goals, the volleyball net that would be brought out for the games.

"You should see yourself, Gruen." His beloved teacher pushed him aside, reached for towels, a blanket, his teacher of math just out of Har-vard, the man he wanted to be. Hans did see himself in the humiliating moment, a deserter unable to feel, not the pain of his childhood sweet-heart who lay quiet as death, but to feel at all. He had watched himself walk dutifully toward the accident.

The young teacher found him out. "You're a cool customer, Gruen."

Thanks to a woman he would never see again, the lost moment has surfaced. What was it after all? An incident from grammar school in which he was the absentee, his cowardice a small cut that never healed, like the gash in a plaster statue of a martyr. But martyrs have a cause beyond self-protection. Gruen looks at himself—weary, aging, un-shaven—reflected in the night sky, first class brightly lit behind him. Tears well in his eyes, blurring his image, yet he is giddy, delirious. He orders another half-bottle, toys with his food, perhaps he's healed, whole—not quite himself.

This time out, the shortcut home proved the long way round, a trans-formative journey. In the past it was easy, maybe too easy, leaping the distance from there to here. Tell, tell all—the runty black boy's laugh-ter, flames licking the clear blue sky, attaché case as sharp object, mar-malade diplomat. Tell the cut-and-dried calculations far from anecdotal, his figuring Absolute Poverty of that country, percentage of AP per million, into the Deprivation Measure. He had been in the hut all his life, hiding in the shadows with figures rounded to the hundreds and smooth committee-speak, escorted to scenes of suffering and degradation as safely as to his place at the conference table. At last he had taken the dangerous journey, somewhat dangerous, somewhat farcical, Terry Coyne his companion. Brave going back to her lover, unearth the argument or whatever set them apart. When the blanks are filled in, she may retreat to Evanston. He will edit out only his embrace of the injured woman in her silky turban, when he tells Claude. Two days late for their lovers' tryst, and it is gone now, put on hold, his urgent need of her body. Still, he can't do without her. They've come a long way since their practice session in the Hyatt. At times, when they are reading—his reports, her student papers—they look at each other, nothing said, simply a wonder they are together in clear lamplight. Too late to find her in that house where she gathers scraps of memorabilia that can't possibly cure the slights of childhood or contain the weight of history, only make-believe in stories of a vanished world.

The *International Herald Tribune* picks up the story from *Reuters.com*: the closing of the American embassy and the further destruction of airport facilities. Weeks later the *Times* alludes to a previous incident in an article on the withdrawal of the peacekeepers. No mention of the distinguished economist or little bees.

BRUTE NEIGHBORS

The mouse. Did you think I was alone?

I believe he was a city mouse, not a woodland creature. Only one small grey mouse who found his way to the tower, nesting in the window seat. Prince of a fellow, as if in a kid's book—velvet britches, red suspenders. Something like that, a loner, and I had nothing to fear, knowing his extended family owned the place downstairs. And that the ants were a danger working noiselessly behind the scenes, so that the shingles, the pillars, the beams were thin as this paper.

So—not always alone. I held a compress to Chris Sheedy's head. At command central the authorities have not shut off the running water in my house. The towel I pressed against his forehead was linen worn thin, embroidered with a swirling *B*. Poor Sheedy had cracked his skull on that lethal low header of the door leading into my tower. I was sorry, sorry he was here at all. I had waited for Hans, testing, testing, and what did I get? Boy lawyer in a flashy silk tie. I loosened the tie, unbuttoned his shirt where dark hair grew thick, springy to the touch. I did not intend to stroke him, only to nurse the injury of the welt rising.

"A shithouse." In some pain, he repeated that appropriate word.

"I know." I did know and was ready to leave, pack up as soon as Hans . . . who might not come for me. I'd known that for a while, perhaps known it all along.

Running water. No phone. No way for Sheedy to warn me of his arrival. In a flapping accordion file with the name of the senior partner now dead, he carried the papers he would hand over to the judge of probate to make final my shithouse inheritance.

"You could have put them in the mail," I said.

"But your week's up." Yes, it was Friday. Chris Sheedy did not thank God. The established men in his firm went home early to their wives and kids. One by one, they'd invited him to dinner, their obligation soon over. He was plain lonesome, on the prowl. Later tonight he would try the cabaret, but for now . . .

"Now it hurts?" I addressed his sore head, but imagined the discomfort of striking out on his own, the bleak small town adventure.

It was the early dusk that lingers into Spring. I had lit my votive candles bought at the store across Park Street, candles for prayer or for emergency. I counted this evening an emergency, with the rain lashing the windows again, streaming through the hole in the ceiling until my pot ran over. Hans was to come at midday, this day or yesterday. Hadn't we figured all likely delays into our pact? My pact, which was holy. I'd

let the hours pass until it was too late to go down to the car and call
Gruen's office, listen to the Foundation's tape, *press one, press two, press
the extension if you know your party*. I knew my party, the man I trusted
above all others. All the others—the slalom champ at that prep school
in Vermont where the Sixties gasped its last in a curriculum of fucking
and folky music, the naval attaché in need of Christmas comfort in the
tropics, silent college hunks and noisy strummers—easy lay for any guy
with an amp and a pick, the philosophy TA who should have failed me.
So many nights in a peripatetic life with my nice little jobs in whichever
city my mother was stationed, though I did not think of Molls as I held
Chris Sheedy in my arms. Sighs, heavy breathing—absorbed in our
abuse of the client/lawyer privilege.

Bottom line: I loved every one of my romantic encounters, each
time believing in a small investment of the heart or else it would only
be bodies, only the nipple erect and the rush of need down there, down
where I wanted them to want me. As I now wanted Sheedy, his head on
my little cupcake breasts, bulky torso on my spindle legs held akimbo,
a pathetic *pietà*. I am not old enough to be his sorrowing mother, only
moved by his self-imposed exile and the years it will take before his
name will be on bumper stickers, a headshot of the candidate garroted
on posts around the city square.

We drew apart, knowing we would go on with our business of making love, cosigning on the dotted lines, we unbuttoned, unzipped, only
to tidy ourselves quickly when we heard the call from below.

Hans, I thought, Hans, how this episode would end in bedroom
farce—weakness of the flesh, lightheaded betrayal. A Molly story, I
might call it.

But I was saved. Down the first flight of stairs I heard clearly—the
grumbling Billy Goat Gruff, Captain Abriola in a yellow slicker, his
flashlight playing over the stained wallpaper. We presented ourselves:
attorney and legatee.

"Now, didn't I tell you to get out of here." The fatherly cop on TV in
a series faintly remembered. "We can't handle the calls."

"From my neighbors?"

About to say I was packing up, on my way, when Chris Sheedy stepped forward. I was proud of my boy handling the situation. Such political skill—the winning handshake, male camaraderie. Abriola was in his corner.

"Thanks for your concern." Oh, in that moment I heard Sheedy deliver many stock phrases at the podium—in the regional high school, at graveside, weddings of every denomination, the VFW hall—working his constituency, a Bobby Kennedy touch in the toothy smile, the honest listening-I'm-listening thrust of the head. Chris Sheedy's banged up forehead cleverly disguised by a flop of black hair.

Abriola left us to our legal affairs. Packing up, I displayed my heirlooms. A pamphlet found in the shambles of the library, *Ferns for the Shady Garden, Julian Baird, 1935*, publication of the Brooklyn Botanical Gardens. *There are two native bladder ferns: C. bulbifera, which must have a moist-rock position so that its tender tapering leaves may cascade* ...

"And look here!" Program of the Eastman Conservatory, student-faculty recital, 1943. *Professor Zak will be accompanied by his student Rose Baird in Brahms' Violin Sonata No. 1 in G, Op. 78.*

"Hey!" Chris Sheedy strained to attend to my discoveries.

I descended to supplementary materials—much like the time lines, portraits of presidents and soldiers—documents scanned off the Net to keep my class awake. My instructional tone: "You will be interested in this map which depicts, more or less, your congressional district, your chosen poltical base." And I showed my student, now alert with self-interest, the topographical map found in an empty closet. On its lakes, rocky outcroppings and elevations, someone had charted the Baird holdings, which ran North through the Housatonic Valley, West to the foothills of the Taconic Range.

The man who bought these many acres was clever. His property skirted the mills, never interfered with local commerce, though he banked on its growth, Banker Baird. With my scholarly nose I had poked into town records to find many acres sold off in the desperate Thirties, then tracked the erosion of fifty years until there was only a back yard, no bigger than any plot on Park Street. Lily and Rose lived off the land. That was personal, not in my lesson plan.

"See the black dot on the river, that's town, but there was nothing out this way, not even a hamlet, until the mills, then General Electric and the prosperity of the Second World War. You will want to know when the blacks came up from the South for work, when the mills began to fail, when the Mass. Pike passed us by, making Jimbo's and The Till and your cabaret an off-ramp experience."

"You're some teacher, Miss Montour." As he studied the elevations and wetlands with great solemnity, I saw that, to Chris Sheedy, Tilden Swamp and Berry Hill, the valleys and fertile meadows spreading out from the river were as remote as some Biblical land.

"Is this where she was from?" he asked. "Your Eliza?"

"Different course entirely." Then we blew out the candles and Sheedy carried my treasures downstairs with the help of Abriola's torch, on loan, to light our way. We said we would be in touch.

But I was not much of a teacher, for after I was informed that Hans was no longer among the missing, when Spring break was over, when I was sleeping in my own bed, when I was finally back at school, on that Monday, Rashid came to my office toting all the books he had borrowed. Not my excitable scholar hot on the trail of our colonial misdemeanors, a slick fellow with downy mustache, his thick body stuffed in a menacing black leather jacket. He would complete the course with the lady professor, but was switching his major—history to communications.

"You don't mean it."

"I must get on," he said.

I recalled the extra hours we spent together, his enthusiasm for Thomas Paine, the son of a maker of stays for women's corsets, that he had dwelt on all such details of class, but Rashid cut me off in mid-lecture.

"I liked your American history and thank you." This formal declaration from a kid born and bred in Jersey.

I could no longer look at my darling student, but turned to the books he thrust at me, *Common Sense* among them. "Then I'll see you in class."

"I must get on."

He joined his pals—thin mustaches, leather jackets—waiting in the hall outside my office. My last view of him that day—he turned back to me with a wan smile decidedly uncool. I refuse to believe in this Rashid who must get on in this world.

That night Hans Gruen called. Now I wanted to know every danger he had faced. He's not a man to linger on the phone. There was a settling-in to our brief talk, a presumption not in need of a clever word, no hint of flirtation. We must each be about our business. We arranged to meet on the weekend.

"And your house?" He asked as though after an invalid parent.

I had nothing to tell Hans, who had flunked my childish testing, my lover who'd been to the wars. Cop stories, a dalliance fit for the soaps. A wicked woman spinning her tales.

Each day I met my classes. At night I gave myself fully to the documents.

Like our common lady fern, Athyrium iseanum *is deciduous. Each frond ends in a graceful taper. The rachis and midribs are blood red blending into the soft grey green of the leaf.*

After the intermission, Professor Emil Zak was accompanied by his student Rose Baird in Beethoven's No. 5 for Piano and Violin in F Major, "Spring."

A Liberty Bond issued in 1918 with only one coupon cashed in. Holding it to the light, I saw the delicate silk threads, red and blue, that defied counterfeit. On my sprung couch I propped up the Japanese screen stuffed in the window seat of the turret, torn once again when Chris Sheedy stowed it in the back seat of my car. Extravagant women are balanced on a boat which may be moored or gently floating downriver. Some display the rich embroidery of their kimonos, some sit on a bamboo bench and fix ornaments into each other's hair. On the fore-deck at a proper remove, a fisherman scales a bleeding fish. And in the rippling water golden and silver and cupreous fish look like a string of jewels.

Only imagine the fool who cruelly folded this scene away, thrust it in with old dress patterns, remnants of rotted silk and a cracked demijohn. Perhaps the fish were an annoyance, a reminder of the scummed pond, or of the day when Glo-Glow Bigelow crossed the spongy lawn in her hobble skirt, exhibiting her pretty ankles, hobbling right over to George Jr. The first warm day in the foothills of New England and Julian, the younger son, caged at Baird Bank and Trust, could not believe his mother had asked that woman to tea, that she'd do any shameful thing to bring her dearest boy alive. The pale young man, still in his overseas cap, had no recall of Mrs. Bigelow's abundant red hair, was dead to the memory of a truant boy who shtupped her when her children ran off to school. George Jr. rose unsteadily, left the women to their gossip and biscuits and walked to the pond, where the rushing rivulets of Spring thaw created trenches in miniature. The sludge sucked his spirit down, down, until he actually lay on his belly and grabbed for his father's prize koi, the bully chasing his fellows' tails. And when he returned to the ladies, he threw the fish gasping its last onto his mother's plate.

I suppose that the trunk with the stickers belonged to Rose, that the Zaks sailed now and again to Europe after the next war, that he toured in a quartet to many cities hungry for the healing music, that his wife ironed his dress shirts, kept track of his scores, got the best rate of ex-change for their dollars. She was a banker's daughter after all. And then one year Emil did not accompany her home on the *Normandie* and that was the end of it, the end of Rose and the gloss of her black hair turned to dull pewter. Lily—oh, Lily stayed on at home with her father and the Irish mill girl, his second wife. Happy as if she'd died and gone to heaven, hemming her flimsy scarves, trimming Mamma's church hats, encouraged, I suppose, to sell them from the parlor. And playing peekaboo with the baby, my mother, who already found these games an endless yet endearing bore.

SOLITUDE

I passed each night of that week, still waiting for Hans. Calm, waiting alone for the end of our story. On Saturday I would go into New York. The day came and I packed my overnight case, then unpacked all my souvenirs. *Their* mementoes. The car choked and I turned off the flutter of my ailing transmission. Waiting, I had always been waiting. The morning, empty of neighbors and dogs, newspapers thrown on stoops, news of the day waiting, I idled and the quiet seemed to me a gift wrapped fold upon fold. No way of knowing if Cracker Jack worthless or a casket of gold lay inside, inside a tissue of memory.

First—I remembered the day of my departure from the tower as a child, how I set my small suitcase by the front door at dawn. Dressed for the journey in my plaid skirt and Expo cap, I took up my post in the parlor, from time to time stealing across the slippery waxed floor to lift the window shade. A grizzly bear man in an undershirt waved from an open window to a woman with a squirming child. Later, kids were hustling to school, the big yellow brick school with an asphalt playground. A bright April day much like this, too warm in the parlor for my Irish sweater, but I believed my mother would come at any moment. The hours slowly ticked by. Aunt Rose with excuses—poor Molly stuck in traffic? Farther South inclement weather? A look of alarm settled on Aunt Lily's placid moon face.

Marie Claude, as I was then, perched stiffly on an ottoman, a sticky toadstool sprouting from the musty Oriental carpet on which I plopped myself each evening for the dread musicale, waiting for Aunt Rose to strike the last dim note, close the lid on her instrument before I was served a plate of the sweet sloppy dessert that ended the day. My beautiful mother did not care to come on time. Did not care, would never come, never. The aunts smiled anxiously over many cups of tea. Stealing to the window, I saw business pick up at the corner grocery, men lolled against cars with the first beer of the day, a scene I had often watched, pulling back the green linen shade. At the end of morning I saw the littlest kids picked up by their mothers from school. Lily, given to giggles, said: "Goodness! You will stay on with us, Marie Claude!"

It was then I ran up all those stairs, slammed the door. There were no shades in the tower. From those windows I saw only the garden, the dark woods which offered no escape, and there she found me in the last light of day, a child steely with grief.

"Why, darlin', what a long face!"

And then such a party! You brought a pink azalea blooming in a pot, a lemon cake with marzipan chicks roosting in the yellow frosting, a crate of miniature eggs, and when I bit their sugar shells they oozed the richest chocolate. You brought Spring into the somber house. So joyous a holiday, though it wasn't quite Easter, but Molly Montour never cared for Lent. Stroking Lily's artistic pillows—silky patches of ecru, violet, mauve—you said, "Like faded petals pressed in a book."

Dead colors I hated.

And wouldn't it be swell if, for old times' sake, Rose played a piece, the Schubert. Rose demurred, so you twirled on *the tippety old piano stool*, thumped out a Gershwin tune half remembered.

"And how was my pigeon?" Cooing, not looking for an answer.

"We will miss her tricks," Rose said. Lily popped another chocolate and I could have kissed her for not telling that I ran away through the woods, that I caused the scene with sirens screeching through the night and worse, much worse. Surely they would tell about the ruined gardener's hut, the fireman come to the door, the besotted Kelsos, the boy with the flinging knife. And they would tell about my Sissy. But the aunts did not tattle. Rose winked as though to say, *Our little secret*. Then wasn't I happy to be going off with you and actually kissed Lily's plump powdery cheek, Rose's chin with wisps of brittle white hair. How rotten I'd been, abusing their kindness. I would write to them from

Paris. End of the spook house, though not of that day, that day, Molls, when you drove your child back into the city.

I remembered you so clearly at the wheel of a rented compact, the kind of tinny car you hated, driving fast, too fast, down the Interstate and a trooper pulling you to the side of the road with no more than a warning, but there were tears in your eyes as you slowly, obediently drove on. Odd, for sure enough you had charmed the big bozo out of the ticket.

"So what's wrong?"

"Lily and Rose"—a sob caught in your throat—"they have loved me since the day I was born."

Given my release from the tower, I was not entirely happy. The tiny sublet on Beacon Place was a bandbox—chintz and delicate furniture, pastel landscapes—a store-bought foothold on impersonal ground. I awoke in a strange bed fashioned like a sleigh to hear you on the phone, a plaintive arguing well into the night, and sometime later, closing my eyes against the murky light of city dawn, I heard the latch on the door, whispers. Your bleating voice and the hoarse displeasure of a man. In the airport, you fumbled through our passports and tickets. *Belle maman*, you looked suddenly old, though you would never be as old as your ancient half-sisters. I was ten, no eleven, able to detect a pattern— party-time high followed by exhaustion.

Waiting, I turned the key in the ignition and my car turned over with a purr. Still I waited for some revelation, but I was no wiser than I'd been as a child, only guessing at the sexual component in my mother's despair.

I wrote one letter to say lessons were real hard at the *lycée*, that on weekends I rode in the Bois de Boulogne. *My horse is a grey mare.* I thought of nothing more to report to these peculiar women who had taken me in. I could not tell them my parents were, or were not, divorcing. How could I second-guess the brass of Molly Montour, or Jack, plain Jack's official delight when you decided to stay. *I hope you are both well.* At the end of the page, I marked XXX, which was improper, avoiding *Love*, which was not my true feeling for Aunt Lily, Aunt Rose.

Idling at the curb, I felt this time of recall to be like the endless hours of retreat at the convent school in Montreal, a time of strict silence meant for the examination of past sins and for future resolve.

PHILANTHROPY

Tonight we ride our hobby horses. The guest with the deepest pockets is seated at my right. Hans has the Senator at his end of the table.

My father is placed between two women charmed by stories of a *Hiawatha* beauty—half-breed, he calls her—the grandmother who went to Michigan or Wisconsin with one of the Montours. (It's the Homestead Act he speaks of, and he's off by fifty years.) "Pardon my French," he'll say, telling the one about Lyndon's rosewood crapper, set up like a throne in the anteroom of the Senate. For all his off-the-cuff anecdotes, my father has believed in the business of this Republic from his first pledge of allegiance in a chill schoolroom in Maine where the American flag stood in the corner next to the Rand McNally globe. Jack, looking good in his pinstripes, unbearably happy to be at Hans Gruen's table.

Plain Jack, but tonight, though we find ourselves on place cards, we might as well be nameless, each playing our set role.

From the grave nod of the Senator's head, I believe my husband tells of the incident, of the child's face distorted with laughter as he spent his ammunition, a small boy eminently replaceable. Hans will push for the demobilization of these children, which is not what the Senator came to hear, though he could bring a proposal to the floor. Hans pressing on—the UN Convention on the Rights of the Child—while our honored guest turns to a woman draped in pearls, fund raising at our table. My husband failing as he has at the Foundation, his cause set aside as single-issue activism. Failing, he will bravely try again, fire his blanks like the kid soldier at the pocked airstrip. *Not toy soldiers,* he will say, pressing on, *children abducted, sold like slaves.* Compassion, not Gruen's known area of expertise, is a very untenable ground, so he will switch to the instability of investment flows. Knowing full well the Senator, chair of the Finance Committee, has heard it from rock stars, from the Pope of Rome, Hans will chitchat, display his irrefutable figures supporting the mutual benefits in debt forgiveness for the poorest nations. Or, he will fall silent, his silence not without pain. Prince, lover, nothing left of the phantom boy who hid in a dark shed from a nasty scene.

Service is first offered to the woman on the right of the host and proceeds counterclockwise around the table.

Though it's small change to my Rich Guest, the man on my right, he's shocked at the cost of the new roof and the reconstruction of the solarium no longer mine. I have willed it away, Mercy House. Yes, my castle in the air remains costly, an expensive pit, why I'm still teaching. The house is now the property of two dedicated nuns—one lean, one stout—who offer it up, their huffing, puffing up the stairs to the office in the turret. Mercy House of Learning, where women, several from Park Street, are taught math and reading, English as a second language, where their children are cared for while they work in what's left of the mills and in the kitchens of the tourist-trade restaurants. Mexicans, Colombians, Asians—cheap labor again in New England.

At the end of the meal the hostess makes the move to leave the table.

"What a splendid piece!" My Moneybucks is a collector. He examines the Japanese screen over the sideboard.

"It cost a fortune to restore. Moronobu?"

"Without doubt."

Ah, this is the way to beg, with my little learning. "Late seventeeth century?"

"Absolutely. A day's outing for the courtesans."

"Are they moored or floating?"

"Not moored," he says. "The lap of water, petals drifting. The fish moving."

"Look at these two whispering."

How shy when he corrects me. "They are kissing." And indeed, they offer their painted mouths to each other, these delicate creatures of the bordello.

I dawdle with him in the doorway, as Molly as I can get, listening to his rap on the floating world of earthly pleasures—

> What's the good in clinging to branches—
> Plum blossoms withered, fouled by birds?
> Petals falling are blessed,
> Drift with hope for a short season.

Fragility of life, he informs me, *ukiyoe*, an elusive term later demoted to describing bourgeois—alas, even pop culture. Then, because the story is not beautiful until added to, I tell about my great-grandfather taking the screen as collateral from an impoverished missionary returned to a stark New England hill town, a nice deal Banker Baird pulled off. I have flattered my Patron with this homey revelation as though I were trained by one of the lovely ladies floating downstream. He will send me a check to prop Mercy House, rebuild the rotted foundation.

It is advisable for any guest to leave a party at a reasonable hour, no matter how pleasant the company may be.

WALDEN, IS THAT YOU?

I will have my garden. A place to sit, read, play with children. Their yard, call it a yard, front and back. What was all that waste space for a circular drive? The *porte cochère* torn down, there is ample room for parking. I have plotted it out, the swings and slide, sturdy benches. All in the sun, the drooping old pine no use at all. My bulbs poking up.

Here and there a blue flower on the periwinkle, pretty name for vinca.
I do not aim to be a real gardener when I visit their yard.

We live in the city. We rent for two weeks on the Jersey shore, but
mostly we choose to travel, not always for Hans' work. For our pleasure.

Question: who will I put the touch on for a shade tree full grown?
Outrageously expensive. All in the unforgiving sun, no timber trail
here, no sign with that tag burned into a cut of hickory. For one year,
my grandfather was president of the American Daffodil Society and had
the right to any name he wished to call his woods. He would disapprove
of my first planting, my bulbs coming up in a regimental row.

I decided against Baird, that name no longer in it. Names are troubling until they settle in. The Sisters requested Mercy, though they
have no cross, no Virgin in the turret.

Things do not change; we change. The words of one of our greatest
pencil pushers. You may have guessed I'm bringing my class, as I do
each year, to the eve of the Civil War with snippets of supplementary
material. I once had a student, Rashid, who would have devoured
Thoreau whole. So—rereading *Walden*, and here I beg to differ. Things
do change, the house with its airy rooms is bright, every aspect inviting.
Children grow simple bean shoots and baby lettuce in the solarium.
Computer screens glow in the library. Though, of course, the Pond
Pundit is right. I have no idea who she was, Marie Claude, that sullen
girl. Bury her in New England earth with Eliza Tibbs.

"You must publish her story," Hans says.

"I'd rather perish." But publish I must:

> *Whereas Eliza Gee, Wife to me, the Subscriber, hath not only
> eloped from my Bed and Board, but otherwise behaved in a
> most unbecoming manner toward me; and as I am apprehen-
> sive that she may malign me, I am obliged to take this public
> Method in hopes that no Person will encourage her Willful
> Absence and return her to Hearth and Rightful home.*

Hundreds of such advertisements for runaway wives in the mid-years of that century. But it was *her* hearth, *her* dwelling house. Were Gee's children intolerable? Eliza's escape was not from coverture, and where did she run to, ruining my story? What of the black woman, property of Schoolmistress Tibbs? Was she set free to ply her useful trade of Fancy-work upon Muslin? Publish I must: to the scholar it is not allowed that all things be mysterious and unexplorable.

No sapling for me, I have priced a large sugar maple. A cool forty, fifty thousand to transplant. Then the deep watering. We're on city water here. Spring—the invincible old pitch pine spreads pollen on the depleted soil, a gift of false gold on a patch of bare, unshaded land.

Question: a fountain? A wading pool for children?

Or imagine carp—flickering metallic orange, not gold. Their movements delightful to behold as swamp grasses swaying on the edge of an ornamental pond. Natural, by design so natural.

MAY

The Magdalene

Woe to the youth or maiden,
who did but dream of a dance!

—Nathaniel Hawthorne
The May-Pole of Merry-Mount

QUEEN OF THE ANGELS

You'll not have noticed her though she held her head high in the gift shop of the hospital, in the chill entrance hall of the museum and in a dark side chapel of Ignatius Loyola. Such public places were her sanctuaries. Head high, the posture of a well trained child—*Here, I am here.* Still, you might overlook Mae lighting a votive candle, her petition one of many. Wandering the galleries of medieval Virgins and martyrs, she appeared to be a lady with no pressing obligations. Mae was all of these phantom women and her given name was Mary.

On her birth certificate and marriage license, she was Mary Boyle.

Born late to her parents, born into a sporty Irish family on the rise, she seemed forever to wonder if she was allowed. *May I? May I?* As a girl she begged permission in a childish bleat so plaintive, her brother and sister aped this gentle singsong and she became—their Maesie, their Mae. The spelling her own invention. They took no notice of this small act of rebellion, which came about in grammar school. She knew they mocked her and would not be their May.

Her sister was Jane, dimple tucked in her cheek, pale violet eyes, fluttering lashes of a shameless flirt. She was Jane, plain and simple but ready for any man's lap, for any woman's envy of her golden hair, pleased to be so admired by the men who came home for a drink with Frank Boyle after a day on the Street. Home, that would be Park Avenue, the big apartment where a daily maid with a scrap of dimity apron and a frill of white cap answered the door. Out on Oyster Bay, Jane twisted from her father's strong hands, ran down the lawn to the Sound lapping at his dock or made a dash for the shed where her pony pawed the dust, begging for her attention. Now that she was sixteen, a sweetheart full grown, she'd bathe in the sun, look up to see Frank Boyle's eyes on her, disappointed if he turned away to speak of golf or listen to her mother's gossip of the club. Her brother, Jane was sure of—Lawrence, called Law. He was in it with her, their conspiracy of being Boyle kids, enviable for their spiffy good looks and their sass, for their place in this world where the tennis court was chalked and rolled by the gardener, where their catboat swayed by the pilings at Daddy's dock. Superior children—but what of the tagalong, the pesky small sister?

"May I, *please*," Law taunting. Mae perched on the threshold of his room, looking at the boyness of his bats and balls, real Yankees cap, sailing trophies, the promise held out in the orange triangle of a Princeton banner. This room, smelling of brine and sweat, was in the seaside home, the big shingle house called The Merrow.

"Go way, Maesie."

She was eight years old when she understood that Law would never get into Princeton, that he had peaked at fourteen. Bronzed by the sun, her brother was like the naked statue of some god or prince her mother brought back from Italy. Law's body was certainly that perfect, but he would never wear a silly hat. Years later, when she discovered Donatello's David stomping the bloody head of Goliath in a coffee-table book, a Christmas present from her husband, she thought it couldn't hold a penny candle to the half-scale knockoff that once graced the turning of the stairs at The Merrow. And her brother killed no one, not even in the war. In fact, she recalled that he never killed her in croquet, but knocked Jane's ball to kingdom come, into the thicket of rhododendrons with undergrowth of poison ivy. She was dismissed, outside their enduring competition.

In the Society Page photo which Mae destroyed, her brother and sister lean into each other like lovers. All of them on the wide veranda, *The Boyles of The Merrow*, their rambling house on the North Shore of Long Island. All in white linen, the mother and older daughter in long skirts shaped to their slim bodies, the men in floppy white trousers of the Thirties. The mother wears a hat of Milan straw with a pointed Peter Pan crown and narrow brim that casts a shadow across her face, one of those lanky Irish faces not markedly feminine. The father's hair is a thatch of pure white, early white, his brows black over lively dark eyes. Dad of all he surveys, a man to trust. Not weathered like the Boyles left behind in the West of Ireland. Though it's only May, he's smoothly tanned for on weekends he cuts a deal or two on the golf links. Boyle looks younger than forty, has been married to his handsome wife with the strong jaw for twenty years. It is 1938 and Frank Boyle is one of the few survivors who heard the faint strains like the groaning of a ship way out at sea, then detected rot, fissures in the market that preceded the Crash. Holding steady, Boyle went safely, fairly safely, into bonds, owes no man a dollar. Though there are weeks when he shuffles the cups—monies here, monies there—to meet his payroll in the city, one clerk and a loyal secretary stationed like department store dummies in the empty rooms of his office; a con-artist game to keep it all going these years—the gardener, chauffeur and maids, the pretense that he is crude King of The Merrow. Sitting for the society photographer, he is a likely ruler of his idling family—the wife delighted that they are to be in the Sunday Supplement with news of her charity tea for children stricken with polio. His own big kids, Jane and Lawrence, are healthy with the confirmation of Thoroughbreds, the horses his father curried for the pleasure of real royalty in Ireland.

But what of Mae? A prim child in a starched dress placed on the bottom step with a panting Skye terrier, her brittle red hair plastered into stiff pipe curls. Skin white as her dress, fair Irish skin that will not take the sun, heavily freckled on cheeks and button nose, on frail arms, on what can be seen of her stick-drawing legs which she tucks modestly out of sight. The Boyles pushing the season in all that white linen, but the photo will not appear until after Decoration Day. Then they will be perfectly correct. Ellen Boyle, who knows Jane and Law's wild ways, insists the rules be observed at least in the matter of dress.

That year the peonies and iris came on early, a fine display for the charity tea, their blowzy pinks and strong purples circling the terrace where scones and little sandwiches were passed by the maids and the two older children bribed to play no tricks on the guests. While in the dark parlor where the glass curtains fluttered like wings above her, Mae crouched on the carpet, took scissors to the Sunday Supplement and cut herself out of *The Boyles of The Merrow*. If that wasn't enough, she snipped them to bits. Then she was the only figure complete. She did not rescue the Skye terrier from her wrath. If it was wrath. The Boyles never had a straight answer, most certainly not from the sealed lips of the young priest who gave Mae absolution, and not from their family doctor who proposed internal confusion—perhaps rich currant cake or the many strangers wandering the grounds led to the child's upset. Frank Boyle did not hold with the recommended doctor, the one who fiddled with the mind. So what was to be done with Mae, who smiled faintly when she was confronted with her party dress all smeared with newsprint, with the head lopped off her mother, the sturdy limbs severed from brother and sister, her father spliced in two? One thing the Boyles knew, this daughter so tentative in her life among them, good in every ordinary way, was surely not envious of aid to crippled children.

There were signs. Throughout the month of May, the girl worshiped at her altars—in the city, little arrangements of paper flowers and beads, offerings of velvet hair ribbons set before the Virgin Mary; at The Merrow, she scouted the woods and shoreline for wild flowers—mustard, daisies and rocket set in glasses filched from her father's bar. At first it was amusing to see Mae kneeling before the plaster statues illuminated by flickering candle stubs.

Then Law said, "Creepy."

And Jane, "Is she taking the veil?"

In the city, Mae woke at dawn to tell her rosary, bead by crystal bead through the sorrowful mysteries, before the hour for school when she must throw off her ghostly white nightie, put on her navy jumper and walk behind Jane to the nuns at Sacred Heart. Her mother had no satisfaction from Mae's teacher, who did not disguise her pleasure in fostering a spiritual child. Mrs. Boyle then charged up the marble staircase and presented herself in the sanctum sanctorum of the Mother Superior's study.

Mother Clare, officially kind, listened to the complaints against the child's piety, then smiled the beatific smile. "Well now, May is the month of the Virgin."

"I know that," said Ellen Boyle, "but we've found her picking weeds, wandering at night, bloodied by thorns and nettles."

"A pity. It was never intended that she suffer."

"Dandelions, wild garlic for her unholy altar."

"Mrs. Boyle!"

"Unholy. Buttons and pigeon feathers."

"In the Spanish countries"—Mother Clare rose from her desk, pacing as she did in the classroom to deliver her instruction—"in the Spanish countries such altars are common in the houses of the poor. The poor give what little they have to the Virgin."

"We are not Spanish."

"And not poor." To Ellen Boyle, the nun's sigh sounded like a laugh. These women had dealt with each other. There was the matter of Jane smoking Luckies in the toilet stalls, flaunting her painted mouth at the communion rail, tucking her skirts high. As for that empty vessel's studies, one must beg the Lord's mercy. Ellen Boyle knew what she had in Jane, that her daughter was more than passing pretty and clever enough to get by. Yet these encounters with Mother Clare did her in. The firm authority of this grand lady with baby-smooth skin, the steady regard in her cool grey eyes, the protection of her gossamer black veil and the concealing folds of her habit were a great annoyance. In her dignity, she was apart from the many sisters in her care, amiable yet markedly superior. Ellen understood that Mother Clare placed the Boyles as recent arrivals to the niceties of their daughters' lessons in French and deportment, to the persuasive arguments of Augustine and Chrysostom concerning the mysteries, and understood her own faith was got by rote in an immigrant parish, her early wisdom of the world picked up in shopgirl jobs.

"Mrs. Boyle, the child has lost proportion. I will speak to her."

Ellen Boyle's patent purse and shoes glistened in a ray of sun streaking through the heavy blinds that closed out the business of Fifth Avenue. She composed herself, but her words erupted high and strident: "We are at our wits' end with her humming that song. Her father forbids her yet she will not leave off."

Shocking when the nun rounded her pink lips, sang softly: *"Oh Mary, we crown you with blossoms today, / Queen of the Angels, Queen of the May!* What a jingle. And what a trial for you. The church in this country has no respect for sacred music."

Then Ellen Boyle took an envelope from her purse, shook out the scraps cut from the Society Page. Her family dismembered, their white linen gone milky beige in rotogravure, their faces dark as Gypsies'. Her own head with the impish hat, cruelly detached from her body.

"My dear." Mother Clare watched silent tears trail through the rouge on this woman's quivering face. The poor Boyles hadn't a clue to the swank of their life, the power of their worldliness over a helpless child, nor that the girl's morbid piety was a feeble attempt to be free of them. What might she say to Mae?

Ellen Boyle walked out into a bright June day, powdered her nose and headed straight across the Avenue to the Metropolitan Museum. Something shameful in Mother Clare's favoring the Spanish, their gaudy decoration of Virgins and martyrs, household saints stuck right in the parlor, if it was parlors they had, if *parlors* they called them. She began her ascent of the broad steps to the museum and at the first landing turned back to look at her daughters' private school in the Beaux Arts mansion, then at the great houses and fine apartment buildings all down Fifth Avenue, at trees fully leafed out in the park softening the classical grandeur of the Metropolitan. Her world now. She was glad of it. *We crown you with blossoms today.* How could the Mother Superior sing it like a nursery rhyme, mock the church in this country? And guess at how little she knew of music beyond Broadway tunes? In the dark wood paneling hung with portraits of bishops and the etching of St. Peter's Square, Ellen Boyle had been simply cowed. In the light of day she took offense, for after all she'd been to Rome and to Florence with Frank in his first flush year, dancing their way across the ocean— first-class. Before the children came. They stayed at the grandest hotels. In Italy their driver spoke fair English. She turned her back on the museum, not knowing why she stood there with a tramp sharing his crumbs with the squirrels, a guard looking down on her from the big open doors high as the portals of a cathedral. Two delicate old ladies, threadbare Spring coats and tired hats, headed past her to the lofty rooms of paintings and statues. Well, it was cheaper than the picture show. She thought to go home to Park Avenue, dismantle her daughter's altar, speak sternly to Mae. Why give her child over to the nuns?

A taxi drew to the curb, scouting a fare, and she ran down to the pavement. "Russeks," she ordered, sliding onto the leather seat. A women's shop she had liked even as a girl from Queens without a spare dollar to her name, a comfortable store with good service, and there she bought quite a smart Summer dress with white bertha collar to show off her tan and, though extravagant, an evening wrap of yellow silk petals for Jane who would dance at the club this Summer, night after night, with a lineup of boys.

Mother Clare tossed the shredded Boyles in the wastebasket. Strange — this proof of iniquity left behind, evidence in that woman's court of unacceptable behavior. She called the child down to her study at once. Mae settled on the edge of a big brocade chair. Her red hair, the only bright thing about her, was pulled tight into braids. Brambles of wild roses had scratched the child's face, angry weals of insect bites scored her pale arms and legs.

"You've been in the country?"

"Yes, Mother."

"The mosquitoes have made a feast of you."

"Gnats."

"Gnats?"

"Yes, Mother."

"Gathering flowers?"

"Is this about my altars?"

A fair guess and a bold question. The nun was encouraged. She stepped out from behind her desk and came to Mae with a dish of hard candies. Glistening in a cut glass dish, set for eternity between Mother's pen wiper and her box of rubber bands, the candies were famous. No girl at Sacred Heart dared to untwist their cellophane wrappers.

"I know they are said to be poison, but they are fresh from the soda fountain on Madison Avenue. Try a lemon."

Mae's hand hovered over the dish, then snatched a yellow candy. Mother Clare chose lime, popped it in her mouth. "My indulgence. You know what that means?"

"Like a vice?"

"That is one meaning of the word." She faced Mae in the second brocade chair. The two chairs, also famous, where both parents sat when there was trouble, real trouble. "The month of Mary is over" — Mae heard the click of the sour ball against Mother's teeth — "though you are perfectly right, it seems arbitrary, you know what that means?"

"Odd?"

"That will do. Odd that the church limits a time for our deepest devotions."

The bell rang for recess. Mae was trapped, clutching the slippery arms of the brocade chair. She yearned for the release from her desk in the classroom. Mother Clare saw that the child was dazed, no longer following her instruction on the liturgical seasons. "So tell me, Mary," she asked, "why are you called Mae?"

"A nickname, I guess."

"And I am called Clare, the name I took with my vows. Clare was a wealthy girl, follower of St. Francis, friend of beasts and birds. Well, her family did not care for that at all, but she ran from them and founded the Poor Clares, Sisters who could not own a stick or a stone. They lived by begging. That is called the privilege of poverty. When I took her name, I knew my life would not be hard, but I liked Clare's story."

Mae twisted the wrapper off her candy, smoothing the cellophane. At first suck it was sharp, then sweet. Her mouth puckered as she listened to the tale of Clare's perfection. The Poor Clares went out from Assisi founding convents. At times they punished themselves with no mercy.

Mother asked, "What do you pray for all those hours?"

"To be the Virgin's child." Mae sucked hard. "And to wear steel braces on my legs."

"Why should she love you less if you are healthy and run free? *Our bodies are not made of brass*, that's what Clare wrote to her Sisters." The Mother Superior now stood, folding the black serge of her sleeve so it would not flap at the child. "You understand" — she drew her finger along a track of scabs on Mae's cheek — "suffering is not required."

Mae promised she would attend to her neglected studies, offer her homework as prayer proper to her age. As she slipped out of her chair she asked, "Was it my mother?"

The question required no more than a tilt of the nun's head. She dismissed Mae Boyle who ran out to the playground though recess was nearly over. The bell rang for afternoon classes and Mother Clare turned to her desk. She taught the seniors their religion, a tribe of good girls nicely turned out. In this class not one soul able to distinguish her social position at Sacred Heart from an allegiance to her faith. She opened a leather portfolio embossed with a gilt crown of thorns and scanned her notes on the difficult matter of the Immaculate Conception, then recalled it was Friday, half-day toward the end of Spring term. May was indeed over and the excessive adoration of the Virgin, folk custom with no place in the church calendar, could be stowed till next year. Small blessing, that there was but one Mae Boyle attempting a childish ecstasy, kneeling early and late with fetishes, wishing herself in an iron lung to punish her robust family. Mother Clare knew the troubles were not absolved by her little parable of the Sisters in Prague, she believed it was Prague, who were so foolishly austere. She chose a grape sour ball, her least favorite, and thought the girl's passion must peter out, though no telling who will be ordinary, who will be chosen. A freckle face made holy with anger, nothing to be done for the little Boyle beyond prayer.

Now Mae was a passing curiosity, having been called to Mother Superior's study. Flipping her braids, she mumbled a dull story about poor women, beggars, but it was half-day, that giddy time with sing-alongs, with cupcakes and a bottle of Coke for each girl in the lower school.

Half-day. Ellen Boyle drove the children out to The Merrow. The sun still glistened on the gentle waves of the Sound when Mae looked down from her room at the top of the house. Through the screen she heard the soft bounce, bounce of tennis balls, Law already at it with his coach.

On her altar, the stems of last week's flowers gone slimy in green water. She heard the phone ring for Jane or her mother. They would be getting the events of the weekend in order. Mae tied a ribbon on the slim waist of the Coke bottle slipped into her book bag at school. Next to a blue mussel shell she placed the candy wrapper. It glittered like mica. She was a girl making up a story of the wounds and adventures of the day, this day's great adventure. *I must not sing our song or run into the wild roses or tall nettles.* Making up words for a second voice, sweeter than Mother Clare's, soft words telling her not to wish for crutches, to call an end to . . . But Mae would never know, not even in her dreamy head, what the Virgin—a foot high in her chalk-white veil, blue robe with gilt cincture, chip in her plaster lip, sorrow in her downcast eyes— never know what the Virgin might say, for a third voice rang out, lilting with laughter, "Now isn't that lovely, trinkets and all. Sure, there's not a Lady chapel so fine."

CALL ME NELL

Trash, not trinkets, but I did not forget my position as a guest in this house. I was to sleep in a narrow box room close to the pretty room of the wan child. What with city and country Virgins, their tea parties, cocktails at the club, Jane's Junior Cotillion, Law failing his math, they had muddled the days. I was far from their concern, the cousin come from Ireland, Matt Boyle's girl. My uncle alone kept me in mind. I had seen a photo of Frank Boyle as a boy in the company of his brothers and their father, Old Dan as we now called him. Frank, then a scowling lad in a castoff cap too big for him and Donegal jacket too small. Now he was well set up in a linen suit and panama hat, as though for the tropics. Surely the air hung heavy and hot as we stood on the concrete pier in New York. His chauffeur carried my valise to the limousine. We were to drive out to a place so queerly named, The Merrow.

I had not taken to the ocean voyage. I feared the open sea, though from childhood I loved the bay at Lissadell and went out a fair way in an oil slicker and Wellingtons, out with the Byrnes to their lobster pots. You might say I was granted a dispensation from my age and sex, yet these excursions were thought an offense, one of many which set the women of our village against me. They were glad to see the end of Nuala Boyle. I had sailed to America out of Cobh, a rough boy handing me into the tender that ferried the passengers out to a tramper. Not sorry to be off, for the bus trip with my father from our village was weighty with silence. When I turned to see the last of him, Matt Boyle waved brightly, as though I was off on holiday, waving me off with a kerchief washed clean for Sunday, while the women I was to sail with cried for the loss of home. Belowdeck the ship throbbed with the heat of the turbines churning. Our cabin was fitted out with four bunks for emigrant women. Two lay moaning on their mats with their babes and one, plain as a post, with the promise of marriage in a letter fallen to pieces from the reading, hemstitched her linens the way over. All going to their men in America. Topside the sailors. I did not fancy walking the deck among them. Though I covered my head with a shawl and pulled a blank face, I was prey to their crude admiration.

In the din of traffic that was New York of the films, Frank Boyle asked me news of the home I had left. I did not know what news he wanted, for he had little to do with us over the years. News of his father gone blind but still able to feel the withers of a mare for a sharp trade? Or of Tim working his few acres for the landlord's purse? Or of Jack's wife, poor milch cow of a woman, breeding till wasted? Or of Matt, my father, heavy with drink since my mother's death, half crocked before I had the porridge on? Little to say to this uncle who had made his way in the world, a stranger taking me in. I delivered the news of our trials lightly. "We're all right," I said. "The world's wrong."

I was eighteen years old. They sold the white mare for my passage. I'd been sent off by the lot of them, the Boyle boys, my father and blind Dan, shipped like a parcel, got out of their way. That story I did not tell, only turned to my uncle, smart as a penny, to say how eager I was to start the course in nursing. Frank Boyle took my hand in his, a fatherly gesture. I remember the softness of his palm, the smooth pads of his fingers, for only once had I felt a man's hand that was not rough and callused.

He spoke to me of his wife, a treasure to him, and of the escapades of Jane and Lawrence—cutups, he called them. Little Mae he set apart, laughed at her saintly ways. "Perhaps, Nuala, you will cheer her. Perhaps you can play together." He looked long at me, his first unguarded look at the tangles of my unruly dark hair and at my breasts in a thin white jersey, then fanned himself with his panama, knowing he'd said something foolish.

It was clear within a day that Mae loved me. No vanity in that claim, though at Ballycarne they said I was full of myself. This child was looking for something to care for and lavished dollhouse rites on a couple of statues, punishing her knees the long hours as a way to assign her blame. Mother of God, she was right—the Boyles were a shallow crew, drinking and dancing and playing at sports. Many evenings that Summer the play continued. Bridge for the ladies, silver dishes of mints and nuts—the bridge assortment. Billiards in a barn for the men, a barn with oak floors and electric fixtures, a fridge for their weak beer pale as piss. And in the vast hall and parlors, all of them dancing to the phonograph. At home only Old Dan had a wireless in his cottage. If he could no longer see the world, at least he could hear its music and misfortunes.

"Play with her," Frank Boyle said to a country girl who never held a racquet in her hand, who was shamed by the priest for a game of tag with the lads, who waded with her skirts tied up the once we took my ailing mother to the seaweed baths in Enniscrone. Did my uncle not recall the cold seas beyond Ballycarne Cove? That the Boyles were turf cutters, tenant farmers, traders of horseflesh, whatever land offered for a living. My uncle twisted his tongue smoothly round my name, "Nuala, play with her!" Well we did, Mae and I, play at being friends over the leap of ten years between us.

All a wonder the first days, the flower garden perfectly cultivated, not a cabbage or ridge of potatoes in sight, and the children's red sailboat drifting on the Sound, the dresses of silk and chambray, the soft store bread and cube butter; the men, fine young men in white flannels looking me over, were easily stirred, though I had no use for them. I had been shipped across the ocean to obliterate the sight of me, though didn't I yet know the game—give the wet lick of my lips, show a bit of calf crossing my legs in what I would learn to call a reflex action.

"Noo? Noo-la?" They mooed attempting my name.

"Call me Nell," I said, and in America Nell I became.

The mother was dense, concerning herself with my shabby clothes, but the daughter knew at once I was a danger, that her sleek bobbed hair and sinewy limbs were no match for the curse, as it was said to be, of my black Sligo beauty.

"Nursing?" Jane drew her mouth into a mocking O.

"That's the intention."

"The best intention?"

That first Sunday, sunning myself on their dock in a moth-eaten bathing suit discarded by the mother, Jane came down, time running out before the drive back to the city, waving her brother in, the boy they called Law, who sailed in the pretty boat not far from shore.

But it was "Nell! Nell," he called, "come out to me!"

"I canna swim."

My cousin Jane laughed a dismissal.

Law swung round to the dock. I had sailed under canvas once in my life and that recently, a story of my destruction at sea. Oh, I'd not been consumed in the watery depths, for wasn't I here in a strange land shooing my cousin away.

"Nell," he pleaded. The boy's skiff seemed no more than the small boat I played in as a child and their Sound was still as a pond, so I let him hand me down. We sailed away, to Jane's fury. I saw how it was with

them, for I'd had such a brotherly love which was now damned. Law
caught the wind, showing off, bringing us round till we faced Frank
Boyle and his wife waiting on the lawn in their city clothes, set for the
drive back to town. Their boy was scolded. Being new to them, I was let
off. Ellen Boyle never knew what to do with me—box room at The
Merrow, maid's room in the city.

On the Monday I was driven to the hospital with my uncle in the
limousine. I donned the white uniform, netted my hair, and the Sisters
at St. Vincent's, innocent women, presumed to instruct me on the human body. I am a nurse still, though I cared nothing for the profession
at that time. Nursing—the idea of the scandalized men in my family,
their plot to make me respectable, not to redeem my soul. In the car
Uncle Frank, as he told me to call him, read his morning paper, often
glancing my way. I was dropped at a side entrance to join students and
graduate nurses, who in those desperate days, worked for their room,
board, laundry and ten dollars a month. My uncle paid for my training.
His name engraved on the plaque of donors in the marble reception
hall. He had arranged my post at St. Vincent's as he arranged his kids'
getting out of scrapes, into schools. My training began as their school
year came to a close, and at the outset I joined the Boyles this side of the
Atlantic for their weekends, exhausting ourselves with play.

Except Mae, who glommed on to me. More like work, her collecting the combs and pins which fell from my hair, sipping black tea in
imitation. On a Sunday soon after my arrival, she spread the comics before us, prompting me to laugh. She had stowed her Virgins away and
leaned into me, her breath heavy with hope that I might get the fun of
her funnies, then—

"Nell, I will miss you."

"Miss me?"

"When you go back." The child a quick step ahead of me. "Not to
Ireland. Into town."

How would I know we'd not all traipse back and forth, country to city
and round again to the endless pleasures? That the mother and chil-

dren were to stay at the big house for the Summer holiday and the student of nursing return with her patron to the empty rooms on Park Avenue. The better part of my life gone by, but how well I remember our mutual knowledge, Frank Boyle's and that of the girl they called Nell, the hoor from the other side, or so my uncle would one day maintain. We left, the family waving us off. Mae and the terrier panting after the car as though to keep us in their simpler world.

My uncle and I were driven in silence to the stale rooms on Park Avenue. We ate leftovers. The two of us with our picnic perched in the kitchen he seldom entered.

"Will you have whiskey?" he asked.

"I have no need of it."

On the nights when he kissed my mouth, the needy kisses of a long-married man, he thrust me away. We did not lay together on the cot in my room. That sorry story of master and maid did not further unfold. I begged the head nurse for night duty until I was thought to be the most ardent student of them all.

"You've not told me," he said, "how you're getting on at St. Vincent's."

"I can tuck up a bed with mitered corners, take a temperature, a pulse—though not on my own."

"Fine work for a woman."

Which got my Irish up. I allowed how I was studying the skeletal system, attachment of muscles to the spine. "Coccygeus and gluteus maximus, if I say them correctly. I've little learning beyond the National School."

A hearty pat on my back and a lecture on the noble calling to heal the sick, comfort the dying. Ah, he could keep his distance with such chatter, transform himself to benefactor, leave the sinner behind.

I might have told him I'd seen my own mother out, attended to Old Dan's bodily functions, strapped my father's ribs cracked on his way home from Hurley's Pub. Such stories were close to the bone, so I said, "Tonight I must study. Out at your Merrow I've done nothing to be proud of. In the week you need not bother with me. I'll be on night duty."

"You're no bother," Frank said.

In the wards I walked softly with a nursing nun, checking the chart posted at the bottom of each bed—attending to temperature, blood pressure, intake and output of fluids—all the while praying the night would be peaceful. Not praying, counting the hours till dawn. It was a relief in that underworld of white beds with moaning, lightly breathing bodies when I was allowed to administer a pill, change a dressing. When all was quiet, say in the wing with single rooms, each patient with a private nurse, I waited for the simple orders to fetch or carry. It was then I thought of my father alone with blind Dan, burning the toast on the fire, setting out sour milk for their tea. And Uncle Jack, the lightheaded Boyle brought down, his kids running wild in the fields, for with what I'd seen of ill-nourished women in maternity, surely his wife was now laid to rest.

No news of them and I'm sure they wanted no news of me. I have long put away my sorrow at being cast away entirely, sunk like the cargo of a ship crashed on the rocks. News in the papers was of eight million out of work in the country which I must now call my own, a great misery, though the student nurses I worked with were made happy by a film or a popular tune. Like the verse we were set to learning in school—*For the good are always merry / Save by an evil chance.* The Sisters of St. Vincent's flew down the corridors in big winged hats, white doves dispensing their mercy. They loved a good gossip with the doctors and the private room patients. With the students it was strict rules. Those serious women believed I had the gift of healing. I had only the gift of keeping busy, tending to bodies not my own. I was but weeks into the nursing when a girl's belly strained the buttons of her uniform, a kissing nurse they called her. She had bedded with a patient, and though she left to marry they were unforgiving; not her sin they decried—a lack of devotion to their profession.

I hold to their rules of decorum.

In the city, my uncle continued his annoyance. I petitioned the Sisters for weekend duty, though often enough I must ride out with him to The Merrow. Boyle drove his long black car, the only sign his family had that all was not well. A man not given to failure, and he did not fail with me, for he never attempted more than the lingering kisses. Dust filmed the fine furniture in the apartment, soot on the sills. There were nights so lonely I might have welcomed him, my fear not of Frank Boyle, fear of the stories I could tell myself to make him a hero—working his way to America on a freighter, a penniless boarding-house mick marrying in a romantic fit before he went off to the war. Still no more than a lad, a runner learning the money trade to perfection. All true—and what's more he was handsome, the white ruff of hair topping a young man's face.

Not scruffy like his brothers, who shaved on a Saturday night. I thought how the men in our family thickened, grew stiff in their joints with the years, the skin of their hands and feet tough with the pachydermia. Men satisfied with a pint or a nip of poteen. At times I could believe I was not beholden to Frank Boyle, because he was no longer one of us, this sleek fellow smelling of bay rum, supple and slim, pleased with a glance at himself in a mirror. He was a great man at the New York Athletic Club. I'd not heard of the games that kept him fit. And great with the colored waiters, ordering champagne with the crab cocktail, displaying me to his pals, the one time he pulled the brogue. *Easy lads, she's me brother's girl, the mist of Sligo still on her.* My uncle played at being a ladies' man. Offering me a hothouse rose, a jade bracelet to make good for his misdemeanors, he was innocent as absolution itself and innocent of my desire. He sloughed off his role of lover like the transparent skin of the garden lizards I would see one day in Italy. Driving out with him from the city, I was no more than one of his kids.

Mae—begging for tales of the children in the polio ward, a morbid interest in these unfortunates. Not to speak of their suffering, I told of the nun big as a barrel scouring the patients' trays for a cup of custard, sneaking the lovely Schrafft's chocolates out of their violet box. The dumb Dolly in training who could not tell sphincter from sphinx. How we laughed at mishaps with the bedpan.

"And the children?"

"Enough of those children!" Then I spoke to her of Ireland, foolish stuff—little girls stolen by the fairies at dusk, a creature left in their place ever so like them but wicked or odd at best. How St. Brigid took her eye out of its socket and popped it back in when her father allowed he would not make her marry. And told of the fires at Midsummer, a penny for the fire, the children of Sligotown cried and bought sweets to suck by the fire at night, when the country boys threw firebrands into the air and you carried a coal home to save the ashes that healed the sick. Nonsense. You dare not say it. And Jack, not strong in his mind, my uncle who was Mae's uncle, laying embers in the paddock that his milk cow might come to no evil, and the shed gone up in flames. I found myself full of such stories for the child, stories I'd as soon left behind like the hunger month my mother spoke of, the lean days of July before the crops were in.

"You were poor?"

"We'd the cow and the hens, bread on the table, but your father might call us poor." Which pleased Maesie Boyle as I sat on the bottom of her bed drinking top of the milk, gobbling the butter cookies ever in full supply. And so to sleep with stuff and nonsense.

At St. V's I couldn't get enough of work, nor enough of my studies. In the terrible heat of the New York Summer, I'd fall on my cot, then wake to read, crouched under the dim night-light of the dormitory. We were on to the viscera—heart, lungs, sex organs, abdominal glands. I believe it was that early on, my first season at the hospital, I fell in love—my love of the illustrated body—studying the pictures in my textbook, the heart suspended in its sheath of pericardium like a fist plunged into a rubber ball, and stones lying in the gallbladder, coins in a bag. I treasured the eye's filigree of nerves, firm arc of the cornea, the dirigible of its lens. The wonderful machinery of bodies, each detail in black and white on the page, were of no man or woman alive. At times

I was called with the soft ring of a bell to assist at the bed of a patient in pain, and once, on a night of hell's own heat in August, to witness the rattle of the dying. Only menial tasks I was set to, but I cared for these strangers. My heart leapt to the business of caring for patients who would not enter my life. I knew then that I would care always for the ailing and wounded, and for bodies *in extremis.* Case to case.

"And the children?" Mae would not let me off.

In the end, I told her of the children in their rows of little beds. That Summer, Pediatrics was strained beyond capacity with the poliomyelitis, and I spelled the disease out for the curious girl. I think always to tell patients the story entire of their illness, though in those years doctors and nurses dissembled. Mae Boyle, who had invented such affliction, was better for the truth—fevers, the virus attacking the nerve cells that control voluntary motion, the muscle fiber cut off, wasting away.

"Be thankful," I said.

"I am thankful." Flexing her arms and legs, blotched from the sun, she asked, "May I?" With a brush in hand she stroked down the length of my hair.

"Is Jane pretty?" she asked.

"Indeed, pretty."

"But you are beautiful, Nell."

On in this way, Law mooning after me, taking his pleasure with my body held afloat as he taught me to swim, my hair stuffed in a rubber cap. I took no offense at this boy's fingers fumbling for my breasts, his hands cupping my behind.

By the end of Summer Frank Boyle's fortunes were up, the maid back with her feather duster. One day, properly chauffeured from the heat of the city, I asked, "Why call it The Merrow?"

"The mermaid. I was enchanted by the place."

"*Muruach*—in the Gaelic. Your scaly woman is not always a beauty, more often a hazard, a scamp with green teeth who locks fishermen's

souls at the bottom of the sea." Were it not for the sorry end of my stay
in America, I'd not remember that legend.

I have lived in Canada the greater part of my life.

I no longer speak a word of Irish.

Then it was Mae with the consolation of an embroidery hoop. Bureau
scarves and tea towels sprouting birds, clowns, Bo Peep with a cast in
her eye. One night, while they danced their sambas and rumbas at the
club, she stood in the shadow of my door, handed over a pillowcase
with a winking owl in a tree.

"Now won't I be wise!"

"You are, Nell." We sat often in her airy room watching sailboats
skim the placid waves, though once a storm came up—a trifling squall,
not deadly winds which swell the sea at Inishmurray. That child with
fiery hair set free like her Nell's, with the pitiful look of a kid in the in-
fectious ward, was my only friend in the States. Picking out yet another
design on a huck towel, content with her stitches, pressing work which
set her apart from the sporting life of the Boyles.

"Nell," she asked when I sat on the bottom of her bed, "won't you say
a prayer?"

I gave her no answer.

Now I told no further stories of Druids and evil spells but only that
the hot-water bottle must be 124° for a conscious adult, 110° for a child,
that taking air into the lungs is called the inspiration, that the spoon
must be half full to neatly feed a patient. In that telling to Mae, I loved
the absorbing details, all that I must learn to tend to bodies. Reverent as
a convert, I cherished my studies, though I laughed at the uppity old
nun who had studied with Sir William Osler. Each week at her command we must recite his seven nursely virtues: tact, tidiness, taciturnity,
sympathy, gentleness, cheerfulness, charity. A guarantee of our recovery room in heaven. And I told Mae of the young doctor who took me
to the films at the Academy of Music.

"Do you care for him?"

"Not at all." The child so glad of that she pricked her finger with the needle, but did not fall into a sleep, as the story tells it, went on with her woman's work.

Now the news was all of the Nazi peril, Britain and France alerted for the war. There was to be no argument at Frank Boyle's table about America's duty. He'd had his fill hunting the Huns at Belleau Wood. "Sell arms, cash and carry," he said. "Stay out of it. In the Great War, the Irish got down on their knees to the will of the bloody Brits."

There was talk among the graduate nurses of the Red Cross, signing up for the decent pay. I had no thought of the world. When we were not at the books or on duty, the new girls were instructed in simple methods—boiling the instruments, the use of hot packs and the steam inhaler. Work was a poultice on the injuries of my past, work till I fell on my cot.

At Christmas my father called from the post office in Sligo, three sheets to the wind. The connection was faulty. I heard only that the child born dead to Jack's wife was late buried. No word of forgiveness.

I have never sought their forgiveness.

The New Year—a penance in the streets, snow mightier than any drifts in the West of Ireland. Ellen Boyle outfitted me in a stiff winter coat, gloves lined with the cheap fur of a hare. For herself—she was appointed to the founding board of the March of Dimes, the occasion for a mink to join the Persian lamb in her closet. The dimes were to mount to dollars, to millions for those stricken with polio—to heal, find a cure. At last Mrs. Boyle and I spoke to each other, and that was some kindness, displaying our small medical knowledge of new methods with the wet heat and manipulation of the limbs.

Law's hands on me, pestering in any small encounter, failing his maths, winning his trophies. Jane out till midnight and after, flaunting her small breasts in the strapless gowns come into favor. Mae—what can be said of Mae? Good by default, she busied herself with Chinese

babies, collecting nickels and pennies to save their souls, the coins tin-
kling for holy charity and the babies no more live to her than abandoned dolls. Sitting on the end of her bed, I went on with my news of
the hospital. Now I valued the gossip less, the language of the body
more, all the clinical words as well as the anatomical drawings which
monitored my feelings. And counted that progress of a sort I could not
confess to a trusting girl.

Blessed with the burden of my work till the sun came out for Easter.
The Boyles in new outfits, the mother's hat flopping with daisies; my
winter coat thrown open for the breeze. I went to Mass with them,
though at St. V's I ducked the obligation. Easter had brought my end in
Ireland, a bitter season. I had soothed the festering sick and struggled
with the books, most recently the physiology of ear and eye—a babble
of malleus, incus, blind spot, vitreous humor—to put the tale of Inishmurray out of mind. A silent complaint came upon me in the sweet
smell of potted lilies at the hospital, the yellow chicks chirping in the
children's ward and the baskets of treats handed round by Frank Boyle.
In Ballycarne, during Holy Week we knelt long before each Station of
the Cross. The women of the parish running to chapel until the Resur-
rection, when some saintly soul stuck a bit of green on the altar. No dye-
ing of eggs. We ate them brown or speckled, as they came from their
maker, though once my mother colored them in a stew of beet root.
They sat like rubies on our plates. Such memories led to my keening
complaint.

Only a year had passed since my removal from Ireland. I found no
words to put to my story, though I was sure the women who hounded
me told it as their triumph. Spring once more, and I should have feared
the stirring of roots and blood. By the Ascension on the sanctimonious
calendar of those biddies who ran to chapel at every call of the bell, I'd
again be banished, this time from America. Sign on for my afterlife, as
I signed on for extra duty to serve the term of my days.

This day and tomorrow.

HOME SISTER

My war stories were set pieces by the mid-Fifties, when Mae listened to them with the generous ear of a woman who's had no adventures, eager as the child who feasted on my tales of Druids and tattle of St. Vincent's. We were in an old fashioned sort of place on Madison Avenue, doilies under the teacups, waitresses with frilled caps that recalled the maids who worked at Frank Boyle's establishments. It was the first time I'd seen Mae grown up, so to speak. Except for the bright hair escaping her pageboy in wiry tendrils, you'd not notice her, a dainty creature perched on the edge of her chair weightless as a wren or common sparrow. Boyle was still in the money when his shy daughter was looking to marry a man he did not approve of. He had carted her to the old sod as though she would find distraction in the backward ways of Ballycarne.

"You are a legend to them," Mae said.

"What sort of legend?"

"Your work in the war."

"Didn't they stay out of it, not to give a hand to the English? And too foolish to make a pound off the battle, cash or carry."

"They speak of your professional advancement."

"How would they hear of me?"

Mae blushed at the slightest cut. Yet she'd stood up to her father, fluttering as she told me of the man she'd set her heart on, a young captain, no less, home from that war running its course in Korea. At the wedding, Jane was to be matron of honor in lavender, Law coming in from California, where he'd been stationed in the navy. Where he settled to surfboarding, another sport I'd not heard of. Frank Boyle had voiced his displeasure, then put his boy, who could not add simple fractions, to managing the books for an oil-drilling firm in Santa Barbara.

"I must miss your happy occasion." I spoke to Mae of pressing duties in Montreal, then of my recent travels, a pleasure trip to the North of Italy, the soft Spring days in Florence, how richly embroidered the linens at my hotel, how proper the service. The steaks alone worth the trip.

"By yourself?"

"Always by myself."

"Why is that, Nell?" When I gave no answer, she told of her finger-tip veil. Mae's moment center stage. Her mother would pin fresh orange blossoms in her hair. Doing her best with the delightful prelim-inaries to marriage, but the fuss of seed pearls hand-sewn on white satin was too much for this simple soul to bear, and she turned the talk to me, as she had always at The Merrow. To listen to her Nell, who went to war.

"They say you were in the thick of it."

"Is that what they say?"

In Ballycarne she'd boasted of my nursing degrees, given my legend, as she called it, a pretty twist. In the war I was no more than an orderly with the Canadian ground forces. Tattered Cinderellas, we swept, washed and tidied while the commissioned nurses went to the ball with medics, carting in the dead and wounded. They called us Home Sis-ters. Home—who thought up that one for the tents we pitched in the unforgiving sands of North Africa and on the cliffs of Italy overlooking the bloody strafing of the shore? True, in our grub work we were do-mestics.

Our unit of doctors and nurses trailed the Régiment de Maison-neuve out of Montreal. Scots, Swedes, Poles, Irish Home Sisters who parlez-voused not a word. And did the bride-to-be with her illusion veil, once so curious as to the fate of ailing children, so eager for my bedtime tales of Ireland, did Mae never wonder how I was transported from St. Vincent's to the European Theater?

When I headed North with my valise, I'd not known Canada had its share of Irish immigrants and its full share of the Great Depression. Half trained, fit for nothing, I swabbed the halls of the Royal Victoria Hospital with disinfectant green as bile. A trial looking on as the Nurse Superintendent led her flock through the wards, teaching at bedside.

As though I still held the privileges of a student, I studied my physiology at night in a cold room let to me by a French family, poorest of the poor. I brought them bread and bits of grey meat not eaten by the patients, living for a year in this way before I was rescued by the war. My last flirtation was with a shy Scot, his gentle face an agony of smallpox scars, who adjusted the date of my birth so that I might be taken for a Home Sister. Filling out papers, I named Mary Boyle next of kin. There was no one in the world I'd have claim me. Mae was ten years old.

Housekeeping chores—I might well have been back in Ballycarne with the scrubbing board in the leaky tin washtub the tinker could patch no more. My allegiance was to the care and comfort of my nurses. All commissioned medics were given the dignity of their last names. The doctors and nursing sisters called *Nuala, Nuala* for my service. But my unit valued me. To this day I hear from Ottawa and Edmonton, from the Sisters whose knickers I washed under a spigot and from the head surgeon at Winnipeg General, whose swollen feet I massaged. These were my companions—free of patronage, of any link to the past.

In the commissary I was a terrier procuring the best bedrolls and canvas washbasins when our unit came across to Sicily. Mae would make a heroine of me as though I operated under the marquee with the surgeons. I dished out in the mess, ordered sing-songs to keep the nurses' spirits up. Grimy, tin-hatted girls, sweating in the terrific heat, shivering in the cold, yellow ice forming on the pail of stagnant wash-up water. Still, when we were not moving up behind the lines, awaiting casualties, there was romance in the air. War stories—all rules of decorum suspended, two of our nurses married their fellas. I made them wedding parties with the Captain's Victrola and dago red. One was a Québecois farm boy speaking his vows to a city girl who would never gather the brown eggs of his prize hen. He shipped out on the last hospital boat from Palermo, his bride our only casualty in the approach to Naples.

My nurses worn to the nub, I scouted out a woman in Agrigento who washed and set their hair in ancient aluminum curlers. Fag ends I lit for dying soldiers, passing them from my lips. Cutting a boy's shirt to plug up a wound, I discovered the naked thighs and blooming breasts of a pinup nestled next to the photo of the plain sweetheart back home. Or, waking to a dawn streaked red-gold across a horizon treeless as Ireland, I'd not think there was a war, the din of mortar distant or not at all, then turned to see in the tent not twenty feet behind me, a boy my age, a ruddy university boy with a paper book in his pocket, *Purgatorio*, a title he need not translate, and we laughed at that one before he went peaceful to his eternal rest. My war stories were bittersweet as doses fed to a child. When it was over, names and dates of the Italian offensive in the history books, I found no need to tell of lice swarming in the seams of a soldier's clothes, of the pervasive stench of ammonia and nicotine that masked nothing, not the muck of latrines or foul mess of bloody bandages, nor the meaty sizzle of cauterized wounds. No need to tell that I was among the Home Sisters who nursed against regulations, pressed beyond our janitorial services. You'll not find our story in accounts of Sherman tanks landing at Anzio or the Poles taking Monte Cassino, so I can't imagine what legend Mae Boyle had in mind—that I was in the thick of it and they spoke well of me at home.

I suppose there was glory in cleaning the filth of wounded men, smelling the waste of war, and that I was proud of our convoy trailing the next engagement and the next, the Union Jack tucked out of sight till we came into a battered city—victorious. My memory was keen enough, but when my duties were over the need to return to my books, to the training I was now entitled to in Montreal, was a dull story.

By the year of Mae's marriage, I'd been back across the waters to St. George's in London, where I delivered my first paper—"Nursing Authority: Adaptations of the Nightingale Method." I then made my way to the toe of Italy, crossing to Messina, thinking to see the island cleared of rubble and booby traps. A sentimental journey.

I travel light and alone. Observations must be mine. Go by the books, I tell my girls in training, but never disallow what you see with the naked eye. Agrigento, still in ruins. On the scrubland where we pitched our tents, set up neat rows of field beds for the wounded men, people now lived in shacks built of debris. And my Palermo, where the Italians welcomed us with wine and kisses, was a poor and dirty place. I found no comfort in the excess marble and gilt of the churches. Children in rags scrambled at me with their filthy fingers for a coin. In the cafés, men turned from the sight of me, a sturdy woman in hiking boots and khaki shorts. The street to my grand hotel was dark and narrow. I was not up for the assault of a horsehair mattress or brackish water in the tub. This unpleasant trip to the South was an abiding loss, I should not say it, dispiriting as our Captain's daily posting of the injured and dead.

Speaking of my travels to Mae Boyle, I left Sicily off the map, thought to amuse her with my tourist walks in Florence. I know nothing of art, but claimed to experience a portion of beauty in those three or four days until in a dim churchy cool . . . What possessed me, picking among the jam tarts and iced cakes? A surfeit of refined sugar did not sweeten my words to Mae.

I said that in a cool dim church I came upon a hideous thing, a statue clothed in hair. "An animal," I said, "hair plastered over her body, surely a naked body, the hair covering her shame."

"Nell?"

"You heard me—shame. The guidebook names her Magdalene." My fury shattered the tea shop murmur. "A saint, sorry all her long life, so God-almighty sorry, and if she washed the feet of Christ with that hair why did she not cut it, save it as holy?"

"To cover herself," Mae whispered.

"Save it to sell off as relics. Flowers left at her feet, dying for her favors. Well, don't you know, a guard removed them as I stood there." What devil was in me, telling this girl of an object I'd put out of mind? "Penitent. Is that the ticket? Life given over to starving yourself in the desert? Well, the artist cut her down to size. Withered, she's nothing at all, feet slick as flesh scarred with burns. Her face ruined."

"Once lovely."

"Who'd know it?" I called for the waitress.

"But your trip? You enjoyed it?"

"Yes, I enjoy seeing such things."

"May I?" she said, but I paid for our tea and wished her much happiness, sorry I would not see her with the aromatic blossoms in her hair. Did she not understand, that though sorry, I must live up to my legend, could not traffic with the neutrality of Park Avenue? I'd broken with Boyle, the fence sitter who procured a desk job in intelligence for his son in the United States Navy.

Mae, who would cross her father in the matter of her marriage, kissed me, a glint of pride in her teary eyes for my political principles. Sorry I'd won the day, should I then have asked the bride-to-be, the girl with the illusion veil, did she not wonder what possessed me to carry on about a statue? Or how I came of a sudden from Ireland, came upon her fussing with her Virgin and in a year just as quickly vanished?

INISHMURRAY

Hugh Byrnes was ever my love. His people were fishermen. As children we rowed out for the fun of it, our little tub of a boat built by his father, a plaything in a world without toys. And there was the gift of our wits— dividing school prizes between us, vying to be head of the class. A kid's competition and far from true. We were bound to each other. Granted a dispensation from our village life that was narrow and hard for other children, indulged by the Byrnes and the Boyles as though changelings, once swans perhaps, or naked infants sprouting seraph wings. We caught sea trout in our net and gathered wild cherries walking the distance to Streedagh. On in this way Hugh and I, till the Christian Brothers came prospecting and took him away. I was left behind, at that time nursing my mother. When he returned at term's end, all was the same, our back talk masking affection, our roughhouse the unwitting touches of children. As the years passed, our bodies broke the charm— diddies poking the thick wool of my jumpers, downy hair on his chin.

Strange to each other. At Christmas, arm wrestling on the table rock, I was no match for him.

"You've gone boggy."

"That I have." For I was soft on Hugh Byrnes and filled my head with dreams while I turned my mother's bruised body this way and that in the bed, her flesh rubbed raw from the flour bag sheets. I dreamed of the train ride to Cork where he was with the Fathers who gave him Latin, Greek and philosophical studies. There I'd work in a shop, selling ribbons or farmer cheese or female remedies—what matter the goods. Cook his fry-ups, go about the city with my hair bobbed. Never once did I think I would marry Hugh, the flat clank of our chapel bell ringing. I was well aware the Fathers had taken him to be a priest. He spoke now of theology added to his studies, but never a word to me of his calling. We were eighteen when he came back at Easter and appeared once at our door, cap in hand, to say it was a blessing, my mother gone to her reward, shuffling the worn words from his mouth. On the Saturday he did not come to the half-sets and waltzing. I heard that when he went out for the catch with his brothers, they set him aside like a passenger. Though he lifted a glass at Hurley's, he'd never again be one of us.

But I would not have my dreams done and over. When the Byrnes walked down our lane, I called from the half-door, "Have you no use for me, Hugh?"

"How could that be, Nuala?"

"You might come by."

"I might do that," he said. I cared not at all what they thought of a girl who put herself forward. So it started—our crossing the outfields that led down to the cove, the old haunts. He told me of gods, of their wars he read in the Greek and of the rowdy scholars, not the seminarians, who were his friends. He had spent Holy Week fasting, silent as the grave in his contemplations. Easter being over, he was released to the world. I believed that world was me. April, warmer than April, the broom early golden, birds busy in the hedgerows.

"Let's go out in the little boat?"

"Nuala, we would sink it. The great size of us."

He held out his hand to prove its span, a smooth hand that turned the pages of a book. Then I kissed the cup of it and let my lips stray to the Mount of Venus. He pulled back only to take the pins out of my hair, spill it loose, wild as I wore it when we were children gathering shells. Now, isn't that the darling story? Lovers in a mist by the sea like the postcards with words the tourists can't read in the Gaelic. Inishmurray, the island I had never crossed to, lay before us.

"What a pity," I said, "to have the island so near and never see it." We paused in our kisses, trailed down to the shore. "A pity to always look on."

"It's nothing but rocks. Rocks and poteen."

I stroked his soft hand. "Will you take me?"

"It's more than a man can row."

"You must take me."

"Nuala, don't go on in this way."

But I would have my voyage. "Alf Ternan sails out for a fee."

And next day we found Alf, an ould wan who lived with his yellow dog in a hut of bark and sticks. No one knew how he came to live by the boulders. Some said he was a shell-shocked Aussie who never found his way home and some that he had been a barrister in Westport and some that he was in the Royal Navy, and that Alf once taught at the big houses, children of the gentry, a Protestant who did not choose to come among us. The few words I traded with Ternan, his accent was not Sligo. He carried himself tall, looking sharp at the horizon as if, counting out his pollack and herring in at the dock, he was still out to sea, content with that distance. His beard was a grey thicket, rough as the coat of his dog. The strangest thing about Alf was his boat, fast and slim, built with two masts. The fishermen spoke of it with reverence, an aristocrat among their castle yawls with the single spirit sails. It was said by some women that in summer Alf braved the open waters to Galway Bay, where his wife lay long buried.

I paid him more than he'd fish out that morning, money taken from a little chamois purse, hoarded shillings and sixpence, given to me by my mother on her last day. I rode out to Grange on Hugh's handlebars, the sky a fine blue above us. When we cast off, Alf did not like the undertow or the excitable froth on the water. Later, we would be reminded—sun in the morning, a storm at day's end—but it was more than I wished for sailing away, as though we were leaving the small white cottages, the cattle grazing and the church steeples poking the sky, leaving it all behind. The yellow dog sniffed the air and yowled, then cowered at Alf's feet. Later, they would say the wind picked up from the Southwest. Fishermen let down their sheets and rowed in early. By the end of that day Alf Ternan, waiting for us off Inishmurray, was swept under the terrible sea. We did not hear his masts crack in the gale, nor the dog who swam ashore yapping for his master.

Like all lovers, we thought the island was our own and took no account of the few people and their cattle who still lived on its rocky soil. An old woman with a witch's wen on her nose swatted flies off the cod drying in the sun by her door. She wondered at our arrival and remarked that Gallagher did not travel out on this day. Oh, I'd known supplies came by motorboat from the Killybeg store but wanted to spend the legacy of my mother's purse on my romantic adventure. We walked at a fair pace through the grassland with nothing in sight till a rotted wood post pointed to the antiquities. Hugh knew the sacred books of this place had been destroyed by heathens, knew as much of the early Christians who built these dwellings as he did of the pagan gods he read of in Cork. There was now this breach of his learning between us.

"Sea pinks," I cried, "and bluebells, the field awash in bluebells!" I stooped to show him the soft feathers of an eider duck nesting. I had Hugh and didn't give a damn for the ruins of a monastery, sixth century A.D. It seemed we might be free of all histories, let the present consume us.

Nothing but rocks, he had said, but as we entered the cashel enclosing the ruins he knew the burial places, separate for men and women, the holy wells and the upright slabs inscribed with crosses. We stood by a mound of stones. You could not live in Ballycarne and not hear of these stones. "The Clocha Breacha," Hugh named it with a touch of awe. Some foolishness they told of—walking counterclockwise against the sun, then flipping them, you laid a curse. I turned a stone.

"Nuala," he scolded.

Laughing, I turned another. "No harm."

He pulled me from them, solemn as a saint, then came to himself, and we climbed the highest rampart, ate oatcakes and brown eggs I had boiled at dawn. Sharing warm orange squash, we looked back to the dark bay and out to the moody Atlantic. We were that high on our crumbling wall. At the inquest we would say the shadow of grey clouds upon the sea was at a great distance, that in our explorations we did not track the time of day.

All at once the fierce rain was on us. We ran for a stone hut and there we lay.

"How long would that be?" they asked us.

Time enough for our drenched clothes to come off in a fury. Time for his mouth on my swollen nipples and trembling thighs. I was wet with desire. The exact blue of Byrnes' eyes? I can no longer say. I believe he had the dent of the devil's kiss in his chin. Yet I am a scholar in my own right, and for many years I pictured with accuracy his rusty pubic hair, that particular gleaming shaft, the dark cutaneous pouch of the scrotum, as though a perfect illustration of penis erectile projected on a slide in my classroom. I bled freely on our bed of rocks. His seed sweet to me as honey. Isn't that how I might tell it if I had not followed the practical course of my profession?

"How long, Miss Boyle?"

"Till the storm was over."

And then the sky was strangely bright, the sun still as a brass cymbal not rung. Retracing our path to the shore, we spoke all that nonsense, stuff and nonsense of sweethearts, as the barnacle geese quacked above the moor. The houses were shuttered, but the woman with the wen on her nose was hanging her cod out after the storm. She knew the hour we had come to the island by the light as it fell on her floor and would tell to the minute when we passed again, so disheveled.

The dog yelped when we found him, then fell at our feet whining. His heart beat, beat hard against my hand, yellow dog of mixed breed, Alf Ternan's companion. The mutt led us to the splintered masts and all that was left of the canvas flapping.

"Look what we've done." Hugh's face ashen with shame. "Look what we have brought about, Nuala."

"An act of God!"

Wasn't that the stupid cry, for it was God who Hugh Byrnes chose in that moment, pushing my body from him, though when questioned he did not betray me, not a word of my inheritance spent, not a clue to our carnal knowledge. He spoke of our touring the oratories. "We took shelter in a beehive, as the stone huts of the island are called." Quite the scholar of Inishmurray, master of more than Christian tales. In the barracks at Mullaghmore, Byrnes told these dark legends with authority— from the pulpit as it were. He spoke of our viewing the cursing stones, made it clear we'd not turned them at all.

An oddly pleasant gathering, with the gardaí more curious in the matter of the illegal whiskey of the island than the death of a stranger among us, poor Alf nailed in his coffin boards. Had we spotted jugs of poteen? A still or keg hidden in the boulders? We had not, which was the truth of it, and the Sergeant himself broke into the mockery of an Inishmurray song—

> *We keep our own distillery; no taxes do we pay.*
> *May the Lord protect my island home that lies in Sligo Bay.*

Death was then declared accidental over a cup of tea, Alf Ternan's remains assigned to the Protestant graveyard. I've heard the sirens' whine far, then the swift whoosh of gurneys rushed to emergency with bodies mangled, bleeding, the flesh ruptured, seared. Frayed wire and flame, ice storm, foot on the pedal as the mind wanders. Not all the stories of happenstance nor frail logic of the calculated risk will solve the mystery—why an experienced sailor lost his long wager with the sea waiting among the rocks for two foolish lovers. Alf washed up with my mother's chamois purse in his pocket. I did not claim it. No fault was found in his death beyond the great swell of the sea, but my man walked from me. Escorted by his brothers in a donkey cart, Byrnes boarded the train to Cork, back to his blessed studies.

I went mad with the loss of him and mourned the waste of my body. My ripe breasts, full hips and what lay between were a ruin to me, like the ancient stones of that island. In a week I gained my own story—it's a favorite, don't you know—the girl who failed to seduce a priest from his calling. To prove the brittle shell of my beauty, I offered myself. Any man could have a go at me. Our schoolroom teacher who lived with his Ma, dug her garden—limp till I worked him over. The bottle boy at the pub who took me against the wall, the husband of Minnie O'Toole who butchered our cow, the father of twelve who thought never to take a plunge again and the sergeant who gave me the eye at the inquest, humping me in the back of his Morris van. Feverish with lust, I walked the one lane of our village at dusk, hair down as it once pleased my lover. On in this way, till the women came up to the door of our cottage in their Sunday shawls, women from the village and beyond. I well knew them, but could not name one biddy for you now. They pronounced me a harlot, a strumpet—such old fashioned words. One, a prosperous farmer's wife in hat and crocheted gloves, was willing to pay my way to Limerick or Dublin, a city that could handle a slut. Another suggested the madhouse in Knocknarea.

I had been washing up. With the wet rag in my hand, I shooed them away like chicks at the door, then heard my father behind me, quite sober that morning. He still wore the black band of my mother's death on his sleeve. Matt Boyle turned them out at our gate, though he knew it was true, what was said of his daughter in Hurley's. A woman with a tattered shawl detached herself from the party, ran back up our path. I see the malice in her eyes, tobacco stain on her lips, her skin crazed like the bark of a creel. I hear her whispered secret, "You are the very Magdalene."

A memorable day, sealed slick, tight as a scar. I could not tell Mae Boyle, girlish and rosy, flushing at the very mention of the man she was about to marry, how I was packed off in such haste to live among them and left just as suddenly. Not a trace of Nell Boyle.

When we met those few times in New York for tea or had lunch in her museum, my cousin seemed content if not happy. Mae O'Connor, as she was then, lived on Fifth Avenue, not far from where she was born, as though the great city was a village. She had a daughter, a difficult child by all accounts, who she named Fiona to please her father who'd gone Celtic with Kennedy in the White House and now visited what was left of the Boyles in Ballycarne, dispensing his favors. Before he died, my uncle lost his edge in the market, lost The Merrow. Jane filled her house in Connecticut with the possessions that once proved her family's worth. Mae took only a famine chair brought as souvenir from Ireland. I remembered that rough hewn plank with tilting spindles. My mother had banished it to the loft where I slept. A reminder of plague and poverty unto death, who would want the damn thing? Mae's life of acceptance.

When at last she asked about my disappearance, we were having our tea at the museum, a high room with fountains playing. "Was it the war?"

"That was it, the war."

"You argued with my father. Well, you know," she said, defending the family honor, "he was no longer neutral when Law went in the navy."

False as it was, I called upon my legend, my patriotic mission, said I'd left my uncle's house on principle, took off with the old valise, *Practical Nursing Procedures* and a castoff purse of Ellen Boyle's with fifty American greenbacks, princely savings all my own.

"Took off for Canada?" she asked, knowing the answer. "They had entered the war."

"That's it." I understood Mae to be an innocent, victim of a sheltered life.

She then took me through the halls of the museum to look at a picture of a jaundiced Virgin presenting her child to the viewer, a babe with spastic legs and dull eyes by an Italian, name of Martini. "My Martini," Mae called it.

"The wine at lunch enough for me."

"Oh, Nell!"

That was our last meeting.

DOWNTOWN

You'd take note of a woman clutching her purse to her chest, a bit upper-crust for the subway. Not quite up to date with the pearls and tasteful gold clips on her ears. Mae O'Connor at the end of the come-as-you-please Sixties, her style set. She does not go out in blustery weather without a silk scarf tied firmly on her head. On the subway Mae folds the scarf neatly in her lap as though waiting, waiting like a visitor to be admitted to the company of her fellow New Yorkers. You can't miss the pastry boxes next to her on the empty seat. Thursday is croissants, sand tarts, brownies on the Lexington Line. Her excursion planned for mid-morning, no crush. The weather must be wretched for Mae to hail a taxi. When she first made the trip, the cabbie pulled up to the door of Anima Mundi, where her daughter waited to welcome her. Fiona O'Connor flinched as her mother dealt out an extravagant tip.

Mae understands her daughter lives in poverty, the chosen way of the men and women not of this greedy world, who are family to Fiona now. Mae's husband, a man of business like her father, reads history at night, American history. He has pointed out the failures of such experimental communities—New Harmony, Brook Farm. In his opinion utopian adventures proved to be ethically suspect—elite.

"At least the Shakers sold seeds," Cyril O'Connor said.

Mae threaded a needle with crimson wool, bent over her stitches. Her husband could barely hear her objection. "They are not Shakers," she said.

"Not celibate? Rather free and easy, I'd guess."

"Religious," Mae said.

"Oh well, then."

In truth, Cyril O'Connor is proud of his daughter's retreat from their commonplace life on Fifth Avenue, from the truce of her parents' marriage, which followed no particular skirmish. His careless daughter with burnished red hair every which way has found something at last in this Mundi of a soulless time. He thinks of Fiona as distinct from the masses protesting the war in Southeast Asia, not that she shouldn't march in the streets against the sellout of the country's honor. She has tied up with this Mundi, which hardly displays an independence of mind. He does not care to see his daughter downtown, his unruly little girl, who now lives by the invented rituals of the sect she has joined.

Not a sect, his wife said. Mae leaves the Anima Mundi broadsides on the front hall table.

> *And the multitude of believers were of one heart; nought that a man possessed was his own, but they had all things in common.*
>
> —Acts 4:32

> *From each according to his ability, to each according to his needs.*
>
> —Karl Marx, *Economic Manuscripts*

His daughter knew little of the New Testament, so he doesn't hold it against her—splicing Marx and the Bible into one reel. Cyril misses

Fiona fiercely. From the day of her birth, she's been the great presence in his life. The emptiness of her room pervades the apartment. In their worst confrontations, when she was asked to leave one school or another, he admired her spirit. The spirit that's gone out of him, if ever he had it. If ever he'd wanted more than his cautious playing the numbers on Wall Street, it now seems to Cyril O'Connor the stuff of youth packed away with his college diploma *cum laude*, with term papers awarded B+ for effort. He had stumbled into his line of work through Mae's father and in his way he is grateful. His way is one of accommodation, of comfortable pleasures—a nightly scotch, chats with his wife, sports on the television when not reading his history, a walk in the People's Garden, as Central Park was called by its utopian designer. He takes delight in Mae's ordering her week. Mondays and Wednesdays, helping out in the gift shop of the hospital. Tuesdays, the information desk at the Met, directing tourists to the various galleries. Now Mae comes home in a strange state of exhilaration from her Thursdays with Fiona at this Mundi.

"You've been downtown?"

"Mmmm . . ." Humming a tune she'd learned from the children. Six or seven kids who suffered love with a good deal of uncertainty, in the floating population of the Mundi, as her husband insists on calling the abandoned brick school where their daughter lives. *Miss Milly Teale wore a silly hat*, sings Maesie. The children call her Maesie, a name not in use since she was a girl. She washes potatoes routed from their bin, peels, slices, wild with the knife—wham, wham.

Cyril wanting news of Fiona.

"She's thriving."

"Brought them pastries?"

"She's reading, all sorts of reading," Mae says. "They don't argue. They discuss."

"Reading?"

She sings of Milly asleep in the deep with her brindle cat. "Meat and potatoes," she says brightly, "not the fare at Mundi!"

Cyril pours himself a second scotch, does not remark upon the morally superior diet downtown. "Actually," he says, "the Perfectionists were driven out of New York State, out of the country entirely. They believed in free love."

Mae, contemplating last night's flank steak, mews like the cat resurrecting Miss Milly.

Her husband thinks—*I simplify for her.* Those particular communitarians came up with an apt term for their sexual arrangements—complex marriage. When Mae calms down she might say what she means by thriving.

Mondays and Wednesdays: in the gift shop of the hospital, Mae knows whether a customer buys in elation before heading to view a newborn swaddled in first love, or selects the distracting toy for Pediatrics or pays for useless comforts—scented soap, roses in their paper shroud for the dying. Many gifts seem to her joyless—key chains, puzzles, row upon row of stuffed animals, chocolates (perhaps forbidden), fashion magazines, the weeklies with pressing news of the world; the fleeting solace of mysteries, thrillers. Bogus books to aid new parents in choosing a name. Not bogus, her husband says, in a society without saints or connections, the new world of Presleys, Danishas, Latoyas all one with the reinstated Schlomos, Jorges, Breons. It went the rounds in the cafeteria when a girl barely old enough to give birth called her child Placenta for the lovely sound of the word. Her own daughter was Fiona, a name to please Frank Boyle, the name of a dowdy cousin in Ballycarne who meant nothing to Mae. She could not call her child Nuala. Or Nell, a name never mentioned.

Mondays and Wednesdays, in the smock of a volunteer, she pinned on a tag with her name, Mae O'Connor. The job had its disturbances. A young man cried at the back counter, a tortoise comb crushed in his fist. The teeth had punctured his palm, not deeply. He held out his hand like a good child while she cleaned the wound with cologne.

They spoke not a word to each other. Mae could not intrude on his sorrow. She hovered with a keen eye, and shoplifters were soon gone, though she was blind to the palsied old dame—beaded sweater unraveling, vinyl miniskirt —who swiped lip gloss and *Vogue*. Mae signed on for the gift shop when Fiona entered high school, arranged to be home at three, often waiting some hours till she heard her daughter's key in the door. Over the years, she kept to that schedule, marketing on the way home, fussing over the evening meal to have it ready when Cyril returned from the Street, the same Street with a disastrous downhill slump that had killed her father.

Arranging the shelves in the gift shop, she often thought of Nell, who was now Head Matron at the Royal Victoria Hospital up in Montreal. When Mae considered Nell's skill and purpose teaching the art of healing, her own cheery exchanges with visitors to the sick and dying seemed a drop in the bucket of tears.

Tuesdays: in the great hall of the museum Mae took her place. *Now, those are LADIES*, her husband said of the docents who manned the information desk. They were so intelligent, very pleasant with Mae, who did not complete her studies with the Sisters of the Sacred Heart, left to marry. At lunch, artists of many centuries spilled off the ladies' tongues—Dutch, Italian, French masters, names that came easily to them. She picked up a good deal about perspective, brushwork, provenance. By the end of six months, Mae told Cyril that she preferred the intimacy of the Sienese to the more worldly Florentines. In truth, she knew only as much as a fourteenth-century lady of Siena to whom the saints and Virgins portrayed in altarpieces were real as neighbors, not distant in their storied divinity. Each Tuesday she marveled at a Madonna and Child in the Lehman collection. In his greenhorn days, her father was a runner for the great financier Philip Lehman. He once stood hat in hand waiting for his orders in the hall of the mansion on 54th Street. Then, stealing to the parlor doors, he wondered what a Jew wanted with all those flat-faced saints and Holy Mothers. "But there was gold, you bet, pots of gold in those pictures." Frank Boyle the genial storyteller. Crude, his daughter now thought, pressing his ignorance. She was transfixed before this Mary who brushed her cheek against the child's red-gold curls. The boy pulled at his mother's veil, kicked at her embrace. Their halos were translucent, magic circles set in a field of shimmering gold which was nowhere on this earth. Mother and Child with sorrowful eyes, wide open eyes that knew what lay ahead. My Simone Martini, she called this Mary, and knew that her visits to the Madonna were something like simple prayer. She would never put it that way to the ladies at the Met who made a game of their favorites— my Cézanne, my Van Dyck. Cyril O'Connor suggested, now that Mae favored the school of Siena, she take down the bloody heart of Jesus that hung between their twin beds.

"Folk art," Mae said, counting herself clever. She'd picked that up at the Mundi, where all manner of saints were pictured on colored tin, decorated with sequins, coins, bright ribbons, where a Virgin pasted in a magnetized bottle cap wept on the refrigerator.

"They have their priests and their masses," Mae said, "in an original fashion." When she first went downtown, she had no notion what she might find in the abandoned schoolhouse. The door was always open, thrown open in all weather to welcome pilgrims from the street. She'd gone to see what her wayward daughter was up to. Fiona could not refuse her. Mae said little to Cyril about the rites at the Mundi, spirited Masses with Italian bread, sips of jug wine, their communal songs, readings, good works to set them apart from the world yet to be of it, to be poor as the real poor of the neighborhood downtown. She'd not say Fiona's spiritual striving quickened her heart. Her husband was not a religious man.

Maesie, the children called, running to meet her, their Maesie with the wicked pastries from an expensive shop. She snapped the strings which bound the white boxes, left them open on the common table. Every crumb was soon gone. Her daughter's comrades were strict with their beans and rice, cakes of gelatinous tofu wobbling in water. White sugar and butter were not staples in their punishing creed. The children loved the sand tarts. Mae made herself useful, bathing the kids in a urinal. All the children were quite small, all in need of a good scrub. She marched them to Delancey Street and bought them warm clothes and shoes. Thursdays were stories and the playground with Maesie. The oldest child, Max, Maximilian, a boy got from the Andes with soot-black hair and always a runny nose, his dark eyes searching Mae out till she knelt beside him. A serious little man who spoke in careful sentences, his solemn recitation of when he woke and how he brushed his teeth and dressed and then waited for her under the big school clock. Each week she listened to Max's story. She had never been the event in anyone's day.

Once, Mae took Max round the corner, well out of sight of the mothers, never sure which child belonged to which mother. She hailed a cab and they were off to the Ringling Brothers Circus. She'd thought this a treat, but Max did not clap or laugh. His nose dribbled as he leaned forward in his seat, transfixed by the antics of the clowns. He seemed not to care for the animals and acrobatics, only the fellows with red noses and baggy pants flirting with the audience, whamming each other in timeworn routines. When they returned from their lovely time, they were met at the schoolhouse door, all Mundi in a flap—the boy could not be found! Max held Mae's hand while she took her berating. Did she know how those animals were treated in the circus, made to prance for their meals, sedated and restrained? And the food? Yes, Mae confessed to hotdogs and cotton candy. And then, Mundi style, her daughter hugged her and welcomed her back to the fold. Max was quiet as could be, but not a bit repentant, dreaming of the bozos' pratfalls and blinking red noses. At night, when the grown-ups were drinking their wine and discussing, the boy practiced zany cartwheels and, cartoon style, smacked his frail body into a wall.

Each week he showed Maesie new tricks. "Do you think?"

"I do think so, Max. You're the funniest of them all."

Now she was also loved by a contemplative Fiona, her child transformed. The men, every last one, were stunned by her daughter's self-possession and by the splendid mass of her copper hair.

"You are so like Nell."

"The Irish cousin?"

"She came to live with us one year."

Mae spoke seldom of this Irish cousin, kept Nell to herself the few times she traveled to New York for one of her conferences. Nell was not family in the usual way. She was forever the angel who appeared at The Merrow to save her, though now middle-aged—stout, childless, determinedly unmarried. Marching the children down a corridor at the Mundi, Mae O'Connor passed a schoolroom where her daughter studied the books that set her against the war, against the whole system of getting and spending she mistrusted in America. Then Fiona did remind her of Nell, who in that miraculous year long ago, read late into the night her books with pictures of skeletons and every muscle and nerve in the body. In the light from the dusty school window falling on her glorious hair as she read, Fiona seemed to her mother saved from the worst of the world, and saved as she ladled out watery soup to the homeless. From her small inheritance, Mae made out checks for the poor her daughter lived with. Let's-pretend poor, Cyril claimed, and so she never did tell of her money given over to the priests in charge of their dissident flock. A secret from her husband, a sin of omission.

But Mae's daughter was not like Nell, for the day came when Fiona called her away from the children's play. She took her mother's hand and placed it on the growing swell of her belly. Then the girl came home to Fifth Avenue with her knapsack and bedding, came home with her mother in a cab, leaving behind the books she had discussed with the residents of Anima Mundi, leaving behind the father of her child, a man never named. A secret Fiona kept always, from the world and from her mother. Then the interlude of peace between them was over.

When her daughter died in a boating accident on one of her many holidays with one of her many lovers, Mae took the boy. He was eleven years old. Though he was solemn like Max, she never had the spirit with him, the delight she'd had with that Indian child downtown. When Fiona's boy was settled in his private school, Mae O'Connor went daily to the museum. Her sustaining passion, a Sienese painting with no Babe, no Madonna. A triptych in which first a wizened monk, she did not care to know his name, bends over a girl lost to life in a pool of water. Next, a woman she believes to be the mother reaches her hand hopelessly into the stylized waves of heavenly blue, and in the third panel it's the bearded monk in his brown robes who revives the child. Mae O'Connor supposes the scene to be one of the saint's many holy accomplishments. For a time she believes in the miracle of the painting, then visits it less often, then not at all. Her faith dwindles to observance — Sunday Mass, holy days of obligation. As for the gift shop and the ladies at the Met, she no longer volunteers. When she wakes in the night the dream is with her, a carnival dream: her descent, making her way down, down to the dark tunnel, juggling empty boxes. This is her vision of hell on the Lexington Line: a boy with black hair wipes the snot from his nose, batters himself against the tiled wall. Bloodied, he turns to a woman who is faintly smiling, but he is not funny, not funny at all.

THE CHILDREN OF LIR

When Cyril O'Connor called me I was working ahead on *Bedside Manners in the Technological Age.* Her husband, we had never met, said Mae had died at dawn. I muttered all manner of sentimental things I do not advise for bedside, that the dying often last through the night as though to see their final day. I did not answer when paged — a disembodied voice calling me to my administrative duties. Now that Mae's gone, not a relation I acknowledge other than the nurses under my care. I had a vivid picture of her, not grown but as an awkward child brushing my hair, begging for news of the polio ward and for my patch-work legends of Ireland. I'd not seen my cousin in many years, yet it seemed a great punishment that my gifted listener had gone before me, before she heard the hard stories I was meant to tell.

My year in the States. New York, the chill Easter behind us. The side door of St. Vincent's thrown open to a bright Spring day. I did not want to leave off with my duties yet felt beholden, that I must please the Boyles once again with a trip to The Merrow. I waited for Ellen Boyle and the girls by a frail sycamore tree, a speckled thing coming to life in the exhaust of Sixth Avenue. It was Law who drew in to the curb, show-ing off in his gift of a breezy car. With the tutors laid on it was certain he would graduate, so here was this swaggering boy, an annoyance wait-ing for me. The ride out was merciful. With the top down we could not hear or see each other—my hair flying about. When we arrived at the big house, the empty rooms waited for us in silence.

"Jane had a party in town. Not to worry," Law said, "your Maesie will be out in the morning." He played with the dial on the radio, found a slow tune he liked. I was half up the stairs when he called me.

"Nell, give me a dance."

"I don't know your dances."

"And don't swim. What else don't you do?"

I was two years older than my cousin. It might have been twenty. He was flippant always, attempting to charm me. His gibes wore me down. Handsome, I suppose, with the long jaw of his mother, the black curls of the Boyles, but not our dark eyes. Law's gaze was blue ice skimming the surface, inattentive when he did not have a bat or ball in hand. He had filled out in the year, but I did not count him a man, a boy with ex-pensive equipment, this son and heir holding his family hostage to his empty promise.

"Have a drink." He reached up the stair rail for my hand.

"I have no need of it."

Then I threw off my coat, a grave miscalculation, and we danced to that tune I will never forget though I did not understand a word, a sad French song I would hear all during the war. What was the harm in our dancing?

"The end," I said, brisk when the song was over, and headed up to the place under the eaves allotted to me. I was still in my white uniform, white stockings, white shoes as Law followed me through the upper hall and took me, not rudely, by the arm, turned me into his room. There he conducted a little tour of his mitts and autographed baseballs, his trophies on which golden boys batted or swung a racquet. His grip tightened.

"Haven't you girls enough?"

"Not the Irish princess. Not Noo-lah."

I pulled from him, but did not get as far as the door with the pictures of his heroes on it, fellows in helmets and caps. I bit at his wrist, tasted blood in my mouth. Animal grunts, no words. The little learning of my American year—pudendal nerve, external jugular—all useless. I could not reach for his gullet, his tight balls, and if I'd offered myself at that moment, my body would not have pleased him. He wanted to force me, that was his satisfaction. When a woman violated is brought into hospital, great care must be taken with lacerations and contusions, with bathing the soft tissue of the vulva, which is often torn. The cleansing of the vagina itself is a delicate matter and often cannot be accomplished until the patient is sedated. It was my way to hold such a girl or woman in my arms long before such intimate practice was reintroduced to the nursing profession. I hold these women to me. In shock there are often no tears. The face registers no emotion.

My cousin had the kindness to transport me, throw me on the bed in the box room, and there his father found me in a soiled condition. The torn white garments I remember, too, for I thought to hide them.

Frank Boyle stood over me. I knew at once that the fault was mine. "Tidy yourself," he said

I covered my body from him.

"Your past exploits, Nuala. I've known them from your father. Didn't he send me news so I might pay your passage?"

"They sold the white mare," I said, knowing it was not true.

"Your exploits . . ." Boyle began to tell a sweet version, so I told him the story complete—every man I had ruined, Alf Ternan and the bottle boy, the constable with his polished boots thumping the floor of the district van as he rode me. I told of the morality league that appeared at Matt Boyle's door, of the witch of Inishmurray with the bump on her nose who knew what we'd been up to on the sacred stones, that Nuala Boyle had made a gift of herself to the honorable Hugh Byrnes.

"But your son took," I said, "took what you wanted all along."

And that night I vanished, quickly vanished, not a trace of Nell Boyle. For some months I thought to write comforting words to Mae, that child who loved me, but the invention of that story was beyond me.

At the hospital it came as a surprise, Nuala Boyle having family obligations. I flew down for the burial, a skimpy affair with the husband and grandson, carbon copies of each other, not a touch of Boyle in them. Mae's daughter dead in a speedboat, careless Fiona I never set eyes on. Did Mae have a notion since I never had a child she best not crow about the girl, one up on her Nell? No, I believe she wanted all our talk cordoned off, quarantined as we once were from her family. Recalling each time we met, how we sat on her bed or mine, sat late into the night longing for some cure. My life began with Mae's listening to my litany of each muscle, nerve, ligament and bone in the human body. The drone of my recitation—forceps, fever chart, catheter, the humors of the eye. That sick child was my salvation, and I suppose I did heal her with my stories, for she gave up on her piety, settled to the privileges of her family, to the life of a woman with no remarkable adventures. If I have one fault as a nurse, it's that I care only for the ailing. Nutrition and sanitation, housekeeping chores for a Home Sister. I leave such instruction to others. The well patient is no patient to me. Nurse Boyle's miracles, as they call them, are with bodies broken, diseased.

I had not attended the funeral Mass, met the mourners at graveside. Jane, wouldn't she say it, "Mae died of a broken heart."

"Of heart failure," I said.

And had I known that Lawrence skied off a cliff in Tahoe? Yes, indeed, Mae had written—*Poor Law grew plump sitting at a desk in Santa Barbara.* Jane, bottle blonde, suburban. Divorced, she has reverted to her maiden name, so it was Jane Boyle who told me her kids were scattered, that she'd be sending them the memento she distributed at the cemetery, a card printed according to Mae's wishes with the date of the death and a mealy-mouth prayer. We were of an age, their Nell and my surviving American cousin. Jane leathery, left-over pretty. It was during the war I let my looks go. Square-set, substantial, no longer the lithe creature who could barely heft a man off the rubber sheet in St. Vincent's. My hair white, cropped out of the way. We no longer wear caps, once the pride and distinction of each school of nursing.

"The dear departed, Mary," the priest called her, a man not known to Mae. When it came time to head off to the ritual luncheon, I said I'd take a car direct to the airport. The car waiting for me patiently as a black car waited always for my uncle Frank Boyle. To tell truth, I was not up for their anecdotes that bring the dead back in a humorous vein. Easement for the living. The fawning undertaker and his crew drove away. I sat by the stones, each Boyle's name cut into the polished granite. On the very island with their Merrow, row upon row of stones marking the dead, and if in some almighty sweep I flipped them, they would not lay a curse. Still, I could not breathe for the weight of them. My body was lost to me then. I did not feel the cold ground beneath me or the warmth of the sun.

Then I came to myself with the roar of planes rising through puff clouds from LaGuardia. Mid-May, brilliant in the city, the season far ahead of our weather in Montreal, the land greening, though it would

never be as green as the false turf masking the raw earth of her grave.
Never green as fields that ran down to the sea in Inishmurray on a day
when bluebells carpeted our way to the crosses marking the burial site
of early Christians, fields fresh with dew, though we found the holy
wells dry, and when the rain came upon us we lay in a round hut, busy
with our life in the beehive. I sat on the mound of her grave, better late
than never told all of that story to Mae, and told her that the stiff floral
blanket that lay upon her could not compare to the first petals of May
we sprinkled on the doorstep to keep the fairies out, but then I could
not fully bring to mind the many stories—that nonsense of boys with
firebrands, or to what purpose you could sting your lover with a nettle,
or the one about St. Brigid's cape, and told that I instruct my nurses: Do
not judge a patient's pain. The pain is real. And that they must honor
the sacred moment when the clothes are neatly folded and presented to
the family of the dead. I recited Dr. Osler's seven nursely virtues, which
make my girls laugh at me, I know it for sure. And did she recall the
children of Lir? Those kids turned to swans, comfortless and cold for
nine hundred years. And you asked, *when will they be free?*

When the religion of love comes to Ireland.

Then their feathers fell away, but by then they were withered and
old.

Nell, will you not say a prayer?

I can manage an *Ave*—in Latin, no less.

Then say it. There's no harm, no more than a legend.

On the holy card Mae's Virgin is not pictured. St. Clare, a pale nun
with a lamp. Patron, it informs me, of embroidery and television. I believe that was all of her life in the end—handiwork and the evening's
entertainment.

JUNE

Big as Life

A Story in Three Panels

*You're painting a shoe, you start painting the sole,
and it turns into a moon; you start painting the moon
and it turns into a piece of bread.*

— Philip Guston

LAFOREST

The sealing wax is unbroken. By the time Audubon's letters arrive at Beech Woods, the seal is often cracked with North Atlantic cold or melted to a blur in the bowels of a steamship coming upriver from New Orleans. By law in the State of Louisiana letters to his wife should arrive from the post office in St. Francisville for delivery by way of a black courier who knows every plantation and every jerry-built settler's house in the environs. Audubon's letter lies in a grass basket on the Postmaster's desk until he takes his pleasure riding out to Beech Woods, the Percy plantation on Bayou Sarah, where he settles to coffee with a dollop of fresh cream served in a thin china cup. He delights in gossip with the mistress of the house.

Lucy Audubon will reread her husband's letters and journals when her son is finally in bed, when Celia wanders down to join her children in the slave quarters, when lessons for the next day are charted. Often her eyes stray from the flourish of Audubon's pen, for she has memorized every word of his trials and adventures in England and Scotland where he sells subscriptions to his book, a book still in the nest, promise of a book in which John James Audubon will describe, by way of his art, all the birds of America. He travels with a portfolio of his paintings which display nature's winged creatures—feathers, claws, beaks, bills, scales—resplendent as God and Audubon design them. And as they will now be engraved and most beautifully colored by the London firm of Thomas Havell. The letters to his wife smell of shipboard, musty and dank from their journey. When the seal comes cracked, Lucy fears his words have been read, not his boastful reports of drawing room triumphs or the niggardly account of his expenses, it's his endearments rounding off each letter that shame her. Sweet words she no longer takes to heart—*My Dearest Lucy may heaven's pleasure be around thee for ever and ever. . . . I am thine own true friend and husband. . . . Do take great care of thyself and of <u>thy intellect</u>*. Transparent words flicker in candlelight, fleeting as moths mindless of their destruction.

This letter arrives on a moody afternoon in the Spring of the year, before the summer heat settles in this country of mold and damp, arrives ceremoniously by way of the Postmaster himself with a tip of his planter's straw hat. "Ma'am?" A question put to her, something he dare not ask. He recovers himself. "How's them boys?"

Before Lucy has time to answer, he turns the rump of his serviceable mount to her and trots toward the gallery of Wyanoke, the grand house of Beech Woods, for his visit with Mrs. Percy. Lucy knows she is a subject of their pity, that they will speak of her husband's long absence, but will not give way to such disheartening thoughts. The children run wild in the dusty patch behind the schoolhouse where she teaches them spelling, ciphering, history and geography. Music and drawing too, most naturally drawing, for she is the wife of Audubon who must be the greatest artist of nature in the world. Must be, she believes, and that the widow Percy, employing her to run a school for her own girls and girls hereabouts, has been decent to her at Beech Woods, if not always kind. Lucy Audubon must continue to think well of those who have befriended her and her boys. She has been raised fair and friendly in a Quaker family, the Bakewells of Derbyshire, in the West of England, more recently of Fatland Ford in Pennsylvania. She cannot help but smile—a tight-lipped smile, to be sure—at her husband's tribute to that heritage, his *thees* and *thous* which adorn the intimacies at the end of each letter. If her heart were not broken, she might write to LaForest, as she calls him, her letter finding him in Liverpool, Manchester or Edinburgh. She might make use of a sharp Quaker maxim: *Things which hurt, instruct.* His reports of brilliant new friends and professional acclaim are hurtful. In some way yet unknown to her, Lucy is sure his letters instruct.

Quickly she cracks the seal, scans his first words to know that all is well with LaForest, who has traveled to France, by his miscalculation six thousand miles from Louisiana. Letter in her coverall pocket, Lucy Audubon rounds up the girls she let out of the classroom. Looking up from her desk, she'd seen the Postmaster parting the dense willow path, whipping the weeping branches away. She could not contain her anticipation and rang the bell for a recess.

How's them boys? Perfectly well, thank you, as all in the Parish of West Feliciana know. Gifford, the elder son, in business with his uncle in Shippingport where Woodhouse will join him to further his education. She calls her sons by these family names, though in his letters her husband underlines their Christian names—*Victor* Gifford, *John* Woodhouse—a sharp stroke against the Bakewells who consider him an idler, a failure, a fraud. Well, *Woodhouse* will soon be gone. Then Lucy will be truly alone. Still, she will earn her keep. She will not pack up, live off the charity of her disapproving family.

She skips the dusty path back to the schoolhouse, and John Woodhouse laughs with the rest, for his mother is always prim in her demeanor. In her long suffering, some would say. She looks to ring the bell hidden under a bucket. Little Percy, bubbling with laughter, gives that great secret away, then ring Lucy does, as their Miss Audubon rings to end all their games. Geography at this hour for the middle students. This day she does not want to contemplate the world, spin the globe with its green isle of England, the blue channel crossing to France, or trace a finger over the sketchy, emerging map of America.

Later, many years later, she will be asked to write of her experiences with the American Woodsman, John James Audubon. She will demur, only edit a discreet biography of her husband with the help of the Reverend John Bachman, his admiring friend. It may be read on microfilm if you have the patience. Expect no revelations; the admiring friend bathes the reader in his reverence. Lucy appears as *a wife willing to sacrifice her personal comfort at any moment for the furtherance of Audubon's great scheme*. Nothing is known of her true sentiments, only that a dutiful widow approved this pious version of her husband's life. Still, if Lucy had been given voice, she would not have disclosed that Jean Jacques Audubon was born obscurely (not so obscurely, now the scholars have got at him), illegitimate son of Audubon *père* — seaman, slave trader, adventurer — who encountered Jeanne Rabine, an astonishing beauty, on his way back to his sugar plantation in Saint-Domingue. Jeanne — a serving girl out of Nantes, hired to a wealthy French planter, a contract she never fulfilled. She was with child and died soon after bearing her son, Jean Rabine. If the sickly infant had not turned out to be Audubon, she would be forgotten entirely. Audubon, a figure so illustrious the last name will serve as it does for Franklin, Whitman, Darwin and Sinatra. Yes, John James (he preferred the Anglicized name, though he never abandoned his charming French accent) could sing and dance to Mozart in the parlor, belt out frontier songs round the campfire. If he'd been born in the time of moving pictures, not in the old days — freeze frame of sketch, still life, copper engraving — he'd have been a star. Well, he was a star, but as Lucy well knew, not always in ascendance. Of her marriage to a man obsessed with his art, she will say, *Every bird was my enemy.* That judgment is not to be found in the bogus biography of *delightful reminiscences.* Nor will her pride in her years as a schoolmarm: *If I can hold the mind of a young child to a subject for five minutes, he will never forget what I teach him.*

But on the day of the reception of LaForest's letter in June of 1828, Lucy's own mind wanders from the next task at hand. No clock in the schoolroom; she tells time by the sun in its provincial course, rising in streaks of gold through the dense magnolia forest in the East to its bloody setting in the shallow waters of Bayou Sarah. For weeks it has been unusually dry and still. She prays for the heavens to burst in a Spring shower. Sharpening the lead pencils for drawing, Lucy thinks of her husband's complaint of damp weather, his fine new coat and weskit soaked with English rain. And how is that, she would ask him, more a trial than sleeping in wet buckskins in storms that plague you in all seasons when in pursuit of your American birds? How is it that you solicit my sympathy for your slight discomfort? That you think to amuse me with news of the grand times you enjoy in England, the country of my birth?

Twelve black plumbago pencils in a row. She will list the cost of this instrument of instruction in her bill to the parents of these girls. Drawing, the last lesson of the day. Until that time Lucy will listen to the youngest reading from their primers while the older pupils write themes on a subject she has set—*Assume a virtue if you have it not, for use can change the stamp of nature.*

Lucy stops Little Percy in her reading to correct a word. "*Buoyed. The prince was buoyed by silver waves.*"

At the back of the room, Woodhouse, too old for these lessons yet too wayward to let run free, draws from nature. He has propped up the limb of a magnolia tree. The waxy petals droop. He sticks them to his drawing board with bits of wet clay and wires the branch much as his father arranges the bodies of dead birds to simulate the breath of life.

When Lucy sits on her high stool, the letter pokes out of her pocket, a personal matter pressed out of sight not to interrupt her lessons. As the children read, the sky darkens. At long last there will be rain. If LaForest were here he could tell to the second when the first heavy drops will fall. The schoolhouse is not glazed. Lucy steals about to close the wooden shutters.

"Porpoise. A porpoise swam. . . ." The story about a porpoise and a prince is the one fanciful tale in the primer without the weight of a moral. Light splinters into the classroom, not enough for drawing. She nods to Woodhouse, who strikes a flint, lights a candle for his work, then comes forward to light the oil lamp on her desk. Rain beats against the roof. Little Percy raises her voice to be heard—"A *poor puss swam.*"

Rain or shine, Miss Audubon will finish out the day's lessons. When the story of the hunter prince and the clever fish—*You understand a porpoise is a cetacean, not an intelligent being as in the higher order of mammalia*—when that distinction is made clear for the Little Percy and the primers closed, Lucy places a darning egg and her sewing box on her desk, which is no more than a discarded deal table, one leg propped with a flat stone. In drawing the egg, the children will learn to see the shading of its dark underside, the elliptical shadow of itself. The box is an exercise in perspective. Box and egg are staples which must be drawn many times until the lessons which they impart to the eye are learned. Little Percy, who is ten, can render only a flat oval and one side of the box. The child has sleek black hair, slanted green eyes. Perhaps, Lucy thinks in despair, she sees like a cat. Perhaps a cat does not see us in our full dimension.

As she marches the aisle distributing pencils, one rolls to the floor. She looks to Woodhouse to retrieve it, but he has scooted out in the dim light. Stooping, the letter in her pocket crackles. She calls out, "Woodhouse!" For weeks he has been observing a family of herons (*Hy-*

dranassa tricolor, Plate 217, *Birds of America*) and knows that in the rain they will be roosting low in the cedar swamp. If she'd not been so flustered with the arrival of the Postmaster, Lucy might have noticed the powder horn poking out under her son's drawing board. He is a rambler like his father, whose instructive voice she hears from afar: *Draw, my dear boy, and study music. You will soon now be able to assist your father very much in our project.* And how, Lucy may ask, is your project of the birds *ours*? Nothing in her son's empty head but hunting the winged creatures that call him away from his books. The boy worships his father, wants to be him, but there is only one Audubon. The wide world cannot tolerate one more. She flings open the schoolhouse door, "John Woodhouse!" Her cry shrill, shrill as air blown through a dry reed.

Woodhouse has lit out again. The Percy girls, all three of them, and their classmates take care not to laugh when Miss Audubon patrols the schoolroom. In the wavering light of the oil lamp they draw the egg and box, egg and box, over and over. The oldest Percy, Sarah, has a long sullen face, pale lips pressed in a perpetual pout. Audubon rendered her in pastels at the command of her mother, as well as the second daughter, Margaret, with forehead flat as a paddle, cast in her eye, no hint of a chin. When his portraits were presented, Mrs. Percy flapped about the parlor in a state of wild disbelief, as though she had never laid eyes on her unfortunate girls, and ordered the artist off her property.

The truth—what was the truth? The girls were infatuated with Audubon, twittered in his presence. Sarah's bosom rose in great gasps of admiration at any wild story LaForest told, and Maggie's eyes teared when he played a simple tune on his flute. Girls quite destroyed by her husband's charm was no news to Lucy, but this post was her living—indeed, the living of her family, for they were penniless when she took on the work of teaching these children at Beech Woods. And so she had sided with Jane Percy, more or less. Let her husband go downriver with his watercolors and dreamy prospects. Who was to feed and clothe the boys? At that time Gifford still at home, if you call the cramped rooms tacked to the schoolhouse a home. Well, Audubon had quite enough of those fawning girls in the Percy parlor and was not one day departed on the flatboat headed for New Orleans before he wrote to his wife of his delight with the great variety of waterfowl skimming the shore. A letter now tied with many letters in a length of blue ribbon.

Maggie's eggs are real, as though popped from hens in the barnyard. "Fine, remarkably fine." But her box is squashed into a parallelogram. Lucy squares off the lines. She has not drawn since she was a girl, was never deft with a pencil. There is little art in her lessons, accomplishment only, as in music and dancing, where once there had been pleasure. "If at first!" No need to finish the adage. She takes such patience with this girl who looks a fishy sport of nature. In fact, Margaret is the brightest of the dull Percys.

A gentle brush of wings under the eaves where phoebes (*Sayornis phoebe*, Plate 120, *Birds of America*) have built their Spring nest, a flash of sun, the storm over. When the shutters are opened, Lucy Audubon and her pupils blink in the sudden light, see each other for what they are—dutiful children and a skinny schoolmarm engaged in a tiresome exercise. Soon they will slip their drawings into their portfolios with the many ill-described boxes, eggs, leaves, bowls, pitchers and blossoms which aim to instruct them in perspective, depth, light and shade.

Miss Audubon says, "You may go," before she has checked their work, before they have handed their pencils in. Only Maggie, the homeliest girl in Feliciana, does not run for the door. *Homely* is not the word for her unfortunate face, the broad span of forehead, the wandering eye. Mag Percy watches her teacher clutch at her black coverall as though pain has struck her sunken breast, sees the thick foolscap poke into sight. A letter. The beautiful man has written his poor wife a letter. Then the girl bolts, runs up the muddy path, the thin leaves of the willows showering her with the aftermath of rain. The Postmaster's horse is being led round to the gallery by a black boy with a cancer on his leg.

Mag's mother is laughing with that bloated fellow who dresses himself like gentry with worn leather boots, soiled white stock, yellow britches bursting with the sack of his belly. They've had a good tattle and look to the schoolhouse, ever curious about the deserted wife of John James Audubon. The postmark on his letter noted as London.

"London?"

"London!" the Postmaster exclaims as though it is the moon, a stupid man for the population of Louisiana is favored with many Brits who clip the long vowels of the American language. He observes that the date was barely legible, eight or ten weeks back. So it has traveled swiftly by packetboat to New Orleans, then idled for a week in a basket with nuts and bone buttons on the Postmaster's desk in St. Francisville, until it pleased him to ride out from his general store, which doubles as the office to receive the post.

Saving the best for last, with a flourish of his hat, he notes that Audubon's letter bore a red seal. "Imprinted!"

"Imprinted?" Widow Percy sees nothing strange in that.

"Stamped and sealed, Ma'am, with a wild turkey." (*Meleagris gallopavo*, Plate 1, *Birds of America*)

"Feathers! All in the world he cares for."

"And a legend."

"Legend!"

"Took up the magnifier to make it out."

The black boy steadies the horse, receives a swift touch of the crop for his trouble. The fat man mounts; hand slapped to his breast in mock heroic, he delivers Audubon's legend: "America, my country."

So—the afternoon may be counted successful. Throughout the parish, they will have this tidbit to tell. "His country! Why don't he come home?" That would be our Postmaster. "He can no more speak the language": Jane Percy's Presbyterian censure addressed to the chosen few in Feliciana, the rich land grabbers, who, like most of her neighbors, are immigrants staking their claims up and downriver for rich fields to grow cotton, sugar and tobacco. Brigands, pirates and good souls alike look to make their way on the vanishing frontier. Louisiana, a world of refugees from wars in Europe, from political and religious constraint. Royalists out of France, prospectors from England,

Acadians driven out of Nova Scotia—all speak a common patois of get-ahead with a genteel varnish.

Audubon shipped (with fake passport) out of France by his father to avoid Napoleon's conscription. The Bakewells, Quakers—suspect of antiroyalist sympathies—were made uncomfortable in Derbyshire. Such a muddle of motives for coming to this new and promising America. History placed Audubon and Lucy across a valley from each other in Pennsylvania, but that is a love story in which a girl with serious green eyes looks up from her sewing. She is alone in the drawing room of a pillared mansion, the main house of her father's elaborate establishment grand as Tara. Fatland Ford, a farm with outbuildings and walled gardens, is a mighty spread, fat as in the fatlands of Egypt that brought forth Biblical plenty, gifts of a merciful God. She looks up from her stitching and finds him, the Frenchman she will marry, a big boy with curly hair streaming down to his broad shoulders. When the leaves fell from the trees in Fall, as they name it in this country, she had looked across to his stone house, but never dreamed of the young master, reported to be a fine shot and horseman though arrogant, something of a dandy, who hunted in black satin breeches and pumps. The dark stranger who lives at Mill Grove might be the handsome brute in a romance by Maria Edgeworth, or a fellow with his nose in the air who gets his comeuppance in a moral tale by Miss Austen. But Audubon's life was never to be contained within the covers of a book, unless the book be the extravagant work of his own making.

So—within weeks Lucy Bakewell was reading him Thomson's *The Seasons* to improve his English—

> *As rising from the vegetable World*
> *My Theme ascends, with equal Wing ascend,*
> *My panting Muse; and hark, how loud the Woods*
> *Invite you forth in all your gayest Trim.*

She stole away with him to a shadowy cave on the banks of the Perkiomen Creek, where he showed her the sturdy mud nests of phoebes. He taught Lucy to pick up the quivering fluff of a baby bird. The year of his arrival at Mill Grove, 1803, he banded a soft grey creature with a silver thread to prove it returned to its home each year. Ornithologists had not yet figured the mystery of migration. Ha!—Spring again, and here was his phoebe returned, its silver thread the worse for wear. Sweet and intimate hours in the cave as though they were nesting, Audubon and his neighbor, the English girl. His first love was for the birds, but her father would not believe that, and Lucy was ordered back to her room at Fatland Ford, where she sewed with a vengeance.

"What were you sewing," a granddaughter asked, "when he first came into the parlor?"

"I no longer remember. I have been sewing all my life." And sewed through her blindness to the end, feeling her way along a straight seam with careful stitches, perhaps seeing in the darkness the miniature of her husband, painted after the engraving by Cruikshank, R.A., in which he wears a starched white shirt with Byronic collar, most assuredly not of her making, or seeing a cartoon in the *London Illustrated* of the American Woodsman parading the streets of London in buckskins, his hair dressed with bear grease; recalling that in the same year she sewed scraps to outfit Woodhouse for the world and stitched her own black dress and coverall for the classroom. Or mercifully, while the inquisitive Maria Audubon threads her grandmother's needle, Lucy may close her useless eyes to view the many birds as though they are projected on a stereopticon device. They are splendid—fluttering, pecking, feeding their young, devouring their prey as they did in life on the double elephant folios bound into Audubon's book which will sell at auction for $8.8 million, March 10, 2000.

Perhaps her blindness is not a curse, as it is for others. She can just make out the white shadow of cambric that lies on the negative of her black lap. Miss Audubon—so called by her pupils, as though she were a maiden lady—always wore black, a ruff of white collar, the white muslin cap. Widow's weeds long before LaForest's passing. Mourning her two little girls laid to rest in Kentucky? Her Lucy, who died in winter, planted in the kitchen garden until the earth thawed and the small wasted body was transplanted to a raw cemetery where, in three years, she would bury Rose. Death was her intimate. In one desperate season when yellow fever came upriver, her husband's business was deathbed portraits, capturing sunken cheeks and sweaty brows, mouths mumbling prayers—faces so alike at their end it was not easy to draw a likeness, five dollars a head. And once a father, wild with bereavement, ran after the journeyman artist to beg for a portrait of his daughter who was interred. That man was a minister, and it was a great sin to disturb the child's rest in the Lord, but dig he did and sprang open the coffin where the girl lay fresh in death; then Audubon arranged her angelic hair to portray her as everlasting in crayons, but would not take a penny and rendered the dead no more.

Death, the settler's companion, unwelcome guest at every door, the date of each loved one inscribed on the back page of the Bible. Perhaps Lucy wore black not in sorrow, but as fitting to her age and station as a gentlewoman without means. In the darkness of her last days, her fingers feel their way down a seam. No memory of what she stitched when the French boy stood in the parlor doorway, but she recalls her dress was of fine linen, Quaker grey. As still, as still as if sighting a bird, Jean Jacques Audubon took her in.

The old woman preens, "My waist, let me tell you, was slim," giving this prize to Maria, John Woodhouse's daughter, the only child who pries into the past. Maria Audubon, afflicted with gentility, will edit out the exuberant bits of her grandfather's journals, take liberties with his vigorous prose. Biographers have worked a hundred years to undo her mischief. To me, her greatest sin may be that she did not catch her grandmother's wit with its sharp burr of pride: "Oh, I was slimmer still in Cincinnati when we did not have enough to eat."

Maria Audubon took as gospel her grandfather's written account of his first meeting with Lucy Bakewell—*She now arose from her seat and her form, to which I had previously paid but partial attention . . .* He had written so much—journals, letters, bird biographies, tall tales of the frontier and that memoir called simply *Myself,* an account for his sons so they might receive the controlled version of his life. *Myself* was written for everyone, really, testimony of the famous man in which he is born, as in a fairy tale, to a woman both beautiful and wealthy in the French territory of Louisiana. Transported to his father's estate on Saint-Domingue, his poor mother falls victim to *the ever-to-be-lamented period of the negro insurrection.* But it is Lucy I must not leave behind, as Audubon did so often in the passionate pursuit of his birds, Lucy who *showed both grace and beauty; and my heart followed every one of her steps,* Lucy of the slim waist thus added to his collection, one more feather in his cap, a ground dove (*Columbigallina passerina,* Plate 182, *Birds of America*), plain and grey, *the tamest of winter birds.* In his *Bird Biographies* he would write of this species, *feeds mostly on weeds.* She was indeed slim at Fatland Ford and slimmer still in their vagabond life, living wherever some small commerce would support them before the next failure, then the handouts, living on the charity of family and friends. That cruel Winter in Cincinnati she was a wraith buying day-old bread, as the poor did in my industrial city in the Thirties, stale bread and cheese rinds all that she had to put on the table for Gifford and Woodhouse. She roamed the markets on the banks of the Ohio scavenging fish heads and bruised potatoes. The boys on their uppers, Audubon shot a rattler down by the river and fashioned shoes of snakeskin, as the Indians taught him. Her husband had come to this city to stuff birds; taxidermy, the stiff project of closet naturalists, was against his nature, against nature itself, plumbing birdskins, painting background, mere background for the Western Museum, an establishment run out of funds. So they taught. Audubon, who claimed to have studied with the French master Jacques-Louis David (untrue, as so many nice details in *Myself*), taught drawing, and Lucy took in pupils whose parents could not or would not pay the tuition.

There her husband exhibited his first birds of America; the beautiful aviary creatures—pecking, clawing, flying, supping, singing, nesting, mating—now came alive in his paintings and there was praise, though no money in it. He left Cincinnati in disgust, traveling with a surveyor and his one talented pupil, a lad of thirteen, on a government project that didn't work out. But the boy, Mason, was useful to him, drew in and colored splendidly the flowers, grasses, trees and berries that were proper to his master's birds. So they went on together, paid their passage to New Orleans, going ashore to kill fish, fowl, venison, otter—any creatures to feed passengers and crew—all the while Audubon drawing new and wonderful specimens killed for his art. Now, sure as come Sunday, he would make his book, not that all else had failed, though all else had—the farming at Mill Grove, which he left to his father's hired folk and self-seeking partners while he wandered in search of geological curiosities, woodland flowers, nests and eggs—not having settled to his single obsession with birds, American birds. And the lead mine back on the Perkiomen that did not yield; the store in Henderson, Kentucky, prospering for a while, a comfortable while with a log house of her own Lucy would remember—its parlor with curtains of her making, her vegetable garden, a cow in the pasture. Though he was often truant, off to the woods with his gun, sometimes camping for days with the Shawnee, learning the ways of cougars and wolves in the winter camp of the Osage. Not to forget the mill in Henderson engineered to run by the new steam engine, grinding the Audubons' capital to silt, little grain to mill for want of farms in the county; or the riverboat purchased innocently with George Keats, the poet's brother. *Tell Mr. Audubon he's a fool* (Lucy in for a scolding, too), the famous letter that would have made LaForest a footnote to John Keats (who wrote to a nightingale, complaining of his own mortality), if the American Woodsman had not painted with such accuracy his marvelous aviary, among them our native nightingale, commonly called the speckled hermit thrush (*Hylocichla guttata*, Plate 58, *Birds of America*), a shy bird whose phrase of mellow notes in an ascending scale is finer than that of the celebrated English bird.

Such a wealth of failure, their log house seized, Lucy's every treasure sold, her mother's china, silver, their beds, dressers, linens, the pianoforte—*all my drawings, crayons, Paints pencils Drawing Paper*—ah, the bitter stroke. He was granted one gun, a bag of shot, bit of powder, but all else gone in the roundelay of disaster that led to Cincinnati, where Audubon's wife heeled in, stayed on to press for payment from her pupils and the Western Museum, Gifford delivering her notes (haughty yet begging) to save the penny to a runner, Lucy dressed now in black, having buried both little girls, waist and sleeves hanging loose from her body, loose as a birdskin her husband might prop like a puppet and paint as though alive. From their first days in the cave, when the banded phoebe consumed all his attention, Lucy knew his dark eyes were drawn from her.

And the promise of the book came out of the depths, not that all conceivable enterprise had failed, but the depths of his need for the birds, for all the *thees* and *thous* of his love talk were only words of human affection. Art as refuge from despair? I do not believe it happened that way to Audubon. For twenty years he had taken a detour, not a wrong turn—lover, husband, father, teacher, merchant, itinerant painter, entrepreneur—in all roles a touch fraudulent, incomplete. An amateur at the life he had led. Though he convinced others, did he fail to convince himself playing LaForest or Papa? Did he look into yet another empty purse and figure his art was worth the gamble? There had to be a moment in Cincinnati when he mounted that first gorgeous display of his birds, marveled at his new technique of melding oil with crayon that captured both depth and translucence of a songbird's feathers and knew, as if it were his very self so truly depicted, framed and hung on the wall with his warblers, there could be no half-measures in his final transformation. So off he went, an artist, with the first of many assistants, young Joe Mason who would provide background—trees, sandbars, stony outcroppings, grasslands—for his birds to live in nature as his master saw them. In New Orleans every indignity served his purpose—portraits solicited door to door, lettering shop signs, gilding the flashy woodwork on steamboats, instructing sweet untalented girls. Now he was certain of his investment: he would paint the birds of America, recoup the loss of himself. There was no other way to be Audubon.

When Lucy settled to teaching for her yearly stipend at Beech Woods, her husband joined her. Chronologies vary as to the exact date he came upriver to Bayou Sarah in pursuit of the Great Idea that now determined his days. He was on foot, of that I'm sure, for his sturdy nag, Borro, was gone in a trade as well as the fine Spanish mounts he favored, long gone with *our dear old happy days* in Kentucky.

Jane Percy of Beech Woods, once a plain Scots girl with rusty hair, face round and common as a penny, was more than ready for the American adventure when she married Robert Percy, captain of the Royal Navy. Sailing the North Atlantic, crossing the country to St. Louis with her King James at hand, she believed God called her to live among the heathen, to administer Christian ways like a comforting pot of tea. During the British squabble with the Spanish for West Florida, Robert Percy sailed into the Gulf, made his way into the new territory of Louisiana and purchased his acres for a pittance, the land he called Beech Woods. He made his first fortune on cotton, returned to Scotland for his bride, who gave him a house full of daughters and one son before he died. Jane Percy had not counted on the subtropical heat, the long rainy season of midges and mosquitoes breeding in the swamps, the everlasting sweat of every day indistinguishable from the sweat that brought on her husband's yellow fever. Widow Percy's plump turned to portly, her consolation—sweet biscuits with cream and honey of her plantation gobbled with Creole coffee shipped up from New Orleans. A Negress washed her hair in magic roots steeped in river water, but the bright head faded to yellow-white of old linen. When Lucy Audubon was employed to educate her girls, the mistress of Beech Woods was then a woman alone, bolstered by money, land, cattle, slaves and full knowledge that she could manage the business of her plantation until the Frenchman, hung with guns, walked up through the magnolia forest toting a portfolio of dead birds.

How she feared Sarah and Mag's infatuation with the entertaining Monsieur Audubon who danced with them in her parlor. Feathers—all he was good for, hunting the creatures down. Still, she was sorry for Lucy, the dreadful small rooms in which they lived with the boys, their straw beds pushed aside for his rotting birdskins propped in effigy; now wrinkling her nose at the foul smell, which is only a memory, for Audubon has been gone for two years. His letters from England are all of that punishing man that invades her property. Jane Percy was pleased to say she never savored his bold spirit (or his flesh, with its musky, male scent of the wild). Her days had been all turned round with his coming and going in the woods, on the river. When he danced to his violin in the evening, all of Beech Woods seemed out of her control, bagged like his daily kill. At end of day, when lessons were over, her girls ran down to the swamp to meet him, their dresses torn in the brambles. At dawn, Sarah loitered by the stables to see Monsieur Audubon mount a borrowed horse, observe him hitch himself in the saddle, settle his privates. Jane Percy ran breathless in pursuit of her daughter who traipsed after this prince of a fellow as he rode away.

Prince, she never believed it. This cock of the walk the lost Dauphin? This scoundrel who could not support his family, this vagrant who would not observe her rules against backwoods stories in the parlor, this Jean Jacques pretender to the throne of France? He let the legend stand when it served him, let the aging refugees from the guillotine in Louisiana believe it, tattered children in need of a story. Now wouldn't Jane Percy be pleased to know geneticists have sliced the dried heart of a child with razor blades and determined (Spring, 2000) that the authentic Dauphin died in prison—neglected, mad, diseased? Her own husband, an aristocrat by nature, who made his way up through the ranks of the Royal Navy, provided for his family from the grave.

When the Audubons swam at night in the stream that cut off from the bayou, she heard laughter, yes, Lucy's squeals of delight and the braying of that bull of a man. One balmy night under cover of darkness, the shame of it called to her as a soul who must bear witness to evil before the Lord, drew her through the willows where she looked long upon their cavorting, his great chest gleaming in moonlight, long hair plastered back from his handsome face. She would grant he was handsome—the strong Roman nose, firm sculpting of the brow above deepset eyes, soft mouth pliant, almost girlish. Widow Percy devoured the sight of this man, his loins clothed only in shadow as he scooped his wife out of the water. Lucy Audubon's thin shift stuck to her body, the whole form of her buttocks and thighs revealed, her thin white legs protesting against him, and then he let her go in their play, threw her back like a fish into the moon streaked water.

The widow had seen enough. From that night in every encounter with the man, she plotted against him. Her daughters smelled her suppressed fury, acrid as smoldering ash. So it was not surprising when she commissioned the painter of creatures for portraits of her two eldest girls. Now she had Audubon in her employ. For several days he must cut short his tramps in the woods, come to Wyanoke when his wife dismissed her pupils. He must closet himself with Sarah and Margaret, for if he was such a master at his work she would purchase a sample of his genius from him. He accepted her offer for pay as he accepted his wife's position at Beech Woods, the contribution of Lucy's savings to the purse that would send him out to show the world his paintings of American birds.

On the final day of this chore, the humiliating hours spent with Mag Percy all asquirm with the joy of his attention, he put the last stroke on the downward slope of the child's nose, packed up his chalks and dismissed her. In the dining room, not to disturb the sitting, Jane Percy was serving tea to the Protestant preacher and his wife, the purveyors of morals in St. Francisville. Audubon stepped into the wide, airy hall with his work in hand to see the preacher tilt his black-suited body toward his hostess in some flattery. He looked a snapped twig next to his corseted wife. Between them Jane Percy, preening in plum silk with a collar of ecru lace, was, to the artist's eye, a forced hothouse fruit—split with her own girth, decaying. He did not go to her for the tea and sweets she would offer, would not entertain them with his accent or some slip of the tongue that might add to his colorful reputation. Unseen, he returned to the parlor, set the portraits on the piano, made his way to the schoolhouse, took supper with his family and went to his drawing board.

He had pinned a red-tailed hawk (*Falco borealis*, Plate 51, *Birds of America*), a precious item killed in open prairie land to the North. The tailfeathers were fanned as though in flight, but how to display the spread of the white-tipped wings as it soared and dipped for its prey? There was no story in his arrangement of the hawk, no setting other than the blank white page replacing the blank blue sky. Beyond the tar paper wall that closed his workroom off from the school and the common room where he slept with his wife and sons, he could hear Celia cleaning up in the classroom and Lucy reading this chill night by the Franklin stove—the *Fables* of La Fontaine to Victor and John in an English translation, a book borrowed from the lending library in St. Francisville, for she owned nothing but schoolbooks, all their books sold in the days of his financial disgrace in Kentucky.

Lucy reading La Fontaine's *Fables* because Jean Jacques, their father, learned many by heart when he was a boy in Nantes. He loved the beasts of nature portraying the harsh and hilarious truths of mankind, and better still loved the Granville illustrations that dressed birds in the demeaning finery of humans. The steady glow of lamplight on his pots of watercolors, his wife's gentle voice pretending the rasp of a peacock or the glum gloat of a greedy frog, the swish of Celia's broom all presented a scene of domestic tranquillity, yet Audubon was disconsolate.

His red-tailed hawk, a male, was unyielding as a taxidermed bird behind glass. Some years earlier he had attempted the red-tail and come
up with the hawk in stiff profile. On this old drawing he finds the notation in faded ink: *20 inches, span 48*, the measurements which he took
of each specimen—length, wingspan, weight, his inclination toward a
scientific description. He had long kept notes in his journals on the

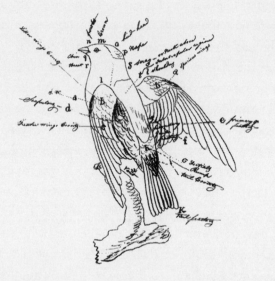

nesting habits, flight patterns, mating and migrations of his subjects,
but when the Great Idea blossomed he understood that a record of direct observation must be a part of its accomplishment. In the cause of
science he stalked a bald eagle (*Haliaeetus leucocephalus*, Plates 11, 31,
126, *Birds of America*) for three weeks observing its habits with a tele-
scopic microscope, making detailed notes, then shooting our emblem
of freedom to paint it upon a rocky cliff. The authority of the bird with
its white head and tail is magnificent, never mind that the artist mistook
the young eagle, all brown in its plumage, for another species.

As a boy he had studied one short season with a gentleman ornithologist in Nantes, read the great Buffon and, in the manner of an auto-

didact free of scholarly systems, hoarded whatever was inspiriting. Classification was a useful tool, but each bird had its own story that could not be seen apart from its habitation of woods and water, from the seasons and from the cruel necessities of its natural life. If his interest in the daily, yearly, morning and nighttime life of his birds marked him as an amateur, then so be it. He had lived as his hawks at the very edge of civilization, a raptor in for the kill. *I hardly call it a day if I have not shot a hundred birds.* The kill was his survival. He turned to a canvas sack and found a female that would do to portray the red-tail's mate in the painting. She had been eviscerated, dried and stuffed, a pretty specimen, though the cap of her head was eaten in patches by swamp midges, her breast, puffed full and fair, scored with the trail of his shot.

Celia came round the tar paper partition. He never did mind her quiet intrusion, her quick touch with the lamp wick, refreshing his jars with clear water. She was Lucy's Negress. Celia's frail husband had been sold, no longer fit for the fields. Her skin was the color of milky coffee Jean Jacques had been allowed to sip in Saint-Domingue, the three years in which he was raised by his father's Creole mistress, the years never forgotten which he would write out of his life. Celia had come with her mother as a small girl to Louisiana with a French family fleeing Touissant's rebellion, so they were of an age, and though he never spoke of his past on the island, there was that history between them revealed only in language. Monsieur Audubon had let slip some response in the patois of his childhood when she stroked the throat of a warbler he had pinned to a branch. He knew this about Celia: that she was as foreign as he was but did not love this America—why should she?—And that she had children in the quarters. Her boy, Hebediah, was *le petit nègre* who led out his horse, the brindle mare on loan from Widow Percy.

That night, Celia came to where he'd set out his colors. Often she reached to his subjects as though they might spring alive with her touch. *Ah, pauvre, pauvre.* But when the bird came from his brush, she would stand aside and say, *Bien sûr!* On the night of the red-tailed hawks Celia stroked the female's white breast eaten by ticks—*Grand mangeur de poules*, she called it—but there was not the slightest jot of a picture for her to admire and she left. It was seldom Audubon could not draw. He drew in the woods at any moment, on the river with the most awful distractions of passengers gabbing, selling themselves and their wares. He had wasted himself these past days, prancing to coax a smile from the Percy girls. He heard Lucy giving bedtime orders, John Wood-house playing with the percussion lock of the double-barreled shotgun he must not touch without guidance.

He came round the partition. "Celia," he called. She was half out the door. Lucy and the boys, these three were his audience and would recall their servant came back at his bidding. "Run to Wyanoke," he said. "Say to Madame . . ." He then ushered Celia out of their hearing. Lucy knew it was money, their life more than ever beholden to money—more than the folly of the steam mill in Henderson or scandal of the boat at the bottom of the river sold to George Keats, more than her disgrace foraging for food in Cincinnati—the getting of money was now for his dream of a book. In the morning she remembered that, though the boys were in bed, they could hear Celia on her return— "Madame say"—but they could not comprehend Jane Percy's words translated into Creole, and then her husband ran off, ran up the willow path to Wyanoke. She called after him, "LaForest, LaForest!," the old romantic name of their courtship. He was in his shirtsleeves, the tail out of his britches as he wore it when at his colors, and she thought—a prim, unforgivable thought—it was not proper to appear before Mrs. Percy, shirt open at the neck.

Audubon stomped onto the veranda. Mistress and hireling, they argued—presumably, fantastically—about art. When the widow looked upon her girls as the artist drew them they seemed stunted as little women in the traveling circus, Maggie looking the fool as always, Sarah's petulance captured in his jaundiced chalks, his keen eye predicting a bout of fever, roses gone from her cheeks. What had their mother wanted, pretty in neoclassical wash? The truth was not *pree-tee*, *pree-tee*, pecking at her, hovering so close she tasted the spittle of his rage, felt the heat of his breath on her cheek. Then he stepped back, saluted her with a broad grin, his contempt for her kind. In that moment Widow Percy knew she was a woman stuffed as a dry pelt. With a high screech, she banished Audubon from her property. The children and house Negroes hid from her fury.

That night he painted his hawks. The red tailfeathers of the male fan in outrage as he swoops down on the female, beak ready to strike, talons of one foot clutching her scapular. Tumbling in the white void of the page, she is fear itself as she clings to the hare she has ripped, the creature still in its death throes. The male will steal it from her. The strong angle of his attack, the vulnerable plain of her breast with black scoring as though she has already been wounded—by her prey. The streak of blood on the hare's belly repeats the red of bird tail, a dramatic composition, but the touch of true horror—the dying rabbit, let's give it the American name—the rabbit's guts dribble down the page, yellow and viscous.

Upon his return from the fray with Widow Percy, he worked, as he often did, through the night. His wife did not know till morning that he must pack up and leave her once again, that she must stay on to teach school and that she would in her sorrow and need berate him. In the *Bird Biographies*, which he began to write nearly ten years later, *Falco borealis* is an unmerciful killer in both fields and farms. The great eater of chickens makes for fine stories. In one, Audubon re-creates his own drawing of these *powerful marauders*, and advises the kind reader to *perceive the male to have greatly the advantage over the female*; this the observation of an ornithologist, not a fabulist like La Fontaine, yet there is always a touch of autobiography in his narratives of the birds, his life and theirs immortally intertwined.

There was that one small boy, younger than the green eyed Little Percy of Lucy's schoolroom. Rob Percy would remember his slight embarrassment when the energetic Frenchman dressed in a lace jabot and satin weskit to teach his sisters dancing. The son's story does not partake of Feliciana gossip, whispered details of the night of Audubon's eviction—smelling salts reviving his hysterical mother, lavender water soothing her brow. When he was a colonel in the Confederate Army, Rob Percy remembered the naturalist with his gun and bloody bag as magnificent, like Daniel Boone, who was already a legend when he was a boy. The inconceivable carnage of the war brought the brave vision of the artist back to him—Audubon killing for his book, his great purpose. Defending the bluffs at Vicksburg, he told campfire stories of home, of Beech Woods, a frail lifeline thrown to his exhausted men. Colonel Percy spoke of Audubon, who was in the almanacs and schoolbooks, a figure so famous his men did not credit the Great Woodsman squatting with a boy in the reeds, teaching their officer to seal dust-shot with dry leaves for the wadding, to take steady aim, wing your bird clean for the drawing. It seemed a tale of a simpler America, an entertainment.

Many of Percy's men, poor farmers who were not slave owners, did not believe in the war. Desertions from Louisiana forces, rumored to be numerous, were in fact over four thousand which often left Rob Percy telling the wind of the spectacular Frenchman who could dive under the hull of a steamboat and swim out the other side, who dined on dry venison with the aborigines, raised a glass with Sir Walter Scott and sold his book to the King of France, stories out of the popular press, nothing to do with Beech Woods. The approach to Vicksburg went on and on as the generals out-generaled each other, until it was counted the first great victory for Ulysses S. Grant. And the last of Colonel Percy, listed among the dead in a skirmish to the South on the Yazoo River, where Audubon was once outsmarted by mysterious blackbirds who evaded his shot but not his inquiring mind. Snakebirds (*Anhinga anhinga*, Plate 316, *Birds of America*) merit one of the lengthiest entries in his Bird Biographies, their deceptions and concealing maneuvers exacting in every particular. In this manner he got the best of those birds, brought them down.

Perhaps it was not strange, the colonel having no memory of Audubon's dramatic dismissal from Beech Woods, for the magic man of his boyhood turned up on Lucy Audubon's doorstep again, settled to teaching jigs and gavottes, drawing and fencing to the children of wealthy planters who despaired of their lost gentility. He did not instruct at the Percy plantation, but lived in the back of the schoolhouse, shot birds, drew them with a purpose a child could not understand and then was gone to England, which folks said was a folly.

Miss Audubon stayed on with her boys, schooled his sisters. No reason Colonel Percy should remember the day of the letter with the seal, or the fuss his mother made about the imprint of a common turkey. It was a day like any other, his mammy fetching him from the boys' school he attended. She drew him under her apron when they met the Postmaster on the trace throwing up mud from the storm with the clop, clop of his big-bellied horse. So a letter had been delivered which might be business for his mother or a feeble note from a love stricken beau for Sarah. If it was like many of Audubon's letters, Rob Percy might have remembered, for when Miss Audubon was invited to sit with his mother, he took delight in her reports—*My husband has lectured to the Royal Academy* or *Audubon has been elected to the Linnaean Society*—though he hadn't a notion what these honors might mean or why his mother fanned herself with her hankie as though to whisk such news away. And when, on the day of this letter, the boy went up the grand staircase of Wyanoke, he stole by his mother's room not to have her call him to come lie with her under the netting. He went directly to his studies and looked down from his window to see Woodhouse, a big idle boy he was not allowed to play with, displaying his kill of a heron. There was Mag tapping the crest of the dead bird to show she was worshipful of the hunter and unafraid, not a silly girl. That evening there was no social call from the schoolmistress with news of her illustrious husband to mark the day.

The day of the famous letter: Jane Percy loosened the stays supporting the flesh of her ample body and lay under the mosquito netting.

The air was dense and humid after the rain. She did not call to her boy as he tiptoed by her room. The Postmaster, a common person trading in weevily flour and the cheapest corn whiskey, had come with Lucy Audubon's letter sealed with a gobble-throat turkey. A scandal how that man abandoned his family, more than two years since he sailed out of New Orleans, the lost prince abandoning Beech Woods. When he was last in the territory, she rose early in the morning to see him ride off, his haversack stuffed with drawing instruments, flute, violin, dancing slippers, gun set across the saddle, always his gun. They say he was the best shot in Louisiana. They say he shared meals with runaway slaves in a cane brake and the beautiful Miss Pirrie, who fell in love with him, extended the hours of her lessons though she never learned to draw. Today Jane Percy has her own story of Audubon's seal, his presumptuous motto. She will bait Lucy with the wild turkey when she comes up after supper to tell of her husband's honors with that air of threadbare pride.

She succumbs to an afternoon doze, to a dream lightly veiled in which she reaches to the piecrust table by her bed—a mahogany table brought to her by Captain Percy from an island with shores more exotic than the muddy banks of the Mississippi, where she is stranded with her children, with slaves working her fields, the first crop of cotton coming on. Reaching for the black weight of her Bible, Widow Percy hunts for a familiar verse, for assurance that she is righteous, she is good.

Margaret Percy squats by the stable. Should be practicing her scales, prattling the French verbs for tomorrow, many *should*s in her life. Mag is mostly obedient. Today she watches John Woodhouse cut open the white belly of a heron. He parts the flesh, scoops the innards. The head with its long beak flops, the eyes bright, fixed on nothing. She touches the crest, soft yet queerly brittle, spiny. When the bird is flipped over with the knife its neck feathers ruffle.

"Whoosh," she says.

"Goin' nowhere"—the stable boy strokes the long blue tail that will be sold to decorate a lady's hat—"that bird goin' nowhere." Well, going home with John Woodhouse, who will attempt to draw it if his mother allows. He will prop the dead thing with wires and draw not nearly so good as his father. He wipes his bloody hands on straw and with care puts his bird in a canvas sack, slings his gun up over his shoulder. His boots and britches wet with crouching till the storm was over and the heron left her nest. He was still as could be in the cattails waiting for his kill until the heron, motionless among the tall grasses, waiting for her kill, stabbed a fish. "Whoosh!" Woodhouse flaps at Maggie as though he will fly away home, back to the schoolhouse.

When she is alone with the stable boy, Mag makes him show her the cancer on his leg. Not black like his skin, rosy and white with tentacles, about the size of a swamp crab growing crabbier each day.

"Come, boy!" His name is Hebediah, but *boy* she says, *you come,* and he follows, for she is Miss Mag. In a rain barrel she wets her handkerchief and ties it round the leg with the cancer, knowing it is useless to stop this thing growing out of the boy's body. Then she is off to her music before supper. The parlor empty, muslin curtains limp in the heat, the satin seat of the practice chair clammy as it will be from now on, through the long days of June and on into Summer. Mag Percy strikes only one note. If she sits quiet enough she may conjure him, watch Monsieur Audubon play his fiddle while dancing, his long hair flopping in tune with a minuet. *Ma petite belle* . . . He will take her trembling hand, sit her in the light by the window, switch to a rowdy repetitive tune of the slave quarters till they are laughing together.

Still as she can be for as long as she can be as he draws her with his chalks. He studies her with eyes that see like no one's eyes, his gaze both bright and dark. He has powers of recall, for at times he looks away; then she might as well be gone. The exquisite moment: he's up from the high stool borrowed from his wife's classroom to draw his subjects, his victims (Maggie this round, Sarah in pink voile completed), and he floats, this large man, across the parlor to raise her chin which is sorely lacking. Her head droops. *Ça va*—searching her funny face, holding her errant eye in his for its tint exactly, observing the pale lashes hardly visible and the flat plane of her forehead. The child, Margaret Percy— twelve, thirteen?—understands that she will never be seen so truly again.

In the parlor with tea table, pianoforte, delicate Adams chairs her father procured in Bristol (a port in a country she will never visit), chairs which arrived at Bayou Sarah by flatboat from St. Louis to proclaim the Percys people of quality—the girl was set on such a chair when she posed for Monsieur Audubon. When he touched her, the pastel powdered her cheek. She did not dust it off. Looking at herself in the mirror above her washstand, she let the smudge of his rough thumb lay like gold dust.

Today, the day when his letter poked out of his wife's pocket and Mag had been praised for her eggs perfectly oval and nicely shaded, she enacts the artist seeing her. Squinting one precious eye, he sighted her with his pencil. *Très bien.* So very good, every moment of her sitting, the silence as well as the race of her heart when he arranged the ribbon on the collar of her dress. But her portrait and Sarah's were soon gone and Audubon sent packing for his efforts. True, he came back to the neighborhood, but Jane Percy would not let her girls go to his lessons where pupils followed his graceful steps so awkwardly he banged the bow of his violin in exasperation and danced by himself, a demonstration to enchant the rough jewels of Feliciana. Or so she heard tell, but once Audubon danced for her alone in this parlor, light filtering in from the gallery. He danced to make her laugh. Then, as though it were not his fault that she squirmed on the slippery chair—

Marrgareet, you will not fidget. Hand like so.

Like so she sat, sits now.

When she is well into middle age, Margaret Percy will look upon her portrait and Sarah's stashed at the bottom of a leather box hidden from the Union soldiers who for one night from hell slept row upon row on the floors of her house. When they first landed on the flats of Bayou Sarah, she removed herself from Wyanoke to the schoolhouse and was regarded as respectful if not polite. The proclamation of General Ben Butler traveled swiftly upriver from New Orleans: *When any female shall by mere gesture or movement insult or show contempt for any officer or soldier of the United States, she shall be regarded and held liable to be treated as a woman about town plying her avocation.* What man would look upon Miss Maggie, always an unhappy sight, now withered beyond her years, as a woman of the streets?

Screened by weeping willows, she watched a boy with cornsilk hair sit at the pianoforte. He played "Jeannie with the Light Brown Hair" nice as could be, an air sweet as once upon an evening with friends in from the parish. Soon the music was shushed with rude words and coarse laughter. They smashed the long windows, threw the Adams chairs to the gallery, making room for their weary bodies. Margaret Percy spied on the Yankee villains with the silver and mother-of-pearl opera glasses which she tucked each day in the sash of her calico dress. The right lens draws the wayward eye into focus. So, when her Negroes, now free men, marched with their children and few possessions away from Beech Woods, she had witnessed their departure clearly. The first Yankees who came burnt the fields and moved on through the parish quickly with their cruel business. Now, watching from a distance, she sees the second wave of brutality play itself out in Wyanoke as she once looked upon the Shakespearean actors who killed each other upon the stage of the opera house in St. Francisville. Then she could see every false whisker of King Lear and a white splotch under the soot black face of Othello. Now it's only muddy boys, hungry as soldiers had been at Vicksburg when the North aimed to starve her brother's men out. Robert Percy had not died hungry. He shot canvasbacks (*Nyroca valisineria*, Plate 301, *Birds of America*), roasted them for his men—*fine table eatin*, or so it was claimed in a kind letter from his corporal. Rob, who never married, had passed his days hunting and fishing like a boy while his sister managed—fields, gin, books in which she noted: *Shipped 104 bales to New Orleans. Shipped 100 bales to market early.* Mag has long been overseer of household and plantation.

She trains her eyes on the pump where the soldiers wash up stripped naked to the waist, their bodies white and frightful bony. Hungry, they devour whatever is left to her, eggs and the meal for the laying hen, then the hen herself and a rancid side of bacon. From her lookout beneath the willows, she can see the officers moving about in her mother's bedroom and her own room with the washstand and pine bed of her childhood. In the flicker of kerosene lamps their shadows are monstrous against the walls, like Barnum's show of freaks in the opera house, a mere peep show compared with the blaze which now sweeps the schoolhouse, hen coop and stables.

Hebediah whispering, "Miss Mag, come away," swiveling on his hickory crutch to block her view of ruination. She spent the night in the fields with him, the last of her Negroes, praying that the Yankees would not torch the house. When they were gone in the morning, she marched past the smoldering outbuildings of Wyanoke, stumbling through broken backs of Adams chairs, trailing her skirts in the piss and shit of her visitors which littered the gallery. The front door stood open. Looking at neither the broken spindles of the staircase nor the defaced murals of an Edenic Mississippi (Greek Revival temple, pickaninnies fishing), she turned directly to the parlor. Horse hair sprouted from crimson silk faded to rose on the settee well torn by a soldier's bayonet. For a long while she sits upright in the print of the enemy's muddy boot. Above, she hears Hebediah thumping from room to room, then hop, hop, hopping down the grand staircase.

"Hebediah!"

He leans on the doorway. Grey-headed scarecrows, the two of them, foraging for wild berries, sharing a cache of moldy yams the first round of fool Yankees did not discover.

"In the root cellar. Captain Percy's box."

Miss Mag perfectly confident he'll hobble round the house with practiced dexterity, lower himself into the dank hole, scramble up and return with his burden aloft like a juggler in the minstrel show.

"Sit."

He turns from her.

"Sit you down."

He obeys, but will not sit next to her on the settee, lowers himself to the delicate chair at the pianoforte.

"For all their destruction they did not find it."

No need to tell him, didn't he fetch it? Not the first time he has witnessed the shufflin', shufflin' through her daddy's box when Mister Rob died. Shufflin' when times gave way and she sold off the first of her slaves with their papers. On some she wrote names of their mammies and pappies and their children, where they might be found if still alive in the parish. Often she kept the families together. When the deserted ladies of Feliciana, many already widows hereabouts, feared their Negroes and in their fear whipped them, Mag let her people walk free to the Union camps without a word, then burned the proof of her ownership, incurring the wrath of her neighbors. Plantation belle no more, was she ever? Then Miss Mag, she went direct to the kitchen, taught herself cookin' and washup in the tub. Miss Maggie shufflin' and there's nothing left but papers that say about the Royal Navy and the certificate of her mamma's wedding to Captain Percy with the Scots piper playing.

"The bags were fashioned of a sheep's bladder," windy music Hebediah could never comprehend. Sitting is no comfort. His stump dangles its weight from the piano chair set in the rubble of broken keys and snapped strings.

"They sailed to New York on the *Britannia*, traveling overland to St. Louis, then down the Ohio. My father did not want to risk the island waters to New Orleans with his bride. Pirates, Hebediah!"

"Shut that old box." He was wild to still her mouth, but did not say, *Hie yourself, go above, look on the ruination, slop pots on your mamma's fourposter, mirror smashed on the cupboard door, Miss Sarah's silk dresses in tatters. Look on the spoilin'.*

Mag Percy fumbles through her documents, wreck of a woman, toothless mouth sucked in. Her houseboy thinking she might look upon the pantry, empty bottles of Beech Woods brandy, shards of the Sunday plates with gold rims. Thinks she cannot read her papers with milky eyes, knows them by touch—honorable discharge from King's navy, fair copies of Grandfather's sermons delivered to his presbyter in Perth, deed to the plantation which is hers by default, Mister Rob dead and buried upriver, little sister with clever cat's eyes run off from the war, scooted with her family to West Texas.

When she exhausts the worn stories, Margaret Percy scrabbles under the evidence that proves her lineage and worth to find some old thing wrapped in sheet cloth gone yellow.

"Come here, boy," unwrapping the last document not paraded the many years with her tales of high seas, pirates, God's deliverance and the entitlement of the Percy plantation. Hebediah thumps his way across the fouled parlor floor.

This is what he sees:

Miss Sarah—mouth in a mean pucker, sallow jaw.

Miss Mag—chinless, the big blank of her forehead hovering over weak blue eyes that tell her belief—no one will care for her, ever.

"My mother was wrong. Audubon knew Sarah was dying, drew her to a perfect likeness. He saw my poor face as a death mask, no matter I was breathing."

"Mag?" The first and only time Hebediah speaks her name without the proper title.

Called to attention, she returns the portraits to their shroud and begins to clear the destruction of Wyanoke. She burns the shambles of chairs and tables. Two of the Adams might sustain some repair and it is a blessing to her—the mirror gone in the armoire. She will not have to see herself again until she is led by Hebediah to the bank in St. Francisville. In the pier glass that stands to the side of the banker's desk (he's a dandy), she will see her lamentable face through the gauze of her cataracts as she begs for a loan to replant her cotton, standing firm with the help of her houseboy. In time, her sister, the once sprightly Little Percy, will come to remove her from the empty rooms of Wyanoke to a long low house in West Texas. Miss Margaret will look out on the vague figures of cattle and horses, of Indian children playing in the dust. By way of her mother's Bible, she will make peace with the Lord who made her as she is. A niece, her voice strained beyond patience, reads the comforting verses to Aunt Mag, who mercifully does not last long in this strange and shadowy place.

The worthless acres of the plantation will be worked by sharecroppers, then sold to speculators, and cotton will be raised again by the freed Negroes who live in shacks along the dirt roads up and downriver. The plantation will prosper until the last decade of the century, when the long-snouted weevil makes its way up from Mexico, lays its fat white maggots that destroy the cotton boll. Then Beech Woods, as it was once called, will again lie fallow.

For a century, the leather box with Captain Percy's original deed remains a curiosity, then it is set out to be admired with artifacts of old Texas—Mexican saddle blankets, silver spurs and the sun-bleached skull of a wild ox—all banished during the high strutting Eighties at the command of a decorator doing up the Tudor mansion in Houston, until one day a smart kid who has been out East to college shuffles through the discarded papers to find the famous signature. *J. J. Audubon.* The bird man? And, being authenticated, the portraits are framed at last. Sarah and Margaret Percy (wasn't she the odd creature?) in their girlish afternoon gowns cannot hold their own next to an aggressive Franz Kline or the gorgeous stains of a Morris Louis. For a while they settle in the dining room with a dreamy Vuillard, the American Naturalist's soft pastels complementing the luminous sunlight of a French garden, but when the Vuillard goes on loan for a post-impressionist show, the Percy girls are relegated to the study, a dark room with pilastered bookshelves, and there Audubon's portraits hang with oils on canvas board of coyotes howling at a lurid moon, Native American women selling beads and pots—regional kitsch bought in an innocent time.

I've wandered from Lucy Audubon teaching school in Louisiana, though not nearly so long as her husband who left her in June of 1826, went off to England to sell subscriptions to *The Birds of America*. All he had to show to prospective buyers was a portfolio in process. His birds didn't come cheap—a thousand dollars for a set which would not be completed for years to come, money up front or purchase on installment plan. He carried with him letters of introduction from honored naturalists, financiers, statesmen. Still, it seems a punk game, selling himself as the American Woodsman to sell the birds of America. Soon after he sailed out of New Orleans on the *Delos*, the ship was becalmed. He lay on deck in the sultry waters of the Bahamas reading Thomson's *The Seasons* for the fourth go-round, sketching dolphins and sailors. Languishing day after day at sea, intolerable for a man with his urgent purpose, but time was slow then, many weeks for a letter to find its way from Manchester or London to Bayou Sarah. It had come round to Spring again when the letter . . .

Possible to see Audubon's life demoted to documentary. Beech Woods, two years later: voice-over delivering facts or near facts; stills of the scientific grandees who honored him in Edinburgh and Paris, cartoon of *The Yankee* (buckskins, Daniel Boone cap) in the *London Illustrated*. An exotic adored by the mothers and daughters who accompany him on country rambles. Sound track of chirps, tweets, honks, a mournful screech of warning, soft rustle in the nest gives way to musicales in English drawing rooms, to London street songs on the pennywhistle, to laudatory toasts delivered at the Linnaean Society. A furious Audubon shorn of his locks, fitted out in a velvet neckerchief for distinguished society, the only portrait in which he is pictured without *fine*

textured hair passing down behind each ear in luxuriant ringlets (his words). Most often portrayed with a fowling piece. To the modern eye, his guns are enormous. I wonder at the weight of them carried for days in the wild, the heft of the double barrel to sight a flock of passenger pigeons (*Ectopistes migratorius,* now extinct, Plate 62, *Birds of America*), as a multitude of these birds darken the sky in flight. Their biography as written by Audubon all that is left of them: his tone more passionate than scientific as he sets forth the horrifying scenes in which the wild pigeons are destroyed by the thousands, captured in nets, beaten by pole men, fed to the pigs. Consuming crops to sustain the energy of their flight, the pigeons have eaten their way into this predicament. They nest in the trees, and *Here again, the tyrant of the creation, man, interferes, disturbing the harmony of this peaceful scene. As the young birds grow up, their enemies, armed with axes, reach the spot to seize and destroy all they can.* Yet Audubon cradles a gun in his arms with such ease the weapon seems an extension of his body. *Cuckoos, killed 5, Painted Buntings, killed 20,* which cannot be excused, even allowing for his collector's greed beyond the call of art or science.

A mediating voice attempts to reconcile such violence to the birds he so loved with our improved sensibilities, reminding us of the common belief that the beasts and birds were given to man for his use in the natural order. Audubon's many references to God, the scene in which he kneels to pray in the noble forest. *The Birds of America* shown on the screen, plate after magnificent plate brought to life with the digital camera; and had I the means, a thousand dollars of 1838 translating to our millions, I would sell my lost soul for that book. That big book, for he came up with the idea that his birds must be rendered big as life. Songbirds may float on their branches in the white eternity of the double elephant folio (29½" x 39½"); but the artist must bend the necks of the Great Blue Heron (*Ardea herodias,* Plate 211), and the Trumpeter Swan (*Cygnus buccinator,* Plate 376, *Birds of America*) to fit the page in magnificent distortion.

Cut to the assembly room of the Royal Institution: *I, Lucy, delivered a lecture this evening!* (Soupçon of French accent.) *Now do not laugh so! I assure thee I understood the subject well, and that is more than one half of the lecturers can assert with a clear conscience. I spoke of Birds, Alligators, Beavers and Indians.* Bestiary of the New World and the Noble Savage, so astonishing to his audience. By how many years in his art and the intimate observation in the *Bird Biographies* did he suggest the struggle for existence, environmental adaptation in the case of the nestless razor-billed auk (*Alca torda,* Plate 214, *Birds of America*), who lays its eggs on the barren rocks of Labrador. Yes, Darwin must come toward the end, not the medical student who fled the bloody sights of the operating theater, but the gentleman scientist who cited Audubon's observations on sexual selection, who let God sit in the lecture hall as he delivered the final word on the harsh struggle for existence, the old man with full white beard clothed for a cold season in black cloak, black hat. His eyes do not engage with the camera, with us, but look inward as he leans upon a stone pillar at Down House entwined with leafless vines so intricate in their convolutions they might be strands of DNA.

Day of the letter, it has come round to Spring again at Beech Woods. Celia sets out beaten biscuits, boiled eggs and a cut of ham. Lucy Audubon calls, "Woodhouse, wash up for supper," calling him away from the measurements of his heron—weight and wingspan of the single bird he brought down this day. He is her darling boy she must send away to school, will not have him a backwoods wastrel. Woodhouse sits in his father's place at the table (and at the drawing board), yearning for his role in LaForest's life.

Nothing is said of the letter in her coverall, a shabby garment Lucy hangs at end of each day on a hook in the schoolhouse, though not this day. She dismisses Celia before the evening chores are completed. Her son at his drawing, the hours till bedtime painfully slow. She stabs a needle into the shirt she is sewing for Victor Gifford up in Shippingport where he is apprenticed to his uncle in a counting house. Both her son and Thomas Bakewell, her prosperous brother, have lost faith in the birds, in Audubon with his portfolio courting yet another disaster—a flourless mill, a steamboat sunk in the muck of the river. Gifford will not answer his father's letters, berates his mother for her loyalty to the Great Idea. Would he be pleased or shocked to know that for many months she has denied her husband the comfort of her words?

Lucy throws aside her sewing, takes up the themes written in class that day. *Assume a virtue if you have it not . . .* Each one of the older girls has written a paragraph. Each paragraph conveys the same sentiment—we must will ourselves to be better. *In the sight of the Lord,* as Sarah Percy puts it, hardly an original thought. *Think!*—the schoolmarm begins her comment, thinking that something is skewed, gone awry in the subject she set, which each pupil dutifully wrote out at the top of the page. She has carelessly omitted a word: *Assume a virtue if you have it not, for use can almost change the stamp of nature.* That *almost* makes all the difference. The sharp words of Hamlet to his mother taken from a blank book in which she has copied out verses and aphorisms since the days of Fatland Ford. The mistake is hers, so she is generous to her girls, noting fine penmanship, a correct choice of words.

When at last, Woodhouse gives up on his heron and lies exhausted on his pallet, Lucy goes round the tar paper partition. She lights a fresh candle—an indulgence, but she knows the night will be long. With each new letter from her husband she rereads much he has written in the packet of letters and in his journal sent to her in installments. The new letter bears his seal, only noted by the unobservant Postmaster this day. She knows it well—the turkey, the self-proclaiming motto—the seal made two years ago from a sketch requested by Mrs. Richard Rathbone of Liverpool, mother of the lovely Miss Hannah. The woman's coy request to surprise Audubon with a present. He records many such tokens from his admirers—a purse and penknife, the gifts of Hannah. And, as in a balance sheet, he lists the gifts shipped to his wife—a number of fashionable dresses, brooches, a set of china, a watch, a piano. Few of these articles arrive at Bayou Sarah, and when they do they are mostly in ruins. She is tired of his promises—oh, not about mere things—has written testily that she would prefer the money to buy her own watch. Her husband replied that it was believed they were people of property, that she must not let on . . . which was the first evidence that her letters were read by his patrons—only by the curious gentle ladies, though she is not sure of that. Well, she won't pretend to be other than she is in her schoolhouse. Tonight she does not at once read the letter from London. She takes all of his letters and the journals out of a pasteboard box, unties the ribbon that binds them. As she turns to the light there is her son's heron, its deep blue tailfeathers and crest drooping against the drawing board, one yellow foot wired up as though she's about to fly off, but her son's drawing is going nowhere. His pass at a sketch can not justify its death, poor bird. Until this moment, she has never thought *poor bird*, would never write it or say it to LaForest. And if Woodhouse has failed to give life to the heron, he has quite nicely sketched in grasses, wind stirring the river, a misty distant shore—background.

Still she does not settle to read the letter from London, fearing his sweet talk, *thees* and *thous* begging for a letter. Easy enough to credit her anger. She has pleaded with him to send money so Woodhouse may be sent off to school. She has complained in her few letters of the piano all unstrung in its journey, of dresses many sizes too large. As for the beautiful daughter of Edward Roscoe—*her hair light and airy in playful curls, some falling on her neck whilst others are viewing the beauty of her circling eyebrows*—she is numb to the annoyance of that prose. Oh, it did rankle when the elegant Miss Rathbone helped him select a cream pitcher to be shipped to her. Lucy has not kept a cow since Henderson, Kentucky, is thankful for the bit of cream Jane Percy sends down from Wyanoke. The pitcher arrived, handle and spout in shards.

The gentle air of the June night blows in at the window, ruffles the heron's feathers, poor bird. Lucy pulls the letter from London out of her pocket, puts it quickly aside and takes up the brown cloth daybook with Audubon's English journals, which she reads often, reads aloud to Woodhouse in the evenings, skipping the bits of her husband's physical desire for his *dearest friend and wife* as well as the many salutations— *my sweetest, my dearest,* and always the closure, *thine husband forever—* editing out prostitutes and ruffians he observes plying the city streets. She has quite liked that the journal is addressed to her, that she is LaForest's audience, takes pride in the notion that when he read passages to those English gentlewomen her name was constantly invoked, almost as though she were there. But she is not, not having tea of an afternoon in the West of England. She is not reading late in a cozy hotel until her husband returns from the Literary and Philosophical Society of Newcastle or Manchester. She carries her candle through the common room where Woodhouse sleeps. In the schoolhouse she collects the plumbago pencils, sharpens all twelve with her penknife in preparation for tomorrow's lesson. Drawing, she will teach her girls drawing, but one small part of her profession. She is alone in her classroom. Perhaps she has not taken full care of her intellect, missing the conditional word, not fully understanding she is but a character in Audubon's story by the name of Lucy. On occasion she plays a part in his scene:

> I received a present of a <u>snuff box</u>.
>   "Why my LaForest thou astonishes me. Not going to suffer
> a vile habit to encroach on thee, I hope?"

Words put in her mouth. Well, she will remain voiceless. He will not have a line from her. And in this state of mind, she goes to the window of her classroom, watches the moon sustain the assault of ravaging clouds. The idea of forgiveness comes to her *like a virtue she has not.* She must try, try to understand, and that is forgiveness, that all of her husband's writing—journals, letters public and private—were never for her alone. They are for everyone, everyone. In time he will be Audubon. He has traveled ahead of this year and the next. In time his boasting, adjustment of the facts, observation of every speckled egg, notes on seed and grains in a dead bird's craw, his alligator lectures and tales of dancing Negroes and wild Indians performed for drawing-room ladies—all of LaForest's stories will ring true, true as the ghosts and wild ambition of that other dissembling prince, Hamlet.

In time—true as the adventures of *the pore disappeared Dauphin, Looy the Seventeen,* shipwrecked on the Mississippi.

Lucy was not afraid when she was thrown from a carriage crossing the Alleghenies on their journey out to Kentucky, not afraid when locked in a room above a tavern of bawdy drunkards waiting for Victor

Gifford to be born, not afraid when beggars grabbed at her skirts in Cincinnati, yet her hand trembles as she at last reads the letter from London. *I returned from Paris yesterday and hasten to inform thee of my Success.* Success deserving of its capital. Audubon has been received by Baron Cuvier, the greatest naturalist of the age, who has escorted him into the library of the King of France, introduced him at the Royal Academy of Sciences. Both the Duke and Duchess of Orléans, the Royal French Institute, Monsieur Redouté (the Rembrandt of flowers) have all subscribed to *The Birds of America.* But this is the saddest letter his wife will ever receive: . . . *do my Lucy understand me well—My Work will not be finished for 14 Years to Come from this very present date—and if it is thy Intention not to Join me before that time, I think will be best off both of us to separate, thou to Marry in America and I to Spend my Life most Miserably alone for the remainder of my days. . . .*

Join him? A course once proposed, withdrawn, now offered as gift and ultimatum. His gifts are a trouble to her. Join him and abandon her boys? Forfeit the safe haven of Beech Woods? Take leave of her profession? Lucy cries, naturally she cries, then stuffs the terrible letter in her pocket. As the night passes slowly, slowly, she paces the schoolroom more dead than alive, then perches on her high stool, which lends her no authority. What can he mean? *Marry in America.* That he will live in exile from her, but surely not from his birds, America is their country. The letter goes on with news of his work, his demanding correspondence, that he will write to her—as though nothing wounding or unjust has been said. She has married in America, married in spite of her father's doubts, married the most charming man in the world. On her first visit to Mill Grove he showed her to an upper room where nests, eggs, feathers, stones, bugs and butterflies and the fragile bones of a squirrel were set on display. He called it *un petit collection personnel.* How could she have known that his amateurish pride in these fragments would grow into a book with more life on its pages than all the dead specimens in a museum of natural history? How could a girl falling deeply in love as she listened to her neighbor, this improbable Jean

Jacques singing the nightsong of the mockingbird (*Mimus polyglottos*, Plate 21, *Birds of America*), chattering like the wren (*Troglodytes aedon*, Plate 83, *Birds of America*), how imagine herself as background? She may be leaves, grass, berries, lizard, fish, fruited palms in the distance, marsh and meadow to him. But she is not his obsession, not a bird.

The phoebes nesting under the eave of the schoolhouse begin their day. In the first violet light the plaintive *pee-wee, pee-wee, pee-wee*. Lucy looks up at their house of mud and grass. LaForest told her they build in a spot protected from the weather—a barn, a ledge, the eave of a schoolhouse, a cave on the Perkiomen Creek—and decorate their nests with moss. They do not mind humankind. He lifted a bird banded with a silver thread to show her it had returned to its home, a sweet parable told a lifetime ago—in her girlhood.

Celia is coming up from the quarters. Her striped headcloth cuts through the morning mist, white, then red, then yellow, as she stoops for twigs to begin the morning fire. Her son limps behind her. She scolds, then turns to pick the boy up, carries him like an infant in the direction of the stables so he may begin his tasks for the day. As Lucy Audubon will begin her tasks, laying out the primers, setting the globe in its place for geography, finding her darning egg for the drawing. She will move on with her life, borrowing money to send Woodhouse to Shippingport where he settles to his studies. She has long wanted to quit Beech Woods and, following some quarrel with Widow Percy, she will move to a neighboring plantation, practice her profession in dignity and comfort. When her husband returns to America, he will spend four months in the East in pursuit of birds he must possess—shooting, purchasing birdskins when necessary, painting, always painting. Though he is at last reunited with his sons in Louisville, his wife will not join him. She remains at her post through the worst heat of August into the Fall, until one day—*It was so dark that I soon lost my way, but I cared not, was about to rejoin my wife, I was in the woods, the woods of Louisiana, my heart was bursting with joy! A servant took my horse. I went at once to my wife's apartment, her door was ajar. She was dressed sitting by the piano on which a young lady was playing. I pronounced her* *name gently. She saw me and the next moment I held her in my arms.* *Her emotions were so great I feared I had acted rashly, but tears relieved* *our hearts, once more were together.*

The story is his. We have no other.

For nine years Lucy Audubon will devotedly ruin her eyes making a fair copy of the *Bird Biographies* to accompany his paintings. She will follow him to Edinburgh and London copying the days away. It will occur to Lucy, for she is his best reader, that often the lives of his birds are akin to human stories. He writes of devotion, jealousy, the love season, the female protecting eggs in her nest, the males preening, killing each other off, the sparse feathers and tough meat of the aging. La Fontaine! She only thinks it, must believe he writes the truth of a naturalist, not fables. Audubon works on his *Bird Biographies* with William Mac-Gillivray, a Scots ornithologist, brilliant young fellow who tidies the science, but does not interfere with the intimacies of the American Woodsman's voice. John Woodhouse, among others, paints marshes and swamps of the Mississippi, the sandy shores of Key West, the terrifying night sky of the snowy owl, while Victor Gifford runs the bird business and launches the next family enterprise, *Viviparous Quadrupeds of North America*. All happy collaborations.

And Lucy is awarded her house, Minnie's Land, which Audubon built for her. Elk and fawns roamed the acres with the domestic animals, and here, overlooking the Hudson, she has her first garden since Henderson, Kentucky. A visitor who worshiped Audubon, the immense size of his life, observed that the artist was *more like a child at his mother's knee, than a husband at the hearth.* Oh, he still roamed— North to Canada, out West to Indian territory—but the show was over. The old man fading, he loved to be out of doors and his wife led him, sightless and crazed, down cultivated paths. He heard the birds, *sweet-*

sweet-sweeter than sweet of the yellow-throated warbler (*Dendroica dominica*, Plate 85, *Birds of America*) but could not see the leafless Spring trees ornamented with their gold.

When he was dead and buried in Trinity Churchyard, his wife wrote that all but her memory of LaForest was gone, *and his goodness to me*.

There was Victor Gifford's injury and death. John Woodhouse had no head for business and once again Lucy was impoverished and again taught school, instructing her grandchildren and children hereabouts. Hereabouts was upper Manhattan, Minnie's Land on the steep rise to Tenth Avenue—Minnie, an old Scots term for *mother* he fixed on her in Edinburgh. There was the war, and the public lost interest in the natural world. *Will not your Society,* Lucy wrote to the New-York Historical, *give me something for all I have, say even a dollar a volume rather than have them destroyed?* Then the house and land must be sold along with the paintings and the copperplates engraved and masterfully colored in London by the great firm of Havell. And one day, the story goes, a boy was playing near his father's foundry in Ansonia, Connecticut, and saw the outlines of wings, beaks and claws on the copper to be melted down and ran to tell this wonder to his mother. It is said many plates were saved and when he grew up, he parceled them out to Audubon's grandchildren and kept just a few for himself.

Imagine Lucy dodging streetcars and peddlers on Broadway, walking from a boarding house in Washington Heights with a few flowers she has grown on the windowsill to put on his grave. She wears glasses, not much help as she crosses to the churchyard, and it is just as well, for she can't see her lost home on the Hudson. She finds her way up the granite steps, then down the path to his stone. The trees in the city are spare, do not muffle the clatter of cart wheels or the cry of a newsboy, but she hears the laughing gulls (*Larus atricilla*, Plate 314, *Birds of America*) who come this far upriver—*ha-ha-ha*. The trees, such as they are, shelter the dead, but they are not the forest. When did she give him that name? Oh, when they were very young at Mill Grove, before they

packed up their wedding presents and headed West. He was like an oc-
currence in nature, or a mysterious place with many stories in which
yours might get lost. Lucy thinks she found her way, though at times the
path was cruel and at times he danced ahead and left her—no, that's
not it. He was the forest. They lived within him—his sons, Victor and
John, the Percys both dreadful and dear, darling girls in the West of England, frail poet, squeamish medical student in Edinburgh, shooters,
stuffers, background artists and engravers, his *Dearest Friend and
Beloved Wife*. They were streams, undergrowth, rocky ledge, bracken,
moss, bears, wolf, beetles and moles, dark of dense thickets, sun shimmering through branches.

He is forest. He contains us.

Audubon Terrace is at 155th Street. It is not a street, though a blue and
white sign is stuck to the side of the American Academy of Arts and Letters to mark where once . . . The Trinity churchyard across the street is
inviting, dangerous, chained off. In the woods he was never afraid. The
neighborhood is largely Haitian and Dominican. The great naturalist
lies among the island people who first nurtured him in Saint-
Domingue on his father's sugar plantation.

So much killing, you say. On a good day he could bring down a
flock, thirty shot to each firing. Though once, *in our old happy days*,
that would be Kentucky, he winged a red-cockaded woodpecker (*Dry-
obates borealis*, Plate 389, *Birds of America*), brought it into the log
cabin. The bird, barely injured, went about its business pecking at the
walls, while Audubon drew its black plumage ringed with white stripes,
its sharp bill and blue talons, the red feather in its cap. He worked
through the night. When he was finished, the artist opened the window
and let his subject go free.

SALVINO

Mid-Island, Long Island, State of New York. Few Summer homes, not fashionable territory, not yet. Small capes and splits in a row, postwar housing, World War II. Industry enough in the sprawl of these early developments—aerospace, electronics—to have brought into being a town with school, library, Catholic and Methodist churches. Lately, The Gingham Rabbit (gifts and collectibles) replaces a coffee shop that's had its day. The last plain place this near to the city, this near to the shore.

Suppose we lived here. The thought of Louise Moffett in a rented cottage as she removes family photos that top the entertainment center. The family, not known to her, are Mom and Dad in the old days of their new VW bus. He is firm-jawed, portly with a gleaming bald head, older than his wife by some years. The missus stands a step or two behind him, smiling faintly, looking oddly out of place, as though she would like to step out of the snapshot. Two sons are double-framed, dwarfed by the pads and helmets of high school football gear. The daughter in collegiate cap and gown, self-possessed in a studio portrait. Nothing more recent, but what does Louise Moffett know? The father is a retired civil engineer. He has taken his wife to Germany to visit a sister, all that remains of his family in Hamburg. The Muellers do not know she's been living here with Freeman and their boy for two weeks. The cottage has been rented, a house that had no comers until Freeman declared he would not live on campus. Campus is a deserted industrial park being converted into a site for biotech laboratories.

Louise has had enough of the Muellers' impersonal good looks and their concealment—medicine cabinet cleared, attic padlocked, mail stopped. She presumes their secrets to be nothing more alarming than a crutch or brace thrown in with the boys' discarded athletic equipment; Mrs. Mueller's cherished silver, the engineer's blueprints in orderly rolls, the daughter's diary with adolescent confessions—things that speak of the family's pastimes and small disasters. Their only disclosure — the photos which Louise now stores in the linen closet, above the sheets and towels she brought out from the city. There now — the bland ghosts gone. The cramped living room takes on its own life with Cyril's Brio blocks arranged in a disorderly village, his trains stalled on wooden tracks, church missing its steeple, Artie's sneakers thrown on the serviceable brown couch.

Suppose we lived here, a peculiar thought. Not that they would be Muellers, though some lost part of themselves might surface: the Louise Moffett, innocent, hopeful — left behind on a farm in Wisconsin; Artie Freeman, the bright loner — cherished and neglected by his loopy mother throwing lumps of wet clay on a whirling potter's wheel. Suppose they were not the city folks they are — an artist on the cutting edge that has dulled, a mathematician in search of a difficult problem. Almost impossible to imagine living without the urgent keeping-up of New York, the metropolitan laws of motion — running to hold your place. Suppose, instead of the Latino caretaker and the costly play group, their boy simply went off on a neighborhood jaunt as he does each day, running out the front door of the rented cottage into the arms of a local girl who takes him to the beach. Enough supposing. Louise stands on the couch to take down The Picture. The Picture — only one in the house — oil painting of rocky shore, turbulent waves, lighthouse at the end of a reef, ordinary to the nth, except when she walks down the block past a row of Mueller-type cottages, crosses the road to a sandy path through beach plums and scrub roses that leads to the shore, she sees the artist's view, the very stretch of Atlantic, rocky reef, decaying lighthouse — unframed, naked to the world.

The troubling thing about The Picture — it's more than good of its kind. A sure hand has laid on the paint, yet there is a disturbance in its flashes of white ruffling the dark sea. The landscape suggests some grief or loss — black rocks thick as dried blood lead the eye to the relic of lighthouse, a beacon no more. This little narrative holds Louise Moffett, but the accomplished brushwork, the careful composition trouble her. The artist backed off from a depth of emotion, made the view sweet with streaks of sunlight on tiny brown birds pecking at the shore. So down comes The Picture. She stores it behind the couch, where the white-capped waves of an oncoming storm face the wall. Louise Moffett might paint this scene. Her concern is real these days, a concern she's only that good. When she was a girl, it was said of her pretty drawings, *Lou has a touch.* It had taken years to overcome that ease, the touch which is second nature to her. Suppose there's no more to her work than a childhood gift. Better to look at the bleached patch on the Muellers' wall than confront The Picture she could knock off as an exercise in competence. Reef, lighthouse, turbulent sea, even the sunshine—she might commit that false note. The Picture hiding behind the couch is unsigned.

In the garage, clean as Mrs. Mueller's kitchen, she puts out brushes, tubes of acrylic, pastels, wet clay, gives herself to the thrill of new materials, first day of school. That trick of fresh start always worked until lately, until these past years when Cyril is taken off to play and she is given the morning hours to make her art. She cuts into a loaf of clay and slaps a hunk on the Muellers' folding Ping-Pong table. Her fingers press into the moist plasticity, a feely, touchy comfort as she forms the clay into an oval, props it on end like a football, which is all it brings to mind, a little football set for the three-point kick. When she lets go, it tumbles.

Thing is, Louise Moffett has been productive, had her hour of fame. She painted miniature scenes, no bigger than postcards, in which nature was demoted; next blew up botanicals on huge canvases displaying the cellular structure of leaves and grass. When the critics were interested in Moffett, they came up with the idea that she was a nature artist interested in scale, the difficulty of placing ourselves in a landscape manipulated by man. Moffett put herself on display in a show of autobiographical artifacts, hers and Freeman's, dead as the documentation behind glass in a musty museum of natural history unless you saw her in the flesh modeling little hearts in the window of the gallery on

Broadway. Putting heart into the archival material of family with revelations of frailty, betrayals, self-deception, and love—that was a risky
business. In a carnival era of self-exposure, the art world, her world, applauded Moffett. The critics had been friendly.

Now she is in an alien garage. She sets the compact oval of clay on
end. Perhaps it is a pineapple, a coconut or an instrument fashioned of
a gourd. Louise likes this guessing game, a sort of foreplay before she
gives in to her material. But suppose her lump of clay is the body of an
owl in need of head and clawed feet. She works away at feathers and
ears, at big owl eyes. As always, there is the pleasure in making. The
bird lists, can't balance the bulk of its body. She has not dealt with the
skeletal underpinning of sculpture since a studio course in college. Her
owl is solid, too heavy. No model to go by, just memory of barn owls
that devoured field mice and the rabbits that plagued her mother's garden. Mistrusting what will become of the bird in her hands, she knows
she can crush it at any moment. Does a barn owl have ears? A curved
beak? Tomorrow she will look in an Audubon Guide. No bookstore in
this town. This far into her work with some of the old concentration,
she doesn't hear Cyril run up the driveway right into the open garage.
He hoots, hoots at her owl. The local girl says it's like, you know, the
one in a story, which book she's forgotten. Yes, the owl is coy, harmless
and plump as a stuffed animal, charming as an illustration in a child's
book. Louise smashes the bird into a mass of wet clay.

Cyril narrows his eyes in disapproval at his mother killing off her
work. His father has taught him to be silent when she is in a fury—it
will pass. A thoughtful child, well aware of his mother's moods and so
much like his father, with unruly dark hair, tall for his age, tall enough
to pat the grey leavings of clay on the green field of the Ping-Pong table,
then turn from her and run for the hose. He sprays the beach sand off,
a rule before he enters the Muellers' clean house.

Suppose we lived here, Louise thinks. Suppose I made many such
rules—no sneakers on the couch, no train tracks on the living room
floor. I would be Mrs. Mueller. I'd tidy up my arts and crafts, go into the

kitchen, open a can of soup for lunch. Which is exactly what Louise does after she pays the local girl.

That night she dreams of the owl flailing about for a perch, not in the dark recesses of the old barn in Wisconsin, in the Muellers' garage or some loftier place brightly lit. Not an anxious dream, but one that wakes her. She finds her way to the kitchen by the dim night-light cast from Cyril's room, stumbles down a step to the attached garage, where the light switch is precisely outlined with glow-in-the-dark tape, so tidy, so Mueller. The Ping-Pong table is her mess, tools not washed off, the dry white scum of her morning efforts. She lifts the wet towels from the loaf of clay, then turns to shelves of brads, nails, bolts and nuts all labeled in their jars. Pruning shears and plumber's helper look like they have just come from the hardware store as does the toolbox, though shame on Mr. Mueller: behind a set of worn tires neatly stored, she discovers an untidy scramble of chicken wire.

Now, the dream has not told her to open the toolbox, take out the wire cutter, scrunch layers of chicken wire until she has built an armature oval as a football for an owl life-size. She tacks this framework to a scrap of board so the owl will perch with ease. Louise is working from memory, not the memory of a studio class at the university, but the memory of summer nights in Wisconsin, the solid body of the bird swooping down, snatching a mouse with its claws. Louise watched by the light of the moon, for her owl was nowhere to be seen in the day. Her owl—she waited at the screened window to hear the death squeal of its prey—mouse, gopher, nest of baby rabbits. A useful bird, her father said, useful for the farmer. He spoke of the owl's good work in his fields of oats and hay, not concerned with the predators in her mother's flower garden.

Her sister, who feared any stray dog or geese flapping in the pond as if she'd been brought up in town, called it a scary thing. To Louise the owl was efficient, spotting its meal, diving for it. Once she saw it fly back to the darkness with a gopher big as itself. Often she heard it hiss when her father stole out to the mechanized barns before dawn. Her owl. She drew it in daylight, recalling the outline of dark feathers round its white monkey face, small powerful eyes. She drew because that was what she was good at and won a blue ribbon at the county fair in a little tent with kids' weaving and carved Ivory soap, the exhibit no one cared about at all. That's when her mother said Lou had the touch, to make her feel better, and that her owl was pretty. Not pretty, just altogether beautiful, with dark spots she speckled on its breast, its head slightly swiveled, on the lookout to see the creature it would devour next.

Lou works through the night—owl time. Moths flutter at the fluorescent light overhead. Mosquitoes are lured to their death by the Muellers' electronic zapper, only their sizzle breaking the silence. At dawn, she hears Artie in the kitchen, her son's happy voice, "Where's Mom? Where is she?" Laughing as though she is hiding in one of their games. Before Artie and Cyril appear in the doorway, she shrouds her bird in a wet towel. He's not perfect, but for a moment she's as foolishly happy as she was when the blue ribbon was pinned on her owl in the exhibit no one cared for. No, as happy as she was when drawing her barn owl, getting him down with charcoal and India ink. Her window was just above the driveway, once cow path, leading to the old barn. The moon revealed the bird's long pale legs, tufted ears, the soft dusting of spots on his chest, his composure—poised and still as the summer night.

When Cyril reaches to unveil what his mother's been up to, she says, "Not yet." A cruel thing to say to a child. "Tomorrow or the next day."

Artie looks sorry about that, sorry as their boy.

Louise keeps the owl to herself.

The town library has three Audubon Guides, one that circulates. The Librarian is a welcoming old lady with spectacles on her nose, her hand unsteady as she makes out a temporary card for Louise, who claims residency at the Muellers'.

"Muriel! Now, *there's* a reader."

Louise wouldn't know. There is a worn *Joy of Cooking* in the kitchen, not another book or magazine in the house.

The Librarian checking out the bird book offers sandpipers, "Flocks on the beach. Plovers out toward the lighthouse, that's not till August, end of Summer."

As Louise leaves the library, old folks are assembling, settling their canes and walkers next to chairs placed in a circle. They are chatty, even noisy, each with a paperback book in hand, all with the same violet cover.

A hearty fellow waves his cap, beckons Louise, "Mystery Club today!"

She waves back, makes for the door. She supposes they read the same murders right through, supposes they all know who done it. Then what can the mystery be?

In the car she opens the Audubon Guide. Barn owls do not have ears. The beak is small and sharp with a lethal downward curve. The owl is more spectacular than she remembered. In the photo black eyes glisten in the flat plane of its white face, so bright, so undisguised for a night bird.

Mid-Island, the aging industrial park, squat buildings sheathed in glass skin of the Seventies, a few concrete bunkers. In the room where Freeman spends his days, many cubicles, many computers. Large screen suspended over conference table. On occasion the mathematicians are set free of their machines. One by one they straggle to the long table, a laminate pretending to be wood. Is it oak, Artie wonders, dark streaks in yellowish grain? He draws with a new pencil on a fresh pad laid out by Matron for the conference, drawing the slick striations of the tabletop. Laughter and words muffled. The carpet and acoustical tiles of the ceiling absorb sound. Nuthouse, he thinks, the walls covered in padded cloth to create an abnormal hush for brainwaves to flourish, to stifle the whimpers and moans of erring mathematicians. They are all lunatics stealing about in this soft-edged asylum on a perfect June day.

Ten of them at table, ten little Indians in their ergonomic chairs waiting for their instructions. A red blip flashes across the screen, then a projection of the building in which they sit—the green lawn with pear trees blooming, daffodils lined up along the drive, pond with outcropping of smooth rocks *à la japonaise*, the façade of the bunker in which they sit, crenellated concrete in friendly earth tone. Someone hums the *Star Trek* theme.

On screen and off, the building they compute in has no visible door. A piping voice cries, "Open Sesame!" Travis, the baby of the doogies here assembled, all babies to Artie Freeman, who is an ancient person, thirty-seven years old. Travis—silky locks of a cherub, no facial hair—a wunderkind, barely able to feed himself like a big boy in the cafeteria. His diet—Pepsi and Froot Loops.

"Open—"

"Shut it, Travis."

Freeman continues to capture the grain of the laminate. His wife draws. Not his wife, she is the mother of their child. He calls her *wife*, O.K.? From the first day he came to the lab, waving bye-bye to his son safely strapped in the kiddie bucket, blowing a kiss to Louise as she took off past the daffs and pear trees in bloom. "My wife," he said to the kids assembled for the security check.

"Wow!" That was a pale boy with a Scooby Doo backpack. Freeman knew it was not Lou's beauty from the neck up, tousled hair, eyes puffy with sleep under wraparound shades, that brought forth this childish cry. *Wow!* was for *wife*, and in the days that followed Freeman never found the appropriate moment to undo the word. Now that he knows Travis, he would not split particles over *partner/girlfriend/wife*. The boy is socially stunted. It's said by the other youngsters that he sniffled when a package of goodies arrived from home. Artie wouldn't know. He doesn't live in the dorm. When he was selected for the Summer semi-

nar at the lab, the simple request to bring his family was met with be-
wilderment, they had never—though there was nothing on the books.
He sensed in the huffing, puffing delay that something like a meeting
of the board had been called to deal with a Human Situation.

So Artie Freeman and Louise Moffett and their son, aged four, with a
clunky hyphenated last name, have been installed in a rented cottage a
universe or half-mile away from the bunker, depending how you figure
it. Lou not pleased to wake Cyril at seven, chauffeur Daddy to Summer
school.

"Middle of the night," her complaint. Each morning Artie awaits her
in his chinos and button-down shirt, eager as can be, his floppy black
hair wetcombed off his forehead. She must stop seeing him as a boy. It's
the long limbs he doesn't quite grow into, the bouncy forward tilt of his
walk as he heads to the car. She is guilty of loving the blubbery tire
around his waist, the strained blinking of his eyes when he's worked
hard at his math, as though her wishing Artie older will make them, the
three of them, settled and safe. Lou's furious at her cheap housewifely
thought. Improbable as he is, all she desires is Freeman.

Artie, who figured to be with Lou and his boy at day's end, now figures he would be on heavy medication living with the doogies. Take
fun, for example. Kids at the lab, as Artie calls it, can't play Frisbee without figuring wrist action into wind current into velocity, forget throw
the damn thing. Take music, bluegrass groove downloaded into their
skulls, beatific smiles on each sappy face when they break from their
screens. Except Travis, who popped tapes into an ancient Zenith, petri-
fied oldies—*Unchained Melody, Hello, Dolly!* It is said that Travis was
a late child miraculously conceived by a vintage Rockette in a retire-
ment village.

"Expunge," Artie commands when Travis-jokes get out of hand. He
hates being cast as Senior Counselor. How he hated those models of
early manhood in his day. His day long gone when you figured math

homework with a Bic on ruled paper. No game, his grandfather ordered, till homework is done. Game was chess played on a wooden board, kings and queens with crowns of ivory. Always beat the old man, like these kids who outfox him at every turn with their swift calculations.

The hovering screen hovers, displaying last month's daffs and dwarf pear trees in bloom. The drive is now lined with red geraniums and an edging of white frothy things.

"Alyssum," said Louise. What doesn't the woman know, and the trees are now green, green as the grass watered each night with timed sprinklers. Freeman thinks the visual powers-that-be might update the picture, bring on the peons in their navy-blue jumpsuits with the clearance tags, show them jumping out of the pickup truck, plopping the geraniums, etc. into the earth, pull back to a full view of the lab with the unrippling pond carved into the smooth undulating lawn. But here ten little Indians idle with a still shot of postdated bloom for a full three minutes of expensively funded time.

The warm moment of the week, Friday P.M. The bunker will shut down, not the minds of the doogies. Matron will lock the lab with the keys hung on her belt. She is all angles, elbows, knees, wrists articulated like a fiberglass dummy in a simulated car crash. Far from dumb, she was Salvino's pet graduate student twenty years back. Dorothy Bunge, sharp-chinned, efficiently helpful, most particularly to her boss whose duties she has assumed in the Summer program. Disappointing to the doogies that Guglielmo, as she affectionately calls him, must, as mathematician of note, go aconferencing, that they must commune with him on the screen while he skips from deterministic chaos in London to complex systems in Milan.

"Soon enough Guglielmo will be with us." Dotty Bunge breathless with expectation. To Artie Freeman she looks like a nun on holiday, in a seersucker jumper over crisp white blouse. In his system she is Matron, Salvino is Leader, bunker = lab, his fellow students = doogies. With such simple equations he gets through the day. *My ten little Indi-*

ans, Leader's warm welcome beamed in the first day. Placed before the cameras in Geneva, he had so designated the young mathematicians in his care. *One little, two little, three little . . .* Artie can't get the ditty out of his head. It has occurred to him he's phasing out, may not stick with Salvino *in absentia* for six weeks of grinding his axioms, but stop, he must stop such nonsense. Nonsense all in his head, for Artie's silent in these weekly sessions with Leader, often miscalculating on his pad. Attention! Now for the jolly-up, the take-home assignment. Only Mr. Freeman will go home to the rented cottage. Chu, Dawn, Vic, Bette, Mel, Shah, Rick, Travis and van Haagen will stay in the dorm—a temporary campsite Matron has outfitted with bunk beds, desks, terminals.

"Peace!" Their Leader's image glows, a gentleman in top form as he lays out the problem to be contemplated in downtime. His fine tailoring, sleek white hair, starched anti-Einsteinian look works well with the devil-may-care manner of a gent who presumably missed Olympian gold by a microsmidge.

"Peace!" A television salutation, the greeting Artie recalls from the spongy politics of his mother long dead, her moody resistance to authority. Leader is authority selling teamwork, concerted effort. He cannot be imagined in younger days, bell-bottomed in mood enhancing fumes of a weedy psychedelic pad, a scene which is beyond even Artie's recoverable past. No trend or passing fashion has ever penetrated the steel armor of Leader's exquisite brain, despite an embarrassing word or two—"Cool! Peace!"—and pretense of devil-may-care. Dr. Guglielmo Salvino in his prime, the father you'd love to replace your own slow witted dad if you were a whiz kid. If you are one of ten little Indians—nine little Indians, Artie has already fallen off the wall. In any case, he's a bastard and so's his son, legally speaking.

Salvino clucking—*no, no, no*—at Dawn, tangled in an algorithmic mess.

"No, you must see the digits of the sum as amended. . . ."

Freeman sees a tough, bright child who leapt ahead of her professors at the good women's college to grad school, Cal Tech. Dawn, a breastless boy/girl with stylish crew cut and sweetheart locket on a black silk thread around her neck. It is said she is sleeping with van Haagen, the bleach blond from Amsterdam, a boy with an affected British accent, but then Artie wouldn't know, going home as he does each night to his *wife* and son. For some days now he has not known why he is committed to the lab, why he applied for the privilege.

On a dreary Winter morning, Artie Freeman came out of the subway at Broadway and 116th Street, made his way through an icy mist to Mathematics, an eccentric building tucked into the old Columbia campus, domed and dark like a little temple of a secret society long disbanded. A notice on the bulletin board advertised Summer programs, one to be held not far from the city, not attached to a university. A photo of students playing volleyball, meadows and soft hills in the distance. Freeman thought of his son, who would be confined to the heat and the grimy playgrounds of the Lower East Side. The seminar was to be under the guidance of William Salvino, a name to be reckoned with, though Freeman could not recall his accomplishments, whether inspectral lines or inaccessible cardinals. *Scholars*, the prospectus read, *will examine mathematical problems, solved and unsolved, in the light of formal and intuitive failure.* He didn't quite get hold of that and put the question to his warmest professor, an ethereal man with crumbs in his whiskers, consumed with nonlinear problems. Would such a seminar be to his advantage?

The professor let go a mirthless laugh. "Salvino was one of the splashy fellows. We called them *near Fields*."

"Near fields?"

"The Fields Medal."

Artie noting his mentor's amusement. Yeah, he was green, not knowing till this moment mathematicians were barred from the Nobel. Story was—Alf's wife was getting it on with a mathematics pal. "This Fields is the jackpot?"

"Only awarded to those under forty."

The professor's pixie smile: "So, Salvino's still at it."

"At what?"

"A genius at writing grants."

"Then," Freeman said, taking the prospectus back, "it's not serious?"

"As serious as you want to make it. Out at Brookhaven, is it?" He was surprised when his student hustling to catch up in pure math was selected for Salvino's instruction in how brilliant men dropped the ball. Perhaps a lesson in futility, nevertheless a freebie, fully funded.

But the Summer program was not at the famous National Laboratory, Watson's domain, of Watson and Crick who unraveled the double helix that nails us all. Closer into the city, yet mid-Island, a small town in the smallest letters on the map. Two weeks of this stuff and Freeman has come to believe that their Leader intends to adulterate math by something like a moral. That's the point, isn't it, Leader's point, that there is much to be learned from others' mistakes?

Chu attempts to correct Dawn's speculation. Travis waving his hand in the air to be called on. The insufferable bright boy in the class forgets the screen is one-way. He can be heard but not seen. Suppressed snorts.

"You have something to tell us, Travis?" Not that Salvino is clairvoyant. The first days into the project, any fool would know it was the littlest Indian who pipes up to correct Dawn, Chu, Vic, Rick, Shah—whoever. Never Mr. Freeman, the nice old student who comes to his defense. Mr. Freeman—speechless, scribbling on his pad—goes home each night to his wife and kid. The oldster who went back to school in his fossilized thirties, his turn away from frivolity to serious business. Smart—he made it to the lab, didn't he? To Salvino's project: A seminar in famous problems which for hundreds of years resisted solution. Fermat's Last Theorem. Mill's Theory, Euclid's Fifth—the Parallel Postulate. A trip, discovering the subtle miscalculations of the great on their way to proof or no proof at all. Watch the masters stumble—ferret out wrong turns, display the gap in their equations. Salvino's trip, his enjoyment.

What Freeman understands: the whole unraveling of past errors might be useful in a classroom, a demonstration of how the mind works, backs up, maneuvers in dead-end situations. What he suspects: he is an element in Salvino's experiment, a mathematics wannabe, slowed by years of flab, running behind the pack. Salvino addresses him as Mr. Freeman. Why should he be so distinguished? Why set aside?

"Mr. Freeman, you have something to contribute?"

"I pass."

But wait, Travis has something to tell us.

"Let's reformulate." The excitable boy bouncing in his chair, if only Leader could see him. "Suppose each term is greater by ten than the previous number in the sequence . . . ."

Groans from eight little Indians who can follow every word, every sine of what they now term *the Travis leap*. The boy always right and proud of it. Fun Friday comes to an end as he whips through the laws of motion, where Mandelbrot's set upended Newton and Lorentz.

"Peace!"

Freeman thinks "Cool!" more appropriate for Travis. Salvino is signing off at this week's confab in Milan. Matron sends them back to their stations, where Mel, Rick, Chu, Vic, Bette, Shah, van Haagen, Dawn and Travis discover the puzzle to chew on for the weekend—mid-Island. Back at his machine, Freeman sees the boggling conjecture, shuts his system down. In this moment, he knows he will give it one week more, not stay the course. Something suspect about his being thrown in with these kids, some plot of Salvino's.

Louise waits for him in their rented car by the geraniums and alyssum, Cyril directing a superhero in the kiddie bucket. An urgent cry, "Mr. Freeman, Mr. Freeman!" Travis, running across the lawn with a printout of the current puzzle.

"You blacked out," the kid says.

"Don't you know it." Freeman opens the back door: "Get in." Nothing in the books against it, the Human Situation of taking the odd boy home for a swim and supper. Travis can't swim. He squats in the sand until Cyril takes him by the hand, leads him into the lapping waves of low tide. Freeman watches as his son demonstrates the dog paddle. The bright boy runs back to shore clutching the waist of the borrowed bathing suit. Freeman gives it a try, takes Travis into the water, holds him afloat while Cyril grandstands with a splashy backstroke.

Hamburgs on the Mueller grill. Louise offers their guest a beer. Travis sips, smacking his lips as though he likes it. Then there is time for the Brio block village on the living room floor. Two little boys right the train on its tracks, build overpass and underpass, set a light at the crossing. The church has its steeple. Until it is time for Cyril to go to bed; then Freeman dangles the car keys to take the bright boy back to campus, but the party is not over for Travis. He spreads the puzzle page out on the serviceable brown couch and displays both algebraic and analytic solutions. Freeman follows, slowly, barely.

Travis says, "One way to the answer is no better than another, but the algebraic symmetry, that's beautiful." On the drive back he asks, "What's doogie?"

"Smart rats. Genetically altered, smarter than other rats."

"So we're doogies?"

"I guess." Freeman doesn't tell the kid he's beyond the geneticists' manipulations, doesn't cite the source—Doogie Howser, a child medic on TV dealing with the bodies and minds of his patients, the sitcom presumed to be hilarious and touching: a little child shall lead us. Looking at Travis, he finds it a bewildering business, the angelic open face, the daffy smile concealing that brain that in a flash can figure two routes to the same elegant answer.

Twilight zone when they drive up to the bunker. Soft lights shine on the trees and flowers, on the slight stir of the pond with the aesthetic gesture of those smooth black rocks.

Travis fumbles with the safety belt. "It's been the best time. Your wife," he says, "she's cute."

He runs across the lawn in the headlights' beam, his limbs floppy, unformed. The sensor detects the arrival of a certified Salvino doogie. Magic as the massive stone in an Arabian tale, the concrete panel of the bunker slides open. Freeman remembers Travis clutching at the bathing suit as Cyril hosed him off, the tough brown body of his son dancing in a rainbow that shimmered in the spray.

Louise in the fluorescent glare of the garage. Her owl, set where the net should be, lords it over the Ping-Pong table, plumage tight to his oval body. Small rolls of clay plopped here and there on the green field. Her hands scummed with clay recall to Artie Freeman his mother's hands, rough and dry from her potting. Fiona's many bowls and mugs were useful but of no distinction. He knew that as a boy. Now Louise has something in the works, a modeling and making that absorbs her each morning, each night. He would like to pack up, scrap Salvino's consuming quest for failure. He touches a tendril of clay, slimy, unformed.

"Stars," she says, "or they will be."

They speak of Travis sipping his first beer, the single track intensity of his mind. He was no more clever with the Brio blocks than Cyril.

"You," she says as an accusation, "Artie, tell me you weren't like that?"

"No, just lonely, smart-assed."

"Good, that's different from smart."

"Quite different." He's about to leave her to her work, which he envies, lie back on the Mueller couch, see what's up with the Yankees. He pats an embryonic star. "He said you were cute."

"Poor boy."

Yes, but Travis was wrong. Lou is the American Beauty rose, the blush still on though her yellow hair is dulling to brown with a streak of early grey. Nothing cute about the hearty farm girl with the classic cut to her features—calendar girl he had called her—softer since their child, an edge of care or ambition worn off. He loved the urgency of her body in bed. Well, in almost any daily maneuver. Right now he admires the strength of her hands, their graceful movement in whatever she is making. He bends down and kisses her fingers, tasting the wet clay.

"Soon," she says, "I'll come in soon."

He leaves her for a long inning, then she comes, holds out her earthy hands. "There will be sparrows," she begins, "that's how I see it now," her voice trailing off as she leads him away.

There will be sparrows, finches in a tree, a tree that will tremble with their song like a toy set in motion. The stars will be scattered on the ground the way you see them reflected in still water at night. You will stand above the stars and look up to the blank heavens. I will sit in my shell of a body on a stone or a chair, I think chair made of wood, manufactured by man. The sky and pond and ceiling will be bluer than the night sky. This universe is new. Or old, old as the golden planets and stars set in intense blue that surrounds the earth in a medieval Book of Hours. The stars will be glass, transparent, nothing to read in them. My body will be wax, perishable. The owl will be cast in brass, an object too heavy to swoop down for the rabbit. The rabbit will be soft, constructed of feathers. The songbirds can't fly from their trembling trees. All else stationary. A Peaceable Kingdom.

Freeman thinks this way: He's got Lou and Cyril out of the city for six weeks. If he cops out he'll be in disgrace with ethereal Nonlinear at Columbia. Third week: for Freeman it's a counting game—one little, two little, three little—crossing out, canceling. The game of gloating over faulty proofs becomes madly competitive. Travis is his tutor. He likes a light beer as he leads Artie (now calling him Artie) through their homework. The Brio block town on the living room floor acquires harbor, town square, suburban sprawl. Cyril teaches the bright boy to play Go Fish. Artie provides the real thing—hook, line and sinker—takes the boys fishing off a rotting pier at the end of the reef, out by the lighthouse, a harmless old structure with a door flapping in the wind, battered signs that inform intruders of danger, high voltage, U.S. Government property. They catch two blues, scale them, cut off their heads, cook 'em and eat 'em. Louise sees this adventure as remedial camp for Artie as well as the boy genius.

Each morning the local girl takes Cyril to the beach. They build sand castles, then let the sea destroy them. In the afternoon Mimi, that's the local girl, studies the Swedish Massage mid-Island. She shows Louise the book with all the muscles, tendons and bones she is learning to manipulate. When she gets her certificate, it'll be a good living. The Swedish Massage is often prescribed for the elderly. Has Mrs. Freeman noticed how many old people live in this town?

"Yes, in the library, all those rubber-tipped canes, aluminum walkers."

"Which they would not need," Mimi says, "if they'd lay their bodies down for the Swedish Massage."

Louise has taken note of the Mystery Club, of the oldsters driving five mph, sunning in their lawn chairs, the energetic walking on the beach, the infirm grazing the supermarket in their motorized wheelchairs. When she lets Artie off at the curried campus in the morning, she drives the streets, many of them roundabout cul-de-sacs, houses and lawns of Mueller perfection in this sleepy town with a full complement of the aged who gave their working lives to the exurban defense industries that dwindled. So there's the geriatric set, and the kids who compute with Artie. By a grammar school, a few children in an asphalt play yard. Each day the sky is bright, clear Kodachrome blue. The Mueller lawn browns out. Louise takes the hose to the patch of yard. As though she lives here.

On a Sunday, the family drive. Other side of the highway, a virtual village of new condominiums. A half-dozen megahouses, baronial colonial, set in a field. Mid-Island mall in progress with promise of cineplex, espresso bar, all the pleasures. Freeman believes the mall is for the biotechs, they've been moving in. Mercedes and Subarus in the parking lot. Black limo in attendance upon executives. Lab equipment hauled into the glass-box buildings. In the giveaway paper, the biotech company lets the town know in plain English that they will enable the delivery to the human body of noninvasive proteins, antisense molecules and genetic improvement. Cable, power lines, the peons leveling out a putting green. The cafeteria in the bunker is invaded. The menu immensely improved.

Van Haagen returns to Amsterdam. It is said that Dawn has shacked up with Chu. Mr. Freeman wouldn't know, going home as he does to the wife and kid. Bette has an allergic reaction to shrimp secreted in a frittata, falls into toxic shock on the cafeteria floor, is spirited off to the hospital by two spry old fellows, the local ambulance corps. It is said she's been shipped home to Columbus or Cleveland. Artie counts himself out, so seven little Indians assemble at the conference table on Friday to hear Salvino proclaim puzzle of the week. On the screen same old pear trees, daffs, pond stuck in green lawn, concrete bunker.

"Open Sesame!"

Groans.

The door to the padded room opens. Salvino in the flesh. Salvino in cream linen, a three-piecer, tummy straining the vest. His face is pinched, sallow, the magnificent white hair unreal. On screen, Leader is blooming, cosmeticized for the camera, so it seems to Artie. Dotty Bunge pulls out Salvino's chair at the head of the table, awaits his uncertain bandy-legged trip across the carpet. "Let us review."

An irreverent doogie mumbles, "Peace!" General laughter.

"Let us review."

An expectant hush. It is known the Great Salvino has entry to their files, yet he might be gazing into a crystal ball, flourishing his bony hands in wonder. He closes his eyes, the better to see an apparition.

"Vic and Rick?"

"Yessir!"

"You have been drag racing in the parking lot. After midnight, quite a stir."

"Yessir! To figure traction against velocity in the Belotsky conjecture."

"Inferior. Applied mathematics. Mel, Shah?"

"Master," Mel, Afro from Austin.

"You are trapped in the forbidden net, stacking the deck against the blackjack game in Wilderness Casino. A corruption of your talents, depriving the house of its take for needy Indians."

"Native Americans." Shah from Bombay.

Artie Freeman is astonished as Salvino lights into Dawn's sexual shenanigans. That finishes off Chu, leaving Travis the only doogie in good standing. The boy squirms in his seat, hands pressed between his knees, no stunning query, no brilliant answer. Salvino has not exhibited the week's mental fault lines, only human frailty. Indignant, Dawn turns to her newest lover, but Chu is transfixed by the screen wiped of daffs, etc. Geraniums blaze up the drive to the bunker. An American flag ripples in the wind, though the pond is strangely still. Dawn, that tough bird with bristle hair, gets her sweet ass up from the comfy chair; her tittery adolescent laugh bounces off the padded walls as she bravely sashays out the door. Not an ounce of shame. Six little Indians howl. Salvino thumbs his vest. Matron all sly smiles. Whatever the joke, Mr. Freeman alone is glum.

Don't mistake, he gets it: their Leader has changed the rules of the game. A well worn classroom exercise: If you are IT playing tag, then you must tag someone out for survival. But suppose that is not your way to play the game. Suppose you invent another game entirely. As in Euclid's Fifth, so often reduced to grammar school truism—two parallel lines cannot intersect. Suppose you depart the flat plane of that world, leave behind the Euclidean dimensions. It's simple as pie to the doogies, who can skip right along to the fourth, fifth, sixth—who knows how many dimensions, or how nature itself is configured in how many worlds.

Artie gets up from his assigned chair, goes round to the foot of the table, faces off with Leader.

"Mr. Freeman?"

Silence.

"You feel left out. Going home to your wife."

"Not my wife, as you know. I misspoke. You know my history," Artie says, "the wasted years." He speaks, now that he finally speaks up, of himself as a mere technician fiddling in cyberspace, conjuring pretty pictures without a clue to the mathematical limits of the marvelous machines. "A convert, Dr. Salvino, I've mended my ways. But I may not be saved, not one of your doogies underwritten by my headbone, you know all that as well as you know my depleted bank account. Louise Moffett, not my wife, will mortgage her loft, our home in the city, to send our bastard to school."

"Doogies? Doogies?"

"Old. I am old, Father William, the young man said. Let's go back, *Professore*, to the level field, flat as the flat earth was once thought to be, another schoolroom lesson." Freeman is stirring in a Jimmy Stewart fil-ibuster—out of reach for all Indians but Travis, nurtured on old flicks. He presumes there is pleasure for their Leader in humbling his sub-jects, these kids who have never known disgrace in the classroom, a cheap cat-got-the-mouse satisfaction in the surveillance of their faults. He suggests the model itself is faulty, equating human imperfection—sins, call them sins, old style—with mathematical failure, and that their Leader should not go for the gag, the hollow laughter of his defenseless audience. He suggests the laugh is on Salvino, if it's laughter we're talk-ing about, not pathology, mad-scientist syndrome, and that we all know, blessed with the bulging right hemispheres of our calculating brains, that we must switch from tag to ring-a-levio, checkers to chess, poker to bridge, to think different and having thought different, invent a new game, a new world which may or may not exist.

"Here's the sting, Salvino, I am unable to adapt, a dying species in your bunker sealed from the world, which is why you have me here, not for my brights, dim, dimmest compared with the brilliance of say, Travis, our shining star. Here, invited to your perfectible world as a specimen of deterioration, sample rat in a cage, because somewhere you lost it, *Professore*. Perhaps you slowed down at thirty, diminishing return on the talent, or simply asked the wrong question, thereby missing your trip to the Elysian Fields."

Dotty Bunge sobs, reaches a trembling hand to comfort her Leader. Salvino shakes her off.

"Still, you're famously funded. It's not even wacko what you're up to here, plain ordinary and instructive for those who make the grade. Keep it sines and numeros, *Dottore*, avoid the personal."

His parting word: "*Cool* is O.K. *Peace* is abysmal."

Louise at work (Do Not Disturb) wonders why Artie is home early, why he suits up to cross to the sandy path that trails down to the beach, find Mimi and Cyril destroying their sand castles. Travis, the boy who tags after him, not with him today. She has fashioned a songbird, a solid body, no need to scrunch Mr. Mueller's chicken wire. The delicate head and body please her, but she's having trouble with the feathers. She looks to the mass of her owl, but the songbird is too small, can't take the bold strokes of his plumage. The little bird rests in the palm of her hand lighter than the shells her father used when he went duck hunting with her brother in the wilds above Lake Michigan. She remembers cradling the shells as she cradles the thrush or prairie warbler, not yet sure what to call it—the bird in hand. Her father said the settlers shot little birds, ate them bones and all when times were hard. His shells and shot were hidden from her. One day she found them buried like treasure under his waders and camouflage jacket. Cool and smooth to the touch, she lay the shells in a row, counted each one a killer. She was no more than six or seven, had no idea that many would misfire. She'd thought twelve shells, twelve dead ducks in a row. The ducks hung by their feet on a crossbeam in the barn until they were seasoned. Once the mice got to them right through the cheesecloth, and once a carrion crow. After that her father strung them on a wire in the cellar. When the day came for plucking, there was a smell of pinfeathers singeing, worse than hair sizzling in her sister's curling iron. The headless ducks lay in the freezer in plastic bags, the prickly skin of their flesh between the blueberries picked in season and the economy vats of ice cream. When one was roasted she would not eat it. Her father pretended to savor the tough meat. Mostly he gave the game birds away.

Louise having trouble with the feathers of her little bird, now calling it a goldfinch according to the Audubon Guide. He is still the dull grey of the clay that forms him, four and a half inches, tip of bill to tip of tail. Accurate, but true-to-life feathers are not working. She molds a number of birds in this way, small grey creatures set out in a row. Suppose she does not incise their plumage, but draws it on after they are glazed. They will be china goldfinch, ornaments. But how to fashion their tiny legs and claws?

Perching birds not about to fly off. Their claws will grasp the branches of the tree. They are settled once and for all as the photographs are in my bird book. Neither captured nor free, that's the whole trouble with art, the endless make-believe, the manipulations. If you look through binoculars to my tree you will be able to see the birds, some with open mouths will be singing. The sound track will be that of the Western meadowlark, which the guide book tells me is used in Hollywood movies, though often the story takes place far away from this country. Nothing is natural, not a leaf or twig of my making. I will hold the glass eggs in the nest of my hands— pale blue, speckled, white. The sky is end-of-day blue, the melancholy blue hour before the birds shut down for the night. Dimmers from the hardware store lead into night, dimmers and a timer. The pond will then go black, that's easy. Christmas lights blink like fireflies, but how to man-

age the bats, nocturnal flap of wings almost noiseless? Nothing natural. Call this piece—Life As We Lived It. My owl will be on a pedestal as in a museum, so twice removed from the natural world. He will be slick, polished, carefully lit to gleam in the dark.

That night a storm blows in from sea. Mid-Island the wind is fierce. From the Muellers' picture window Artie Freeman watches lightning strike, roll in a bright ball down the very path to the beach they walk on each day. Then he is in the dark stumbling through the Brio block town to Louise clutching Cyril, who's not one bit afraid. It's fun with the flashlight and candles. When his son falls asleep on the couch, he whispers to Lou of his break with Salvino, every word of the grand finale, that embarrassing script. . . .

"The whole enterprise, a warped children's crusade with a lunatic leader." He calls his time in the bunker a comic book adventure—The Calculus Affair, Salvino and the Nine Crystal Balls.

"You were serious, Artie. An honor to be chosen."

"Not an honor. I was being observed for my failures, and I did fail, now didn't I? Expelled myself from school. Let us presume that every wrong turn, every weak move of my past is known to Salvino, documented like the misdemeanors of those kids. Seriously brilliant, seriously limited, the Indians who'll stick it."

"Indians?"

As he sings *"One little, two little, three little . . ."* with their son sleeping soundly between them, the wooden trains, tracks, bridges, churches and schools shift on the carpet. The heavens have burst, running down the wall behind the Muellers' couch. Not the end of the world, a soggy situation. Artie pries open the padlock on the attic door to find one small gap in the roof, and by that time the storm's over. It's exactly as Louise imagined under the rafters—the soccer sticks, knee pads, unstrung rackets, prom or bridesmaid dress, yearbooks. Curious, she unrolls the engineer's blueprints—water systems, electric lines. Hidden beneath Mueller's plans for civic improvement, a cache of explicit pornography—graphic, the text in German.

She comes upon a grotesque cartoon, group sex, bodies impossibly tripling—"Picture that!" Louise stows the porn carefully back under the blueprints. No one will know this about the engineer. And no one will know the failure of her own imagination when she discovers the paintings, the many unframed canvases stacked against the chimney. Mid-Island landscapes signed Muriel Mueller. Gloomy salt marshes pocked with snow, the dock Artie fished off pictured on a blistering Summer's day, the back yard in the death throes of Autumn. Mrs. Mueller has painted her dark view of the seasons over and over.

"Look here," she flips these desperately unhappy works, and Lou, given to supposing, supposes the artist knew they were not good enough, not deserving. The Picture behind the couch, now water-damaged, of reef, lighthouse, moody sea relieved with a dash of sunshine—that was the best of them.

Louise Moffett is caught crying in the flashlight's beam. Arthur Freeman holds her tight. The water found its route down to the living room without damaging the Muellers' secrets in the attic. Now the storm is over, still they cling to each other. Without a word said, he senses Lou's spirit is broken by doubt, by the tragedy of Muriel Mueller's nearly good paintings. She knows Artie is prone to failure, that it's all too easy to mock Salvino though he's a punishing piece of work. They are shipwrecked together mid-Island and wouldn't know what to name this primitive place of dependence and brute survival.

"It's only . . ." she says.

"That's it, it's only as if something big happened." He picks her up, carries her down the attic stairs, like a bride over the threshold.

Morning after, the telephone is out. Word comes from the bunker. During the height of the storm, Travis ran out to the pond. It is said the boy was courting danger, fell and bashed his head on a rock before he ever got to swim. Mr. Freeman wouldn't know. He was home with his wife and kid.

Dawn stands in the Muellers' doorway with this official report, then tells as much as she is willing to tell of the story. How Travis had a couple of beers, maybe more than a couple, how they were fooling around. They were dancing, just Travis and Dawn in her room. Dancing. His first dancing, she guessed, wild with the storm out the window, then the music went off and in the dark he was such a baby. Plucking at her shorn hair, much subdued, Dawn looks down at the soggy carpet, at the train wreck, houses, church and school toppled in the flood. "He said I was cute, such a baby. We were only fooling around. Then he said, Let's go for a swim."

"In the storm?"

"Yes."

"And you didn't?"

"Not that crazy." She pulls at the dainty heart on a black string around her neck, telling how Shah and Mel found him as they were quitting the bunker for good, how he bled from the head wound.

Artie finds his way to the hospital through streets ravaged by the storm. In a sunny room there's Travis propped up with pillows, the mother of all bandages on his head.

"Why?" Artie asks. He doesn't want the answer Travis can't give now, maybe never. Why prove himself to that twinkie of a girl? Prove he was one of the pack. He was Travis.

"You were naked? Why, why did you run?"

"Faster than the speed of light."

"Yes, you crashed. . . ."

"But suppose"—Travis holds the bundle of his head, aiming to be funny—"suppose now I can't do Reimann."

Artie wants to say there's more to life than Riemann's Hypothesis,

which has stymied great minds for 138 years, but knows that may not be
true for Travis.

"They call your folks?"

"My mother? Last we heard, she was in Phoenix."

We is Travis and his grandmother, who now appears: "He'll be O.K.
The doc says he'll mend." She introduces herself to Mr. Freeman.
"Bebe Wheeler. Say, what kind of outfit is this school anyway? I'm get-
ting him out of here."

"Good move."

Grandma Wheeler is nifty, strappy shoes, great legs, flirty skirt. Sev-
enty, that's generous. She's driven down from Troy through the night
and has a word or two for Professor Salvino. "I don't look a gift horse in
the mouth, but this is one smart kid to fool around with."

"I feel great," Travis says.

"They've doped you, that's all." Mrs. Wheeler is a sweetheart, tucking him in, finding cookies in her bag bought on the New York
Thruway.

Artie promises they'll be in touch. Travis must come down to the city
and play with Cyril, knowing how foolish that sounds as he says it to the
brainiac, this swollen-headed boy who danced naked in the dark. They
don't speak of Dawn or any Indian, nor of Bunge or Salvino. A manly
handshake.

"Mr. Freeman?"

"Artie."

"You, you changed the rules of the game. Isn't that so?"

At home—that is, the cottage they will be leaving—Mimi and Cyril are
an audience with the neighbors, retired people who have lately started
nodding to Mr. and Mrs. Freeman. All look up at Louise draping the
hole in the Mueller roof with a tarpaulin. When she scrambles down
the ladder, she says it will do. Competent, the handy farm girl.

"How's Travis?"

Artie reports the good medical news. Then says, "He's wonderful, plain wonderful."

Mid-Island, last day. Packed up to drive into the city. Cyril, stashed in the kiddie bucket, puts a silver-helmeted demon, more powerful than any previous superhero, through its paces. Owl and songbirds in bubble wrap. Lou takes a last swipe at the clean kitchen floor. Oh, the Audubon Guide abandoned on the Ping-Pong table! They drive to the library. Saturday, day after the storm. The ancient Librarian closing up for the day. She returns to her computer, checks the bird book in.

"Not here to stay? Not with the biotech folks?"

Louise reminds her, "We were in the Mueller house."

"Then you're with Billy Salvino!"

"I suppose we were."

"Such a reader. That child went through the Oz books, all I had on the shelves. Pity arithmetic was his thing."

"Yes, it is."

"He was sweet on Muriel. They were a couple of readers, but you know, well, you do know—she stayed."

"Stayed?"

The Librarian wriggles the specs on her nose, fumbles in her purse for a small key with an engraved collar like the golden key pictured in the Grimm tale Louise reads to Cyril, the one in which the key fits the lock and opens the chest but the story never reveals its treasures. Steady on her spindle legs, the old woman ushers Louise out the door.

"Stayed?"

"Well, she didn't run off with him, did she? We never saw him after that, except once on the news when he figured something out."

"But he's here!"

"Yes, and won't be traipsing off again. Billy Salvino's here for good."

And when Louise asks why Dr. Salvino would be staying, the librarian whispers, "He's home. Come home to die." The frail old girl finds her way down a path littered with branches. "See our sandpipers?"

Louise allows she's seen flocks and flocks chattering on the shore, but she will not be around for the plovers.

There is nothing left of their duties mid-Island but returning the cottage key, which Artie will leave at the bunker. Four or five of the dwarf pear trees still stand, the rest toppled in the storm. The pond smooth as glass. Artie never noticed the spare arrangement of low grasses and reeds placed among the rocks. They could trip a guy up. Open Sesame with the coded card. A *local boy*, he can't get that out of his head, *sweet on Mrs. Mueller*. The halls of the bunker bustling with men, some with clipboards, some with hardhats working Saturday, overtime. The biotechs urgent to get down to business. In the distance, folk groove from the temporary dorm. Chu hanging in? Dawn packing her bags?

The padded room, off limits for the work crew, is unlocked, deserted. He searches for a fresh pad not scribbled with improbable equations, takes his usual place at the conference table, writes KEY TO MUELLER COTTAGE. The prospect of death with its finite dimension does change everything. He marvels at Salvino's energy, the wounded warrior still in the game, flying off to London and Milan. Then wonders if, in fact, his teacher, his inquisitor, was not enjoying the comforts of first class, just bedded in a hospital mid-Island. Now, if that old number in the library has it right, and he presumes she is privy to all town gossip, Guglielmo is grounded, staying with his sister on Front Street, which fronts the railroad tracks, the house he grew up in. Perhaps he will die in the very bedroom where he first came upon the wonders of the calculus. He must have known the risk, that he might not make it through the project on fallibility, when he wrote the grant proposal, when Dorothy Bunge sent the prospectus to the printers with the seductive picture of meadows and gentle mountains beyond the volleyball field of a New England campus, known that pleasant Summers of conjecture and disproof lay behind him. Salvino had come home to "the place where land levels out," as the Algonquins once called it, to a town laid out on potato fields after a war.

Artie Freeman thinks to write a parting word, not by way of apology, just a word to settle the score between them, to admit he has been out-played. He thinks of nothing better than *Thanks, Mr. & Mrs. Freeman.*

When he leaves the bunker, the peons are out of their truck, re-planting the pear trees. He asks Lou if you can do that, just stick them back in the ground.

"Sure, if you prop them with guy wires, give them plenty of water. Trouble is, they are rather fragile trees, decorative, shallow rooted. So— comes the next storm?"

What he loves about Louise, on the long list of things, is her knowl-edge of the natural world. It seems a gift, her affinity for plant life, ani-mals and birds, something more than growing up on a farm in Wisconsin. Almost a charm, like Travis' way with numbers. In the back seat of the rented car, Cyril mumbles a story of superhuman endeavors. Louise comforts Artie's hand on the steering wheel. They are leaving this town for good. He senses her sadness. And his—as though they had lived there.

In the city a strapping young woman with nerves of steel helps Cyril into a van of screaming kids off to day camp. On weekends his mom or dad marches him by the benches of burnt out druggies to the play-ground in Tompkins Square, where he runs happily through the spray of a fountain. Artie lucks out. His professor of nonlinear comes up with a job, remedial math for private school dummies. Louise carts her owl to the foundry where it is cast in bronze. The songbirds are glazed: yel-low for the goldfinches' bodies, orange for orioles, their black wings and sharp bills perfect copies of the photos in her own Audubon Guide, but the legs and claws have no semblance of authenticity—chicken wire pilfered from the Mueller garage.

The songbirds' throats are pierced, strung on a wire. I will hold their dead bodies up to view in my waxy hands. They are colorful trinkets, memory of flight, a bright necklace of mourning. The sheer weight of the owl will ground him. The rabbit will survive as a plush toy, harmless creature. The tree will be toppled, roots made of wire and string exposed, leaves rusted. The still pond will be blue silk embroidered with green algae, the rocks that surround it broken tombstones—papier-mâché, inscribed but not legible. If I trust myself, I will have a boy squat on the ground. He will be naked as I am, fiberglass, less flimsy. With a telescope he'll look to heaven. But on the field of blue beneath him, the stars will be crystal, many of them broken by the footprint of man. Or I may be alone in the electronic hum. May be, that's the problem with more than one answer. Now I know what to call this stage set of a world. Habitat—that's plain, not preachy. And if it's not good enough, I must have the courage to hide it—glass, wax, scrap metal, wire, china birds, that doorstop of an owl, the whole kit and caboodle, hide it behind the couch.

One day in mid-July, having accomplished the legal preliminaries, Louise Moffett and Arthur Freeman go down to City Hall where they wait in line with fellow citizens to be married. Louise wears a dress from the back of the closet, blue sprigged with white flowers. Cyril holds his mother's bouquet while his parents promise to love each other till death do them part. Death thrills their son, who kills off monsters and heroes, then commands them to come to life for the next adventure. His dad in a suit and tie looks like somebody else's father. When it is over they go to Battery Park where friends have assembled—art friends, math friends and people Cyril doesn't know from the life his father once lived in what is called business. Balloons and unlimited sodas. The grown-ups eat fish eggs, drink champagne and kick a soccer ball around. All in all, not a bad day.

News comes to the Freemans at the end of August. Mimi sends a friendship card. She has been awarded her certificate in the Swedish Massage and manipulates the old folks as well as the biotechs who injure themselves working out in the gym installed in the industrial park.

On a crisp Fall morning, Artie comes into oddly domed Mathematics. He is early in the classroom, alone, the way he likes it. Out the slit of window in this mysterious Masonic building, the leaves of ancient trees are turning loveliest to die. Artie missed their glorious demise as he came onto campus. He'd come out of the subway, walked into traffic, miraculously survived. Waiting at 59th Street for the Broadway local, he read the obituary of William Salvino, *a mathematician whose early work was with complex systems, problems too intricate to be solved by known methods. His contribution to a theory of functional analysis led to an understanding of infinite dimensional space.* In the manner of obits the notice is generous, citing the youthful fame, moving swiftly to Dr. Salvino's administrative posts at Berkeley, a Midwestern university and a little Ivy League college in upstate New York. It mentions his contribution at many international conferences, where he was known for his flamboyant dress and striking refutations. Artie Freeman wonders if in the end Guglielmo was a figure of fun. Leader has died in what was once called the prime of life. He is survived by a sister and his companion of many years, Dorothy Bunge.

It's pure luck that Freeman has been given this course, a miscalculation on the part of his chairman, the impractical professor lost in nonlinear. He writes on the blackboard, $H(n) + T(n) = n$, the old heads-and-tails equation. Today he will pursue the fair coin problem for his class in introductory mathematics, launch a discussion of probability and randomness, tell them it's a hell of a job to set up a system against the infinite toss of a coin. He takes a Kennedy half-dollar out of his pocket and a dime, flips them.

His students wander in, not a doogie among them. On this bright Fall day, he feels their reluctance and his own, not knowing why he is so moved by the passing of Salvino. They copy the equation on the blackboard and still Mr. Freeman does not address them, fumbles through his notes. He would like to tell them the history of a gifted man who lost it, a professor who looked like a fortune teller in a wax museum, but the material he would draw on is untidy, unmeasurable. He could make a hero of William Salvino, who rented an empty building to stage his last show, but there are missing factors. It's a problem beyond him, the size of that life. It seems inelegant, even a false solution, to take a sentimental view of science. Still, he is uncertain. The instructor flips a coin.

Over the years, no need to be exact, Arthur Freeman, as he slowly climbs the shaky academic ladder from assistant to associate professor, noted not for his originality in mathematics but for the inventions of his classroom performance, will read the published papers of Travis Wheeler in math journals and in *Nature*. Wheeler's work is over-the-rainbow brilliant, though he is not the genius who at last proves Riemann's Hypothesis.

Cyril is an athletic boy with no head for math, though he carries the stats of the Yankees in his skull dating back to the great year, 1998. The Freemans' girl, Sylvia, is much like her mother, delighted with drawing, cutting and pasting. She's a fair, sturdy child, fresh as a farm girl though she grows up in the city. Eventually the Freemans buy a summer cottage far out on the North Shore of the Island. When she models a world, Louise neglects her garden. When tending to her vegetables and flowers, she neglects her art. At times Moffett is forgotten. When she is noticed, it is always as a nature artist. She accepts this limitation.

Moving on from the raw emotion, the ruined settings of her *Habitats*, Louise begins to draw—butterflies, frogs, fish, the crabs her children bring to her in a bucket, and wild flowers—each species in its setting. Her drawings and prints are said to be contemplations, intimate and self-reflective, not about plants and animals at all. Moffett thinks this is nonsense. She simply wants her work to be luminous, her color and light more suggestive than digital accuracy. Birds are her banished subjects. When she looked beyond her Audubon Guide, finally discovered the great man's work, Louise saw that his birds were not real—their nesting, flight, squabbles and love stories—the mastery of his craft was coupled with pure magic of invention. Once Louise attempted a hermit thrush that came to the feeder in Winter, sketched its little ball of brown body in charcoal, but could not capture its throat swollen with song or the flick of its tailfeathers, and erased it to a smudge. She supposes it will always be so. Her making will be followed by remaking, even destruction. Sand castles. No, her working life is merely unpredictable—cruel or blest as the arrival and departure of the seasons.

At dawn the Freemans often leave their moody adolescent children asleep in the cottage, Louise leading Artie down to the shore, one of the extremities of America. There they sit on a rock, binoculars poised, expecting piping plovers, sooty terns, hoping to sight an osprey with a fish in its mouth. They have taken up this amateur pastime demanding silence and patience. Once they spotted a Louisiana heron migrating South and, on a day they will never forget, the astonishing mating plumage of a red-throated loon.

MYSELF

The day of my birth was unseasonably warm, so I was told. The end of June in Connecticut leapt into high summer. When her water broke, my mother was showing our new little house to strangers interested in its modern conveniences of sun parlor and breakfast room. Such a shy woman, I imagine her suffering this bodily betrayal, yet how graciously she must have dismissed her guests, then called my father at the courthouse to come home and drive her to St. Vincent's. I know nothing more of that day, only that my brother was billeted at my grandparents' big house next door.

My mother, almost pathologically modest, found it impossible to speak of matters of the flesh — birth, sex, illness, death — still she told me of the embarrassing flood of my early arrival on that very warm day, to log it in as the opening chapter in my record. It was meant to be an amusing account, but when she first told me I was young enough to believe I had botched the departure from my comforting prenatal pool. Yes, I thought, that's it — I was trouble from the start, pushing ahead, the second child, pressing to find my story line in the family romance. Years later (a phrase that lets me replay scenes to my own advantage), I felt it was perfectly natural, what with the very warm day and my mother's descent to the basement where she demonstrated the first automatic washer in North Bridgeport. Her guests watched suds mount in the little glass porthole of the Bendix. I made my move when the rinse cycle swooshed my father's union suits, his socks and handkerchiefs, so I was told. Don't you see? My response was to the oceanic swell. Perfectly natural.

What was unnatural — she'd hung the wash out to dry before her husband turned into the driveway and was at the ironing board in the breakfast room pressing my brother's playsuits, performing these duties before she went into labor with me. So dutiful, wedded to her tasks. Later, I believed that the natural world was missing from the cottage my parents built in the shadow of my grandfather's imposing stucco house. Nature was at a remove from daily life, contained in the two city parks famously plotted in the past century by Frederick Law Olmsted at the North and South borders of the city. On Sunday drives a few miles beyond the city limits, I do not remember my parents ever stopping to admire a sweeping or distant view. The urban scenes of our industrial city claimed us.

FLORA: Twenty feet of grass between our house and the sidewalk, a storybook house with a peaked roof and iron latches on the door like Mary, Mary, Quite Contrary's pictured with the nursery rhyme. No one dare ask, "How does your garden grow?" One red maple graced the front lawn, the only thing my father ever planted in his life. His garden decorations were fortunately set in the back yard—a cast iron gnome with a peaked red hat and bumptious beard secured the cap to the oil tank; three plaster ducklings trailed their mother in her stalled journey to the clothes line. That's it, folks, except for the Victory Garden the size of a throw rug that did not survive the Japanese beetle season, though my brother and I sent the dense metallic bodies of those ravenous creatures to their death in jars of kerosene.

The big house, a narrow path to the right as you faced North Avenue (U.S. 1), with the bus stop at its front steps, sported purple rhododendrons nestled into a side porch. Planted when the house was built in 1910, they were enormous in my childhood. I could hide in their branches and never be found. Prickly rambler roses and a common honeysuckle bush against a fence that marked the double driveway. On Summer nights I could hear the clang, clang of boxcars coupling on the railroad siding which was at the same distance from my room as the iron tracks from Thoreau's shack in Walden. The sound of commerce, which he tells us is "confident and serene," was my lullaby, the nightsong of the neighborhood, with raw goods positioned for unloading the next day by the Brass Company and Remington Rand. No sounds of owls hooting, rustle of undergrowth, wind in the trees—no cart path in the woods. When I came to read Thoreau's great book, I fell for his romantic riff on the railroad, but could not credit his disclaimer: *I will not have my eyes put out and my ears spoiled by its smoke and steam and hissing.* I did not share his pastoral.

"Barberry hedge," my brother reminds me. Yes, but out of the way, its scratches of little account, and there had been my grandmother's garden, an oval the size of the dining room table with the leaves extending it for Christmas dinner. But that garden was let go when my grandfather suffered a stroke and her days and nights were given to nursing him. All that was left—succulents she called *live-ever*, which we killed off with our tricycles and wild chases in which Buck Rogers defeated evil Dr. Zorro. When stunned with the futuristic gun, we dropped dead in the crabgrass that took over the bald spot, once garden. One of the faithful men, who had little or no work from my grandfather's paving company during the Depression, came to chew the lawn with a rasping mower that sat in our garage, unsharpened, unoiled. On hot days we ran through the sprinkler in our bathing suits with neighborhood kids, but no plant life was watered, pruned or fed. So, in its way, nature took its course. My family's adaptation was complete.

Meanwhile, the Italians in the rented two-story houses down Parrot Avenue tended their peppers and beans, onions and garlic, spinach, eggplant and squash. I could look over the fences at the weight of ripeness bowing tomato plants, but never enter. Off limits for all children, even those who lived in the house attached to the sacred gardens. Papa Messinio had fig trees tied up in burlap all Winter and cherries that we scrambled for when they fell our way. Those old Italians, earth was in their blood, so I was told.

I'm not complaining. Our yard with its few neglected plantings is imprinted on me forever, a landscape of enchantment. Impoverished? Perhaps you will find my reconstruction of the city lots, 622 and 630 North Avenue, dreary; I do not. I see only the endless possibilities of mud pies decorated with the bright poison berries that followed the honeysuckle's bloom, and the secret side yard where lilies of the valley spread from the Schacks' ambitious garden, fenced off from the flower-less world of our little house. Every inch of their deep double lot was cultivated with glorious blooms I could not name.

"So much work. Why, it's endless!" My mother's gentle disapproval of the industrious German couple with two maiden ladies for daughters. What else had the Schacks to busy themselves with? Her endless work was all indoors. How she washed and ironed and dusted her nest. With what energy she overfed us. And yet she had been an athletic girl.

The closet in the back bedroom of my grandfather's house was a confusion of heavy wooden tennis rackets, golf clubs, a crop and whip, divided riding skirts and, most romantic, a side saddle like Guinevere's in the Wyeth illustration of King Arthur.

Yes, there had been workhorses for my grandfather's carting and hauling and a pleasure horse for my mother. There had been a legendary farm just North of the city, property owned, not lived on by her family. Surely a trophy for my grandfather, once the poorest of poor Irish, to have a tenant farmer to care for his many acres with an orchard, barns, a chicken coop. They had stashed my ne'er-do-well uncle up there when he married. He did not make a go of it and died in the farmhouse I never laid eyes on in the flu epidemic of 1919. I presume that land was a burden, that by the time of my pestering to know about the cream and the eggs once sent down from the farm, about cows and chickens not pictured in books or magazines, it was near impossible for them to come up with the taxes. Once my grandfather, crippled and speechless, was carried to my father's car, driven up to his land to take a last look before he died. I was told that at the phantom farm my mother was poisoned by daisies, but I believe it was my uncle's death that cursed the place.

"A field of daisies." My mother held her hands up to view, speaking of the plague that came upon her. "I walked through that field and broke out in blisters so painful and leaky I could not hold a pen or turn a page. My eyes were swollen shut." They wrapped her in gauze like a mummy, so I was told.

Cut to the alternate version. She had been accepted at Smith College, but the damnable daisies somewhere on the lush parklike grounds (Olmsted again) did her in. There was a Negro student in Albright House, where she lived that one week before returning home defeated and freakish, as though nature conspired against her departure from the narrow domestic scene in Bridgeport. I have often thought that she was lonely in a room under the eaves in Northampton, homesick for the grey wooden house her family had abandoned, not for the grand stucco house, new that very year. I have seen pictures of the old half-house, a small tenement, with stables across a courtyard and the quarters where the Italian workers lived with their families. The next year she returned to college bravely, and graduated in 1915. My mother spoke often of the colored student who befriended the Catholic girl. She never again suffered daisies, and though she went on long walks with her college chums, whacked an occasional golf ball, her sporty life in plain air was at an end.

I see her always indoors or driving her green Chrysler on errands to all ends of the city. I see her in the big house where we now lived to care for my blind grandmother, the rooms improved with my mother's vases, shawls, candlesticks artfully arranged, shades drawn protecting her from the view of the Texaco station and the factory buildings of Bridgeport Brass. I never forget her consuming adventures with sculpture and painting; still, I was amazed, when in a cold season, I came home from college to find my mother deeply into the aesthetics of Japanese flower arranging. She would in time return to Swiss chip-carving and ceramics, but it was *ikebana* on coffee table, sideboard, in dining room and hall. Pine branch with rose, eucalyptus with chrysanthemum, long fleshy leaves staggered according to rules of *moribana* and *shoka* in low bowls and bamboo baskets. And you know they looked perfectly swell on the mahogany furniture (ca. 1910).

"Isn't that a peach," my father said, always in awe of her artistic leanings.

Not a peach—asparagus fern, crataegus berries, papyrus, strelitzia. Anthurium leaves positioned according to the nine branches of *rikka*— the most ancient art of flower arrangement studied by Brahmin priests and the nobility, so I was told. She drove the miles to Westport, the fancy town within commuting distance to New York, where the artsy shops and florists had a supply of New Zealand flax, lotus pods and Asian pots.

Books on *ikebana,* the revered practice, were stacked on the window seat with my father's *Life, Time* and his occasional descent into murder mysteries, which he never believed, being, in real life, a true detective. I settled to read about the master Unshin Ohara (sounded Irish to me) and the principles which he set forth for his followers. Use space to emphasize form and depth, give great attention to balance and scale. My mother had a near perfect eye, was optically gifted. I understood the draw to this floral art so distant from the potted poinsettias and lilies wrapped in metallic paper that my widowed aunt sent from Bladgy's on holidays, but it was Ohara's fifth principle that made painful sense: *Endow each arrangement with feeling.* Then I saw in her strange flowers and branches not artifice or distortion, but a yearning for beauty natural to her, that she was able to find—I can't say what joy— perfection in the exquisite placing of an aspidistra leaf, the buoyant curve of weeping willow. It was possible to quit her father's house, take leave of us, walk through these alien fields without a single daisy.

Ikebana did not have a long life in the stucco house. Cut off by my father's heart attacks, that art soon seemed no more than one of her many diversions. After he died, a short flirtation with bonsai, but the miniature cypress and pine could not survive in the big rooms which were dry, overheated, as though the oil burner churning full-force would bring life back to the big house which my brother and I had left.

When I was thirty I had my own garden in New Jersey, an established garden with roses (hybrid tea and floribunda), iris (bearded and Siberian) and a great willow that choked the septic tank with its roots, deadly nightshade that strangled the mock orange. There was much to be learned. I took to that garden with a vengeance, as though I could get hold of the natural world my family had left behind, once useful, then discarded like our lapsed subscription to *National Geographic* with its color photos of faraway tundras and tropical forests. I learned to clip the roses a quarter-inch above the first five leaflets, to control black spot and aphids, that lilacs like a sweet soil dressed with lime. Rosemary will winter over in Zone 3. Violets and ajuga are invasive. I studied it up, sitting under the silver maple on a flagstone terrace, and learned that there was no remedial course in seeds and roots, no exam to pass, much failure. I grew tomatoes, red and wormy; pithy, tasteless zucchini the size of clubs to bludgeon the enemy. The enemy was Mama Raccoon, who taught her babies the art of marauding in my vegetable patch, and they were so dear, don't you know, clasping my few ears of corn in their paws, nibbling away till the cob was picked clean.

My mother came once to that garden, bringing me a flat of sweet William (*Dianthus barbatus*). Exuberant blossoms—the full spectrum of reds with delicate sawtooth white edges. William was my father's name. At that time her days were devoted to keeping him alive with a host of medications and the respirator.

"They're biennials," I said, Miss Know-It-All puffed with book learning.

"Yes," she said, "they bloom, go to seed and die."

Now I grow flowers and herbs in the Berkshires. We have frost well after the first weeks of Spring. June is the best month, with lupin and foxglove. Sage comes into bloom, and beard tongue with its delicate pink blossoms above mahogany leaves. Our yard is less than two acres, about the size of the lots where the little and big houses sat side by side in my native city of Bridgeport. That's if you include the double driveway and garage that housed the heavy cars my family favored—the Auburns, Buicks and Chryslers. Where our grass ends there is a patch of forest, mostly white pine. We have made a short path through the undergrowth of ferns, nothing like the Timber Trail coaxed to a state of natural perfection by an amateur botanist, Julian Baird. His woodland in the Berkshires was a refuge from commerce and family life, so we are told in one guide to our habitat by a fellow who is somewhat too chatty, more scribbler than naturalist. His interest in this Baird who made a garden of the woods, a project started in the Twenties, is more personal than scientific. As a boy he had toured Baird's Timber Trail with his mother, then secretary of the Pittsfield Garden Club. *What loveliness this quiet man, a banker in our town, had brought to the unruly primitive growth of New England with a host of daffodils and fields of primula. I recall the ladies in their light Spring dresses and straw hats posing on a rustic bench for their photograph which appeared in* The Eagle.

We figure it would be destructive to impose our will on the scrap of woods that came with our little suburban house. We have no Timber Trail ambitions. I figure Baird's path was cut through boreal woodland where some hardwoods still grew, poplar and aspen, birch. At that time there had been no virgin forest for a century, no primitive growth. But I can't blame the writer of my outdated guide who scants the facts, gives way to memory—like a gap fostering growth under the canopy of trees. A gap may be a disturbance as small as one tree fallen so that light shines through, allowing trillium, wild geranium, starflower—plant life which is called the understory.

At one time Audubon, the bird man, thought of adding vignettes of the countryside in which each species lived, a sort of postcard, mini-panoramic view. He abandoned that idea, having *no taste for landscape painting*. I suppose he meant no talent, for the exquisite details of branches, flowers, berries, grasses which live on the big pages with his birds were mostly painted by his assistants. *Sorry*, he says, but I do not believe him. He knew his book must be bold in design, the Great Idea uncluttered:

> *Sorry, notwithstanding, that as time flies Nature loses its primitiveness, and that picture drawn in ten, or twenty, or more years, will no longer illustrate our delightful America pure from the hands of the Creator!*

The flora of *Birds of America* delights on every page—natural in their depiction, unnatural in their perfect placement. I open my front door in mid-June to see with what accuracy the mountain laurel in bloom was drawn and colored as a perch for Cuvier's wren. But who would have chosen the upright thrust of the branch for this little yellow bird? Who would presume to spin the rosy magnolia blossoms and buds out from center stage of a dark green leaf, backdrop for the female warbler who bears the tree's name—*Dendroica magnolia*. The catbird feasts on a baroque spray of blackberries, and the house wren's nest balances on an ionic pillar of grass—art deploying architecture. The king rail wades in the marsh before an entwinement of reeds that might be the artful tangles of a Morris wallpaper, except that the reeds are freer in their composition and the aggressive forward trot of the male is thoroughly American, not decorative art. Much early flora for the warblers was drawn by a gifted boy, Joe Mason, who studied and traveled with Audubon; later waterland settings are attributed to the American Wood-man's son, John Woodhouse; then there was a Southern lady awfully good at flowers and some were rendered by the Master himself, for we know his wife shipped him branches from Louisiana so that, drawing a flycatcher from memory in London, he would get it right, the scaly bark of an alder. But not a blade, petal or seed would matter a twig without Audubon's birds.

FAUNA: Bootsie, a Boston bull tied to the clothesline. He had the run of twelve feet and a lump of blanket beside the kitchen stove.

"Did we walk him?"

"No," my brother says.

"Feed him?"

"No."

"Did we play with him?"

No answer. I did not ask if we loved Bootsie, who had four white paws, thus his name. He was a well-bred pup my father brought home from the investigation of a crime in Fairfield County. Bootsie was a gift to my father, a man of great charm in the public arena. Our dog was the only pet in the neighborhood. A pet was another mouth to feed.

In our apartment house in New York City, we have poodles (standard and toy), a champion chocolate Lab, a miniature dachshund (grotesquely amusing) and a friendly mutt named Sullivan after the famous psychiatrist, who was nuts, so I am told. I am told there is a society of city dogs who have select friends in the dog runs of Central Park. They have play dates and on birthdays exchange doggie presents, lap up their doggie cakes. These canine bulletins, which speak of good times and indulgent love, are as troubling to me as my neglect of Bootsie.

"The alligator?"

"Poor creature!"

He (or she) was shipped up from Florida by Grandmother Kearns, a frisky old lady who, on a winter vacation, bought a baby alligator, just the snappy souvenir for the kidlets. Our parents thought to keep it at a distance. In the cellar of the big house next door it flapped in and out of a washtub, scuttled across the cement floor to oily darkness behind the furnace. For a few days we fed it iceberg lettuce, and then it was gone. *To a family who live by the shore.* We knew they lied to us, that there were no happy children by the sea who would romp with the bewildered creature. We knew, in those dark days before our expensive subscription to *National Geographic*, before television's benefits of *Wild, Wild World* and *Nature*, that the icy rocks and snowy sands of the Connecticut shore would not comfort that baby. Later, I thought our deception was mutual, a familial law of nature, accommodating fakery between parents and kids.

All goldfish died.

But the animals in the little zoo at Beardsley Park (Olmsted yet again) were healthy in their cages, provided with food and water. No habitat. The monkeys swung on ropes from dowel to dowel. And there were deer, imagine, nibbling what leaves we fed them, deer on display as rare specimens before their dramatic comeback, before their invasion of every farm, garden, back yard in New England. Two peacocks paraded in the dust and there were macaws squawking an inarticulate mimicry, but not the Carolina parrots native to our country. Audubon remarks upon the carnage of these birds who feasted on apple and pear trees, grain and grapes. Planters kept a gun handy—*eight or ten, or even twenty, are killed at every discharge.* From my side of the cage in that sweet, small zoo, I heard the cockatoos screech and saw them fly from fruitless perch to fruitless perch and never wondered where these birds of some tropical paradise, or for that matter the Asian monkeys, were housed in Winter.

Wild for the circus, for the tamed animals. I loved every growl and crack of the whip, the elephant's decorous curtseys, the horse's Viennese waltz, dog's leap through the fiery hoop, the mane of the trainer, the glittering Oriental costumes. With the first piercing tune of the calliope being drawn round the show tent of Ringling Brothers and Barnum & Bailey, I clapped. I clapped through every act, so I was told.

I was only three, that first time at the circus, which came to town at the end of June as though for my birthday. My father had passes. We went every year. I held my breath to bursting for the tumbling, the high wire—every act exotic, familiar, risky and safe. Sort of safe. I loved the clowns with childish passion, their paddle shoes and unbelievable wigs, simpering red smiles, crocodile tears, their assault on our trust in the laws of motion.

"You never laughed at their antics," my mother said. "Solemn, except for your clapping, we might have been in church."

Later, taking my daughter to the circus in the new Madison Square Garden, she was full of wonder at the display of caged animals before the show, but I noted that in this area given to the menagerie no one thought of the giraffe. Its head stuck through a hole in the ceiling, where it viewed the electric guts of the Garden. The tiger licking his paws was weary of us or sedated. I observed the heavy makeup of the artistes, their bodysuits tinseled and worn, the rip-off price of popcorn. The Polish acrobats and Chinese tumblers were authentic, yet their names seemed phony on the costly program. We never had programs under the Big Top in Bridgeport. When appropriate, I applauded a stunning performance with my girl, who had the joy of it.

When grown—that is, on my sixteenth birthday—I went to work in the Bridgeport Public Library, the Reference Room. An old woman with a cloying smell of decay about her put me to clipping notices from the *Post*. It was 1946 and my topics were Europe and Asia—very grand. I took scissors to the Nuremberg Trials and the Communist Party gaining in France, news which our local paper took off the wire services, and I filed these items in manila folders marked *WW II (France, Germany, Italy, Japan, etc.)*, though we had celebrated the Allied victory the previous Summer. A few weeks into the job, I would understand that no serious citizen of Bridgeport, certainly no historian, would make use of these fragments, this crazy quilt of documents. The old woman was very gentle with me, noting with a sickening cough that I must remember to paste the date cut from the newspaper onto each clipping. When I looked back to 1945—German Soldiers Surrender in Ruhr, Okinawa Taken—I saw that the library paste did not hold, but said nothing, for I could not bear her hovering over me. She was a devout Christian Scientist who answered every question put to her by the public and left her post one day in the middle of that Summer to go home and die. Or, as I discovered in research of my own, not to die.

Her replacement, a woman with reptilian braids coiled on her head, was sharp with me, took WW II and its aftermath all for herself and set me to shelving books. I roamed the stacks with a trolley and found each book its proper place, taking great care to observe every letter and number of the Dewey Decimal System. Hidden away from the public and questions I could not field if they were not answered in the *Britannica* or *The Baseball Almanac,* I read on city time. On a dusty metal shelf I discovered *The Birds of America,* volumes V, VI, VII of the Octavo Edition, 1843; Purchased with the Legacy of Miss Catherine E. Hunt, 1892. The birds were of the United States and its Territories as drawn by J. J. Audubon, Fellow of the Linnaean and Zoological Society of London, the Lyceum of Natural History New York, American Philosophical Society, Société Statistique Universelle of Paris, etc., etc.—such excessive self-advertisement. The book was strange and wonderful, yet the beauty of the birds was beyond me. I leafed through Audubon and went about my business, but came back to these old leather volumes when I returned a book where contemporary guides to beasts and birds were shelved. No reader requested *The Birds of America.* I had them to myself. On lunch hour (a sandwich brought from home), I took one volume or another to the dusty window overlooking the parking lot my grandfather had paved gratis as his civic duty.

I tried to understand the much honored man who made these books. Drew them. Wrote them, for there were stories of each bird, how it nested and swam, where it wintered, the color and number of its eggs and how it was considered by man. The episodes of the writer's adventures with Indians and a faithful horse, with wolves and an earthquake, were plain fun, stories about himself as though his life was as notable as the birds. Well, some of the birds, for I guessed that the other volumes of Miss Hunt's legacy had been stolen. I had only the families of mergansers, geese, ducks, swans, and, proud of my second year Latin, was comfortable with the Linnaean classifications. *Fuligula rudiba,* that's ruddy ducks. Perhaps, in the punishing heat of the stacks, I comprehended Audubon's devotion to his task, to an ardor brought to information of feathers, claws, beaks, flight, color, to song and violence, which was my natural world too, though I hadn't known it.

That year I studied biology with Aretas A. Saunders in Central High. It was my first year out of the convent school I had attended with girls from prosperous Catholic families. The rough and tumble of the hall-ways in the public school was not the hush I was accustomed to, and for a week I wanted to run back to the slight irreverence and girlish giggles directed at the Sisters of Mercy. It was my mother who insisted I leap the convent wall into the heartier mix of kids, to study with bright teachers who had been her colleagues before she married.

"Mr. Saunders, what a privilege," she said. "He knows his birds."

A-REE-tas A-RYE-tas, my classmates chanted the name of this mild man who taught at Central for thirty-five years. He looked remarkably like Woodrow Wilson, with a long jaw and steel-rimmed glasses. We thought him a hopeless back number who could not see our superior smiles or hear our snickering laughter. In fact, Aretas Andrews Saun-ders saw and heard with great precision. He was an ornithologist who invented a graphic system of recording the language of birds. I remem-ber nothing of the biology he taught us, tapping illustrated charts of amoebae, finny fish, dissected frogs and the organs of a man discreetly cut off at the torso. Dutifully, Mr. Saunders approached each lesson in the book, but often we could tell he wandered, was not with us. Then a fresh-mouthed boy would call out, "Mr. Saunders! Mr. Saunders! Guess what I heard comin' up from the Hollow." And he'd chirp a gar-bled tune.

"That might be a flicker, Mr. Riccio." We would then have our show. A-REE-tas A-RYE-tas began to whistle the *fret, fret, free, fri* of the flicker's flight, followed by *fri, frish, fri, frish* when it lit on a branch. Shameful, egging him on, and once he started his innocent songs we were through with our study for the day. Mr. Saunders went to the blackboard and drew his bird shorthand.

Song of the Yellow-throated Vireo.

"*Beep-beep*, Mr. Saunders."

"Woodcock. You did not tell us, Mr. Mayer, that you have visited Squantz Pond."

Our teacher was off to the waterfowl world of clucking and honking, and I thought of my bird books in the library stacks, their pictures and stories. One day when class was over, I asked Aretas A. Saunders if he knew the books by Audubon.

"Miss Kearns," he said, but got no further. He wiped his glasses with a spanking white handkerchief, put them back on to see clearly one specimen of the genus—*Urbanis ignoramus*—he dealt with each day of his teaching life, and I saw he was sorry for me. Perhaps sorry that he'd made a fool of himself, for he gave up performing in answer to our impudent whistles and peeps. We did biology according to the book till the end of the semester.

I thought of that day I stopped his birdsong when, a good deal later, I came across the name Aretas A. Saunders in a book titled *Birds of America*, a workaday effort with blotched photographs and illustrations poorly tinted and drawn, a collection of scholarly essays attempting to correct and better Audubon. It was inscribed to my husband by his parents: *Dear Mark, May you in the worthwhile things in life soar as high as the birds and may your life be as free as theirs. December 25, 1940.* Their boy would have been fifteen, already on to the lofty flourish of that language, yet here Mr. Saunders was cited as the greatest authority on birdcalls. Back in the Reference Room, I discovered that he had written many serious works of ornithology. Known for his system of birdsong notation, he was alarmed about pesticides before *The Silent Spring*. With Lady Grace, as he called his wife, he traveled each Summer throughout the Alleghenies, listening and looking, getting up before dawn to write his hieroglyphics. Funded by the American Philosophical Society, scholarships given in his name by the Audubon Society, A-REE-tas A-RYE-tas was celebrated.

I am writing *Myself* for my nephew, Chris Kearns, and my granddaughter, Kate Howard Fudge. They must see that the life of my high school teacher is not a sad story. Years of servitude in the classroom supported his passion. His passionate work. In *Bird Song* he speaks of invention and imitation, tells us that the evolution of song goes on at a more rapid rate than the adaptive coloring of plumage. *It is probably this that accounts for abnormal songs. Abnormal singers are probably unusually inventive individuals. There is a strong parallel here between man and the bird.* Neat, but they will find his graphic squiggles, lines and swoops ancient and more useless than cuneiform in the era of sensitive recording equipment that can pick up the softest quack of a common teal or ruffle of a heron's feathers across a pond. Technology put Saunders' system out of business, but if they will come with me to the stacks and look at the volumes of *Birds of America* which are still there in the dust, still beautiful though damaged—someone (could it be that shrew with the braids plastered to her head?) has perforated every picture with the legend BRIDGEPORT PUBLIC LIBRARY—if they will patiently turn the pages they will see that Audubon's drawings will never be surpassed by the digital camera, because it's art, I will say, somewhat flustered. You can be odd, even unnatural, draw stars down from the sky, muddy the pond, kill off the tree of your making or let it shimmer with song, solve the unsolved. You can draw an owl so fierce it will win prizes.

And I know these children will think Bootsie, the alligator, my mother confounded by daisies to be legends. But legends, I will tell them, are true.

I will tell them of the day when I first went to the New-York Historical Society. A time in my life when I was moving on and afraid that a neighborhood I did not know would never be mine, never compare to the fading bohemian ease of Greenwich Village, where I lived for many years, or more honestly, that this Upper West Side with Central Park (triumphantly Olmsted) would expose me in its vastness and light as a provincial, a woman from an exhausted industrial town. And the park with its rambles and planned groves could offer nothing to equal my landscape of memory—the happy, stifling embrace of two city lots on North Avenue in Bridgeport. I ducked into the museum, walked up the marble staircase. I will never forget my first view of the big birds. I was moved to tears. Let them laugh, I will say it—tears: I had so long been denied this pleasure. It was an exhibit, you see, of the hand-colored plates from LaForest's original elephant portfolio—the turkey in his American splendor, the eagle poised on his rock for the kill, the many songbirds on their bright berried perches. The trumpeter swan must swivel and dip its head, the pelican squat to fit the page, but they are exact—that is, big as life, exactly as the artist knew they must be.

Sitting now at the library table with the children, we will only have our three books with the small illustrations which Audubon's son Victor Gifford, by means of a camera lucida, an old fashioned device of prisms, reduced to normal page size, thus making *Birds of America* affordable and an instant best-seller. He had a head for business, but you—you must never be a trimmer. If we have time we'll read all the *Bird Biographies*, pleased we have this ruined treasure, for in later editing they threw out all the episodes of animals and men in the wilderness to seem more scientific, tidied up for the market. I will admit that some of Audubon's birds have never been seen. At times, not often, he worked from memory, the great distorter.

We will close the books, send them back to the dark. Then we will go home and, with our sharp pencils, crayons and Magic Markers, begin to draw.

Today in the Berkshires: This morning a chipping sparrow walked across the lawn with me. We went a fair way together and I began to wonder when he would fly off to his life. Midday a wild turkey strutted out of our woods with her chicks, gobbling as though the place was hers. Imagine that.